BORN
OF
EARTHQUAKE
AND
VOLCANO

BORN
OF
EARTHQUAKE
AND
VOLCANO

Ester Maria Segretto

BONARMA PRESS

New York, New York

Born of Earthquake and Volcano

Copyright © 2026 Ester Maria Segretto

All rights reserved. No part of this book may be reproduced or retransmitted in any form or by any means without the written permission of the publisher, except in the case of brief quotations used for book reviews. No part of this book may be used in any manner for the purpose of training artificial intelligence (AI) technologies or systems.

This is a work of fiction. Names, characters, businesses, organizations, places, events, and incidents are the products of the author's imagination or used fictitiously. Any resemblance to actual persons, living or dead, or actual events is entirely coincidental.

For permissions requests or information on this title, contact the publisher:

Bonarma Press
Ester M Segretto
P.O. Box 697
New York, NY 10159
www.bonarmapress.com

Book Cover/Interior Design by The Book Cover Whisperer: OpenBookDesign.biz

Author photo by Ebru Yildiz

Bonarma Press logo by Peter Santiago

Library of Congress Control Number: 2025926578

ISBN: 979-8-218-81849-4 Paperback
ISBN: 979-8-218-81850-0 eBook

Printed in the United States of America

FIRST EDITION

For my parents, Maria and Dominick,
I'm eternally proud to be your daughter.

Ti voglio bene, sempre.

"An earthquake achieves what the law promises but does not in practice maintain–the equality of all men."
— Ignazio Silone

"People never believe in volcanoes until the lava actually overtakes them."
— George Santayana

1

STELLA

QUEENS, NEW YORK
DECEMBER 2019

He is driving me absolutely insane! Fumbling with the ancient lock on my father's front door, I tried to no avail to kick it open. The man was so dramatic, especially when he was sick or injured. At eighty-six years old, a fractured arm and a bump on the head had been enough to land him in hospital. First, he'd complained I brought him the wrong T-shirts, then he refused to keep his arm in the *unbearable* mesh sling, insisting on fashioning his own from one of my mother's old headscarves.

As I eventually twisted the well-worn brass doorknob open and almost fell inside, I heard the muffled sound of large feet clamoring back up the stairs. The oafish upstairs tenant, who owed three months of back rent, had been hiding from me since Dad had been admitted to the hospital. I waited until the echoes of footsteps disappeared, letting him believe he'd evaded me yet again. I collapsed, exhausted and overwhelmed, on the cracked and sagging black leather couch in the front room. I'd told Dad I was leaving to grab him some clean clothes, the correct ones this time, but mostly I just needed a break from the sights, sounds, and smells of the hospital.

I dragged myself into his bedroom and rummaged through his messy armoire for some clean clothes. I grabbed another of my mom's silk headscarves, a souvenir with brightly painted images of Venice. *Let him turn this into a sling if he wants. I'm tired of arguing about it.* I pulled out a rumpled stack of seemingly identical white T-shirts to locate his favorite of the bunch. Not the one with the itchy tag or the hard seams, or heaven forbid–the crew neck.

I chose the softest V-neck I could find. As I freed it from the middle of the jammed stack, something else flew out with it. A small photo with a scalloped edge floated at my waist until it landed face down on the hardwood floor. I picked up the discolored and tattered wallet-sized photo, running my finger along its creased edges. Trying to make out the image without my glasses, I squinted, moving it closer and farther from my face until it sharpened into focus. A black and white photo showed a uniformed figure set against a backdrop of Roman columns and laurel wreaths commemorating a date.

"28 October 1922?" I muttered to myself.

I drew a sharp breath as I began seeking to piece together the clues. The darkly familiar arrogant stance of the man depicted in the photo. The ominous date–that day in 1922 had changed everything for Italy. The day Mussolini's Fascists marched on Rome.

I felt a shiver race down my spine.

I threw his clothes and the photo into my bag as I hurried through the house. I'd chase the late rent another time. I hurried down the worn stoop to my little red Fiat and tossed my bag into the backseat. Earlier, I couldn't wait to get away; now I clamored to get back to the hospital to confront him with my chilling find. Still parked in front of the house, obsessing over the photo, I grabbed it from my bag again to make sure I didn't miss something. A handwritten note on the back? An explanation? Nothing. My father hadn't even been born in 1922.

So, why did he have this photo? Hidden away, but clearly too important to discard.

As I drove the familiar route back to the hospital, I reflected on how Dad and I had clashed on all the big stuff–politics and religion–since I had begun to develop any comprehension. But we never spoke about the war in Italy–he couldn't. Holding on to this photo, this eerie memento, seemed completely out of character. Memories of his childhood in the early 1940s seemed too painful for him to confront.

As I tried to remember any story snippet or shred of information that could shed some light on this, my mind went back twenty-five years to the day before my cousin Dino left for boot camp. I entered my living room to find my confused and incredulous mother sitting beside my father, consoling him. My father, whom I had only seen drunk once before, sat sobbing at the end of our black leather couch, clutching a tumbler of Scotch. That irascible man with the big temper looked so small, it frightened me.

Through his sobs, I could hear his trembling, slurring voice, "He's going to die!"

My mother attempted to reason with him, comfort him.

"He's never coming back home!"

Neither of us could comprehend the long-buried origins of his strange meltdown. I knew Dino seemed like a son to him, but my cousin wouldn't be shipping out anywhere. Dad couldn't have been worried about a war, right?

My father was terrified of and terrorized by war. I remember him watching the nightly news, visibly shaken at the mention of armed conflict breaking out anywhere in the world. Unlike most men of a certain age, he avoided all war movies. He refused to take sides in global conflicts, seeking to ignore what was happening at all costs. Sometimes it seemed that making new memories or resurrecting old ones became inescapable, and we'd see him suffer.

As I stepped out of my car, I looked down at my shiny new platform Doc Martens boots. I stood in the hospital parking lot and recalled the day Dad drove sixteen-year-old me to the West Village in NYC, so I could buy my first pair of Doc Martens–the boots of my dreams. The ones I had saved up for all summer. The ones my father could barely look at–they resembled soldiers' boots.

As we exited the Village Cobbler, we were approached by an old woman dressed in Balkan-style clothing. She held up a tattered piece of cardboard with *"War Refugee Please Help"* scrawled on it. The Bosnian War, playing out directly across the Adriatic Sea from his hometown in Abruzzo, east of Rome, had begun that spring. I watched in astonishment as my normally stoic father stopped, his eyes glassy, and reached into his pocket to give her whatever he had without question. The only words he uttered during the entire ride home were, "War is miserable."

So, he was especially terrified that someone he loved would join the military–that they could be deployed to war. That it could happen again. Thus, the reaction to Dino's departure.

Although I can recall the many vague platitudes against any conflict, such as "War ruined my family," I couldn't remember any specific details or epitomizing stories to define the depth of his feelings. There was only one way I could solve the mystery of this photo: I needed to get back to my father.

―

"What the hell is going on?" My heart sank to my stomach. "Where's my father?" I asked as I arrived back at room 407, shocked to find a nurse's aide stripping his bed.

"I just work here," she said as she continued to tuck the fresh sheets around the mattress.

I dashed past an all-too-familiar sad sight–the hospital Christmas tree–on my way to the nurse's station.

"Oh, Stella, there you are! We had to move Domenico to the ICU," said the nurse, pushing her pink eyeglasses up and smiling apologetically.

"What the hell do you mean? He's in the ICU? For a fractured arm? I was only gone for two hours!"

"His blood CO_2 levels were through the roof; he was hallucinating!"

"I have no idea what any of that means ..." I responded, feeling out of breath as my voice trailed off.

"We had to–" she was still blundering through explanations as

I raced down the bleak hallway, fluorescent lights intermittently flickering above me.

Flying down the back stairs, I resented that I knew exactly where to find the ICU. I charged in, demanding answers. I spotted Dad behind a pair of double doors as they swung back and forth. I tried to slip through just as one door flew open, but a large orderly blocked me from entering. Through the small window, Dad looked almost unrecognizable. In two hours, he had somehow transformed from my stubborn and mischievous father into a small and frail old man. Propped up by two nurses, connected to tubes, and surrounded by beeping machines, he looked barely conscious.

The photo seemed so insignificant now. Unwilling to wait for permission, I nudged my way through the swinging doors to be with my father.

2

STELLA

QUEENS, NEW YORK
JANUARY 2020

I had been carrying the photo with me to his bedside continually for thirty-five days. Thirty-five days of waiting for him to be off sedatives long enough to wake up for a moment, to finally talk to him again, to ask him. I shuffled into his room and waved to his roommate like I did every day. The man only ever sat up in his bed, watching the same cable news channel.

"I think he's awake," he mouthed to me, pointing beyond the curtain.

I pulled back the curtain and entered slowly. His eyes were open but empty. I took a seat next to him, but he looked right through me and smiled, "Maria."

"No, Dad, I don't think it's time to see Mom again. It's me, Stella."

"You're not supposed to be here yet."

"OK. So, you're not happy to see me, Dad?"

"Stella!" His eyes opened wider.

"Dad, I don't know if you realize how long you've been asleep."

"Did I miss Thanksgiving? Oh no, I missed your Thanksgiving dinner!"

"Dad, you ... you don't remember? You spent Thanksgiving with me and Michael. But—you missed Christmas."

His eyes turned empty again.

"Dad, can you hear me? I need to ask you something. Can you look at me? Do you recognize this photo? Can you tell me who this belongs to? Why did you have it hidden in the room?" I held up the black and white photo for him to see, hoping to get an answer, any reaction. "I know you really don't like talking about the—"

"No! No! Get away from me!" His voice sounded weak and raspy. That didn't surprise me: He hadn't used it in over a month.

I glanced nervously at the monitor out of the corner of my eye. I could see his pulse rate and blood pressure spiking, racing upwards. Everything flashed red.

"Dad, it's just me, Stella. Look at me. Everything's OK, you're OK. You're safe."

His face relaxed, and the beeping and blinking of the monitors subsided as his heart rate began to hover around normal.

"Dad, try to concentrate for a minute! I need you to explain this. Why did I find this in your house?" The loud overlapping beeps sounded frenzied and insistent again, and much like my father, they were growing more agitated with me.

"Dad, I'm sorry. It's OK. We don't have to do this now. Please try to calm down." I sat beside him and held his hand.

"Don't let me die!" Without warning, his body lurched forward into a seated position like a puppet when someone had pulled the strings. His eyes were crazed and unrecognizable, bulging wide like the villain in a silent era horror movie.

"They're going to kill me!"

"Dad, what are you talking about? It's just me, Stella. Nobody's going to hurt you," I tried to reassure him as I leaned back in the chair, freaked out by his strange outbursts.

He always was a bit paranoid.

"No! Don't go in there!" He clumsily tugged the leads of his heart monitor, but he couldn't even hold his arms up long enough to rip them off.

"It's not mine!" He looked directly at me for the first time since waking up. Flailing his arms, he grabbed the photo and knocked it out of my hand.

"Dad, I found it in *your* armoire when I went to get you some clean–it doesn't matter. But who were you talking to just now? Don't go where? Dad, please, tell me what this means."

Rising slowly from the pink vinyl bedside chair, I picked up the photo and placed one hand on his arm to calm him down. I presented him with the photo one last time.

"I know you've never wanted to talk about the war, but why keep something like this, about such a dark moment–" Two nurses barreled in and pushed me aside as they settled him back on the pillows.

They silenced the beeping but had to restrain his wrists to keep him from ripping out the leads and the IVs. From the corner I'd been relegated to, it felt as if I wasn't even in the room anymore. Everything looked distorted as if being filmed through a wide-angle lens. More people joined the melee, and I saw a small flash of light hit a silver scalpel as a blue-gloved doctor mumbled something behind a surgical mask. "Intubate!"

The photo had been pushed aside again.

3

STELLA

QUEENS, NEW YORK
JANUARY 2020

The smell of lilies overwhelmed me, and the sight of the brown and green patterned rug under my feet made me feel dizzy. My husband, Michael, and I stood at the entryway of the viewing room. I fidgeted with the high collar of my black wool dress as Michael combed his impeccably kempt salt and pepper beard–a perfect match to my silver-streaked black hair–and smoothed out his black tie. Funerary attire would never be a problem for us: we wore black for any occasion.

We waited for the funeral director to re-style my father's hair. I had carefully chosen a photo to best reflect his signature hairstyle, only to show up this morning to find his white hair slicked straight back. It jarred me how much that simple style nuance made him the spitting image of my grandfather, Emidio.

Some guests were already queued in the hallway, patiently waiting to pay their respects. Greeting my cousins Angela and Carmela, first in line, I spotted a man in expensive-looking black frame glasses at the end of the line; he looked familiar. I realized I was looking right through my Aunt Teresa as she gripped my hands in hers, offering her condolences, distracted by the man in black glasses.

Why do I feel as if I'm ten years old again?

As I recognized my grandmother's divergent eye and my grandfather's long nose in the man, I heard someone calling my nickname. Only my father used that.

"Stellina?" asked the man in glasses.

I walked toward him, knowing that only my father called me Stellina. This had to be my uncle Donato.

"*Zio?* Zio Donato! I can't believe you're here!"

I had phoned my father's younger brother, who lived in Rome, with the news of Dad's passing last week. I had gotten the impression he wouldn't be making the trip to New York City, so I hadn't expected him to be there. I had only met Zio Donato once, on his one and only trip to the US over thirty years ago. He looked much the same as he had then, albeit older, grayer, and smaller. The man standing in front of me was all at once my father, my grandmother, and my grandfather, but also nothing like any of them. He'd never said goodbye to his home country. He'd never had to choose between that and assimilating into the modern world. He'd evolved with Italy, stuck with her through her growing pains.

"I'm so glad to see you, Zio. Please have a seat in the first row. I'll be there as soon as I say hello to everyone," I said, passing him off briefly to my husband, Michael, who spoke not one word of Italian. I couldn't worry about that; hand gestures would have to do.

I made my way into the viewing room, which was filling up

quickly. I spotted Zio Donato heading to my father's pale silver casket to say goodbye to the brother that he hadn't seen in thirty years. I hung back for a minute, taking in the surreal scene. I hoped my father would approve of the new navy-blue suit I purchased for him the day before. I felt certain that he, a very picky menswear expert, would haunt me if I'd chosen wrong.

I couldn't help but think of my mother, and how different this would all feel if she were still here, if we'd have gone through this together. Would she think I'd done enough to take care of my father? Had I done a good job planning his funeral? Did I forget something important, something my family was whispering about right now?

I felt confident in my decision to uphold the tradition of the red floral rosary draped on the inside of the casket. I made a mental note to retrieve the crucifix–the same one that had hung in my mother's casket twenty years earlier–before his burial. I noticed Lisa, the funeral director, adding some last-minute touches around the room.

"Lisa, is there any water or anything to drink?" Before I could even finish my sentence, her assistant appeared with bottled water for me. While chugging my water with all the grace of someone stranded in the desert, I realized how remarkably unprepared I was to use my rusty Italian. I touched the small gold *cornicello* charm hidden under my collar, passed down from my mother when I turned thirteen, for strength. My muscle memory had better kick in fast because I had so many questions for Zio Donato. I stood up straight and walked back into the room, feigning confidence.

Was it this loud in here a few minutes ago?

I winced at the sound of many Italian Americans, all speaking over each other. My cousin Dino had slipped in unnoticed and sat alone in the last row. Hiding behind his wraparound sunglasses, I barely recognized him if not for the large *Semper Fi* tattoo on his forearm. *He'll come find me when he's ready.* I headed straight to Zio Donato, now sitting awkwardly by himself in the first row.

"*Ciao Zio.* Thank you so much for making the trip. I know *Papà* would really appreciate it."

"Stellina. I'm sorry for not making this trip sooner. I regret not being in your life. I also regret not spending time with my brother and my parents while they were still alive. Your cousins, mostly Luisa, convinced me to come. She convinced me that your father would forgive me."

I was sitting beside the last link to my father's life in Italy, his little brother. I tried to muster up the courage to ask the questions that had been eating at me. I didn't want to come off as tactless or callous. I know those questions shouldn't have been so important to me at that moment, but I had to know. *He might leave straight after the funeral, and this might be my only chance to get answers.*

I took a deep breath and pulled the photo from the small black handbag at my side. The heavy chain handle fell and clanked hard against the metal frame of the chair. The sharp sound made me feel like the center of attention I didn't want to be. I waited a few moments for people to stop looking at me.

"Zio?" I managed to squeak just as my father's neighbor, Charlie appeared before us, offering condolences in his thick Queens accent, before moving down the row. When he'd gone, still gripping the photo, I opened the palm of my hand and turned to my uncle again.

"Zio, do you know why Papà would have kept this photo?"

Zio Donato stared at the photo with a furrowed brow for a moment, then turned to look at me. He seemed confused.

"Where did you get this?" he asked.

I found it in Papà's house. It was already too late to ask him about it, he was really– disoriented at the end."

Zio Donato's eyes seemed to grow both bright with recollection and wide with fear upon seeing this relic of his past life.

"Domenico held on to that?" he asked, as if surprised.

"So you know about this? Why would my father have this stashed in his armoire?"

My uncle sighed deeply and loudly.

"Stellina, how much did your father tell you about the war?"

"Almost nothing. He never wanted to talk about the war. It upset him too much to speak about it." I paused, feeling sheepish. "And it's just occurring to me now that I may be upsetting you. I'm so sorry."

"Ahh, it's OK," he said, waving his hand at me. "I remember the first time your father laid eyes on this photo." He chuckled softly. "He was so angry. Though not for the same reasons that you may have been angry finding it."

"What do you mean? Where did the photo come from?" I asked.

"There's too much to tell, and yet so little I feel that I can even begin to describe. You would probably think I was telling tall tales, but it's all true. That's the worst part of it all."

"I'm ashamed to say that the few stories my father told me, I did think were tall tales," I said.

While I knew a little about the pain that war in Italy had inflicted, I didn't yet understand the horrors that had been inflicted upon the Italian people.

"I haven't talked about the war in decades. My kids never even ask me about those times. It's as if Italy decided to forget. We collectively agreed to rewrite our history as simply one of art, cuisine, and culture. I guess it worked; everyone forgot. So I pretended to forget as well."

Zio Donato appeared to be lost in thought. I didn't know if he was doing it solely for my benefit, but I had yet to detect even a hint of an Abruzzese dialect when he spoke. He didn't sound at all like my father or grandfather. You could almost believe he had lived his entire life in metropolitan Rome.

Michael stopped by to check in on us. He'd been making the rounds, greeting guests, and collecting sympathy cards. My job. I watched as my husband spoke into his phone, "It's a pleasure to finally meet you, Zio Donato." He proudly held up his phone as Siri said, *Ciao, Zio Donato. È un piacere conoscerti finalmente.* "My new translation app!" He looked very pleased with himself as he sat next to me.

I rested my head on Michael's shoulder and whispered in his ear, "Sorry, I should be doing all of that, playing host." He just gave me a little wink and smiled.

I translated some of my conversation with Zio Donato–I didn't want Michael to feel left out.

"Zio Donato was just telling me about his and my father's experiences in Nazi occupied Abruzzo during World War II."

"Jesus Stella, just a little light conversation for your first meeting in thirty years?" Michael chuckled. My husband knew better than anyone how much I hate small talk.

4

DOMENICO

MONTESCIANO, ABRUZZO
JULY 1943

If Domenico squinted his eyes tightly, the shapes and sounds of his village remained as they had been the day his father left. Before the war, before the world called them the enemy, before the desperation. The town square bustled with the familiarity of neighbors and housewives buying produce and other humble provisions. Women still crossed the narrow *piazza* while skillfully balancing large woven baskets of hand-washed laundry on their heads.

The Gran Sasso mountain range would always rise high above every horizon line, and now and then summertime brought a brief yet so familiar whiff of the warm and humid Sirocco wind that blew from the south, skimming the Adriatic Sea on its way to Abruzzo. Today, the normally dry mountain air was filled with tiny droplets of moisture, making the air feel thick and heavy.

His thoughts were interrupted by a terrified voice echoing through the piazza. When he opened his eyes wide, the present harsh realities came into sharp focus, dissolving the layers of protection he had built for himself.

"It wasn't me! I've never said anything like that! Please, no! I've always been loyal to *Il Duce*!" The young man sounded terrified.

Domenico covered his ears. From his hiding spot on the inconspicuous bell tower balcony, looking down on the piazza from above, Domenico watched in fear as he made out the shapes of a young man and his Fascist interrogator. The young man below began to give a half-hearted salute, stretching his arm straight out and to the right as proof of fealty.

A discordant jumble of voices shouting, doors slamming, vehicles grinding and clunking smothered the air, overwhelming all Domenico's senses. The townspeople were scattering into the shadows and out of the piazza, desperately trying to avoid being witnesses. Domenico decided to use the chaos as a cover, a distraction to flee. He descended the tower and escaped the scene of this latest act of authoritarian cruelty. Domenico knew that the damage had already been done. He knew that no matter how far he ran, it wouldn't change anything. Only a ten-year-old boy, there was nothing he could do or say to save that man. In fact, he'd probably just get himself arrested as well. His father, Emidio, had been imprisoned in Africa by the Allies for the last two years. He thought of his mother, Pasqua. She couldn't lose anyone else to this war.

Domenico clomped down the rickety spiral staircase behind the bell tower as swiftly as he could, before he slipped into the tiny alley leading away from the town square, the main piazza in Montesciano. The piazza bore the same name as hundreds of other town squares around the country, Piazza Vittorio Emmanuele, after the first king of the united Italy. He sped through the alcoves, cobblestoned hills, staircases, and walkways that together created the mismatched and jagged puzzle comprising his family's village.

Rushing through the maze of centuries-old limestone and terracotta huts, he winced as pebbles managed to find the hole in the sole of his left shoe as if they had radar. With a pain in his side and throbbing in his foot, he finally stopped short when he reached the beautiful blue and green expanse of the countryside. He'd made it to the main road, suspended over a vista of farmland, olive groves, and vineyards.

He usually took this view for granted. After all, everyone was leaving for a reason, weren't they? Way before the war took them away and picked them off, the men of Abruzzo were leaving their families behind to go find work in America. Entire families were packing up and emigrating to places like Brooklyn, to be near New York City's garment district, Philadelphia to work on railroads, and Chicago for construction opportunities. Some returned, but many never set foot in this forgettable village again.

Today, Domenico found the majesty of the Gran Sasso mountains and the lush green lands the Abruzzese had been cultivating for centuries, awe-inspiring. Surprised by these more adult thoughts, for the first time, Domenico wondered how so many of his countrymen could have found the courage to leave.

How could they turn their backs on this beautiful land to live amongst strangers, tall buildings, and noisy automobiles?

He touched the palms of his hands to his empty, grumbling

stomach and remembered all the reasons why people desired to escape Montesciano.

With the sun positioned high in the sky, the heat became unbearable as late morning approached. Domenico needed to find shade, but he couldn't go back home. He couldn't bring himself to walk through that piazza and relive the events that he had inadvertently helped to set in motion–not yet.

"Hey, Pepino!" Domenico spotted his schoolmate sitting on the guardrail overlooking the valley.

Pepino hopped down, ran toward Domenico, threw out his right hand with three fingers strategically extended, and exclaimed, "Eight!" Domenico, without skipping a beat, threw out his hand and yelled, "Seven!" He looked down at his five extended fingers, "Ah, you win, Pepino! You're always better at *Morra* than me. OK, let's go again!"

The simple game dated back to the Ancient Romans. All the players would throw out a single hand showing anywhere from zero to five fingers as they all called out their guesses for the tally of all the fingers shown.

"I didn't manage to get my hands on any cigarettes today, sorry," Domenico said, ashamed, as he thought about the young man and all the horrors the blackshirts—Fascists—must be subjecting him to now. Pepino reached into the front pocket of his tattered linen shorts and presented Domenico with one of the bent cigarettes he had stashed away.

"That's OK, I have an extra!" he said.

They continued with their spirited games of *Morra*, warm,

glowing cigarettes dangling awkwardly from the corner of their mouths, until it took Domenico's mind off the disturbing scene in the piazza this morning. "Six!" Domenico called out, revealing three fingers, just as Pepino shouted "Five!" while also holding up three fingers. "Ha! I won again!" Domenico beamed.

They carried on playing while the sun slowly began sinking toward the horizon. For the remainder of their sticky summer day together, they settled on the edge of the road, using trees in the distance as targets to hit with the rocks they unearthed from the sandy soil surrounding them.

Then someone began calling Domenico's name, and he looked up to see his younger brother Donato approaching.

"*Porco Dio!* What are you doing here?"

"Mamma sent me to get you," squeaked the young boy.

Domenico knew he'd be late for dinner, again. Seven-year-old Donato would often be sent out to look for his older brother. Donato was tall for his age, already outgrowing Domenico's recent hand-me-down clothing. Donato's rail-thin, scrawny legs were completely out of proportion with his thick head of floppy dark hair and the giant black framed eyeglasses he was forced to wear.

"You're always spying on me! Don't you have anything better to do than tattling on me?" Domenico yelled over his shoulder as he ran back toward the town square, and the very same piazza where Domenico's day had taken a terrifying turn.

Lagging behind Domenico, Donato's little legs struggled to keep up with his brother, his glasses slid down his nose and fell to the ground. He stopped short and knelt on the floor, feeling around to find his thick glasses. He had already broken them twice before, and he didn't wish to explain another incident to his mother.

Donato shouted out to his brother, "Mimi, *aspettami!* Wait!" It only made Domenico run faster. He wanted to run from the memory of the young man's pleas as much as trying to outrun his brother.

He could still hear the man's desperate pleas over and over again in his head— "It wasn't me!"—and see his weak Fascist salute. "I've always been loyal!" The damned salute flashed in his mind again.

How could this be the same regime my father urged me to respect?

"*Mimi!!*" cried out Donato again. "*My glasses!*"

"*Just leave them!*" yelled Domenico.

"Yeah, you'd love to see me get into more trouble than you. Wouldn't you?" said Donato, more to himself as he found his glasses, luckily not broken.

Neither brother wished to incur the wrath of their mother, Pasqua, a sturdy woman with a tough exterior but a kind heart. She had a divergent squint in her left eye, which she had passed down to her youngest, Donato. Her eyes contributed to her stern expression. Pasqua inspected everyone she met with a look suggesting she had good reason to be suspicious of them. Now and then, you could catch a glimpse of a warm smile wash across her face if you found her lingering in a memory.

Domenico had agreed to run some errands for his mother in exchange for permission to spend the day in town. Despite his haggard appearance, he hadn't completed any of them. His wrinkled white button-down shirt had turned tan from dirt and sweat, his shorts were ripped at the pocket, and his boots scuffed. His mother would be furious, that extraordinary level of furious that only a Southern Italian mother could achieve.

Domenico could see that the last four years had taken a large toll on his mother and their whole family. He knew she expected more from him, her firstborn, than she should from someone still a child himself. He felt guilty because he knew that he often did not live up to those expectations. Every day, he had to remind himself she had no other choice, that she did the best she could, but he always found himself avoiding being at home and any responsibilities that came with it.

As Domenico reached the bell tower dedicated to St. Michael, he could already hear his mother shouting.

"*Domenico! O, Mimi, it's 6:30!*"

He ran through the archway, down the stairs, and onto the long piazza. He could see his mother scowling on their little dilapidated balcony. Pasqua stopped yelling as she spotted her two sons, but now muttered under her breath. Domenico couldn't hear what she said, but he knew it wasn't good. Her short dark hair was slicked back on her head, and she wore her favorite house dress, blue with tiny flowers, accessorized only with her *mappina*, an old, tattered dishcloth, draped over her right shoulder.

Domenico stopped and turned to Donato, grabbed his shoulder, and warned, "You cannot tell Mamma I was with Pepino today!" before running ahead again. Domenico finally reached his front door with his brother ten steps behind and hurried up the two crooked flights of stairs to their apartment. He could hear his mother's voice getting closer and louder until a familiar nausea came over his whole body, and her voice suddenly sounded garbled as if underwater. He stopped as he reached the landing to steady himself.

"Boiled rice," he whispered to himself weakly.

"Rice, again?" he asked his mother. "When this godforsaken war is finally over, we have to move somewhere where rice doesn't exist! I can't even stomach that disgusting smell anymore!"

"You know damn well that there's no pasta out there; Mussolini made sure of that. Even with our ration tickets, we can't afford the flour to make our own. You want pasta, get a job instead of wasting your time at school or causing trouble in town with God knows who!" Pasqua barked back at Domenico.

"I'm not eating that!" said Domenico.

"Mimi, I spend all day cleaning the houses of the *signore*."

These, Domenico had been told many times, were the people who just didn't care to imagine how the rest of them lived. They went on living like the war couldn't touch them. And maybe it wouldn't.

"So, I can't deal with your ungrateful whining about dinner! Again!"

"But Mamma–"

"I'm too exhausted to argue with you, Mimi. I know I'll regret saying this, but your father will send us some money soon. I know he'll figure out a way," she said.

Rage began to fill Domenico's ten-year-old body.

"*You don't even know where he is! Papà is not sending us anything. He's probably dead!*"

Nobody had heard from his father, Emidio, in four months. Domenico feared the worst, but it made him so angry when his mother lied to him. He didn't want to be placated or pacified. He wanted answers. He wanted his father back.

"You better watch yourself!" threatened Pasqua, raising her open hand.

Domenico stormed out of the kitchen, into his room, and burst into tears. From behind the curtain that served as a bedroom door, he could now hear his little brother Donato comforting his mother. His angry tears now turned to tears of pain, knowing how his words had hurt his mother, not that she'd ever admit it.

"Well, at least I won't have to eat rice tonight. I'd rather go hungry," he stubbornly whispered to himself.

He sat alone for the rest of the night in the sweltering room he shared with Donato, angry, upset, and with the terrible pain of hunger in his stomach. He started replaying the events of the day over and over in his head. He thought about how his curiosity and clumsiness had set them all in motion. He thought about the conversation he had overheard the three men having in front of the *tabaccheria*, or tobacco shop, earlier today in the piazza.

He had been lingering nearby, watching them, hoping to snatch one of their unsupervised packs of cigarettes while they weren't looking. The men looked to be laborers, most likely from one of the vineyards just below the town. Their hands were swollen, calloused, and dirty. They were dressed in clothes clearly handed down from an earlier era. Two of the men seemed practically elderly to Domenico, definitely older than his father. Maybe the years of back-breaking work and stress had prematurely grayed their hair. However, the third man was barely out of his teens. He had an oblivious look and goofy grin that Domenico recognized in younger kids, like those his own age. As Domenico waited for the right moment to approach the youngest and least intimidating of the three, he heard him begin speaking about the war in hushed tones.

Each time a customer approached to enter or exit the tobacco shop, the men would stop speaking. Everyone needed to be very careful. There were eyes and ears everywhere, and they had all unfortunately learned what neighbors were willing to do to each other to gain an upper hand in these scarce times. Domenico quickly scanned the four corners of the piazza to make sure nobody was watching and then inched a little closer to the men. He hoped to go unnoticed as he eavesdropped on their conversation, but he became increasingly distracted by the loose cobblestone at his feet. It made him sway from side to side as if moving to a piece of music.

He could just barely hear the young man, who he had just learned was named Antonio, whisper to the others.

"Did you hear? The Allies just landed in Sicily, in a place called Gela. Maybe *sta miseria* will finally be over soon," Antonio said excitedly before his older friend, who Domenico had heard called Gaetano, quickly put a hand over Antonio's mouth.

"Shut up, you're going to get us all killed!" said Gaetano.

"I just meant that there isn't enough food, I don't know how much more we can take..."

"You're a real idiot!" Gaetano muttered.

Domenico froze, trying to decide what to do with this new information. He wanted to stay and hear more, but he didn't want to bring attention to himself or this group of friends. The town square, once vibrant with the chatter of old men and the laughter of children playing, had become somber, guarded, and swirling with suspicion. As he slowly backed away, he stumbled. He felt something underfoot and heard an ear-piercing screech coming from below.

"Damn cat!" he muttered, frustratedly as he resisted the urge to kick the stray feline, one of Montesciano's many community cats. To add insult to injury, it was a black cat, which always made him feel uneasy.

Domenico whispered *"Padre, Figlio, e Spirito Santo"* as he hastily made the sign of the cross.

You can never be too careful.

So distracted, he didn't even realize that all three men had turned around and were now staring at him. Their bodies remained frozen and tense until they realized he was just a child.

"What do we have here, a tiny priest?" asked Gaetano, relaxed and relieved to find young Domenico standing before him.

"A tiny priest!" said Antonio mockingly. "What are you praying for?"

The man standing furthest away, Pietro, strained to get a closer look at the boy.

"Hey, kid! *Guaglione!* Domenico? You don't remember me?" growled Pietro under his breath.

The men had only let their guard down for a split second when a green vehicle carrying a group of Fascist blackshirts came roaring around the corner from Via Milano, just outside the piazza. An oval-shaped, middle-aged woman directed the blackshirt's attention to the group of men outside the tobacco shop.

"That's them, over there." She made every effort not to lock eyes with any of the men at the tobacco shop. "I heard them disparaging Il Duce and the war effort. I think they were even celebrating the Americans' landing in Sicily."

The woman stood holding out her hand, anxiously awaiting her reward. The blackshirts were tasked with eliminating political opposition and stifling dissent all over Italy, which they did violently and with glee.

At the first sign of a blackshirt exiting the vehicle, Domenico panicked and immediately took off running out of the piazza, through the archway that ran under the bell tower. He quickly and quietly climbed up the tower, taking two stairs at a time. He sat perched above the town, peering into the piazza out of sight of the Fascists, watching to see what would happen to the men.

This was all his fault. If he hadn't distracted them, if he'd minded his own business, that young man would still be in the piazza, grinning with his friends.

Maybe if I just go back and explain, they'll let those men go?

"It wasn't me! I swear, I didn't say anything like that!" the lanky teenager pleaded with the blackshirt, clearly an exercise in futility.

A second blackshirt exited from the passenger side of the vehicle. He approached from the opposite side; they now had young Antonio cornered against the stone wall of the tobacco shop. That's when they really began to have their fun.

"I've always been loyal to Il Duce!" Antonio yelled out with his arm raised taut in a salute, just before taking a swift punch to the belly. He slid down along the wall, onto the floor in pain. The ruthless blackshirts surrounded Antonio–they relished violence and sowing fear. The larger the audiences that their violent acts drew, the more compliant and obedient the population became.

Back in his stuffy room, Domenico had spent hours poring over every detail of that day. He repeatedly played the men's conversation in his mind, trying to get every detail correct. Only a few short hours prior, a small but bold cigarette heist had been his one goal for the day. Now his mind raced with possibilities. He wondered just how far Sicily was from Abruzzo.

If the Americans are in Sicily, then that means they might make it all the way up to us in Abruzzo. Is that a good thing? Are they on their way to save us, or to invade? Does this mean the war will be over soon? Will the Americans bring Papà back home?

He wanted to ask his mother all these questions, especially about what would happen to Antonio, because he still felt somehow responsible. But he knew she'd tell him that these were the problems of men. The women needed to work, keep the family together, and pray for their husbands' safe return home. She needed to make sure Papà had a home to come back to.

Domenico got on his knees, clasped his chubby fingers together, and started praying to take a load off his mother. He also prayed to St. Michael to protect poor Antonio and, not least, to St. Anthony to help find his father.

―

FOUR YEARS EARLIER, ON an early morning in March of 1939, when Domenico was just six years old, Emidio had gathered the family in their chilly kitchen. Together, his wife and two young sons huddled around him, saying their teary goodbyes. Frost outlined the little wood-framed windows that illuminated them from behind. Emidio and Domenico both stood proudly in their uniforms– Emidio in his Royal Italian Army uniform and Domenico in his *Figli della Lupa,* Children of the She-Wolf, uniform. At the age of six, membership in the Fascist youth group had become compulsory in Italy. Further illustrating Mussolini's obsession with the Roman Empire, the group had been named after the story of twin brothers Romulus and Remus, the founders of Rome, who were said to have been raised by a she-wolf.

"Mimi, it's just one year. I'll be back before you know it. Il Duce is going to make Italy powerful again, like the Roman Empire!" Emidio assured Domenico.

"Papà, you're a tailor. You don't need to be a soldier anymore. You can teach me to be a tailor too. I'll help you so you don't have to go away."

"Mimi, when your country needs you, you have no choice," Emidio said with his chest puffed out, proudly.

"I–I need you. Please, Papà!" Domenico begged his father in vain.

"You can't keep acting like a child, Mimi. You have to be strong for Mamma and Donato. Make me proud. Remember what I taught you?"

"Yes, I remember. If I feel like crying, make a fist and squeeze it hard until the feelings go away," Domenico recited with his head down, concentrating on his little clenched fists.

"*Bravo,* Mimi!"

Emidio waved as he left his young family behind to begin his week-long voyage, first to Naples and then onto Addis Ababa, in Abyssinia. Domenico felt abandoned, but he had no reason to doubt his father at the time. After all, it wasn't wartime. Emidio's military service had him stationed far from home before, and he always came back. What young Domenico couldn't have known or understood then was that Europe stood at a dangerous tipping point. In one year's time, Germany would invade Poland, and Italy would declare war on the Allies–Emidio would officially serve in WWII.

In school, Domenico learned that Mussolini would conquer Abyssinia, where his father was stationed, as well as Eritrea, Somalia, and the entire Horn of Africa for Italy. Domenico's schoolteachers and his father's letters conveyed the same messages: Italy would be great again. She would be strong. She would be respected. Another empire, much like the one of ancient Rome, would be born.

He also learned that when Great Britain entered World War II, it wanted to stop Italy's powerful empire and steal East Africa from Italy's grip. That same enemy, the British, captured Domenico's father in the capital city of Addis Ababa, and they were holding him as a POW. His father's letters began to arrive postmarked from prisons and internment camps all over Africa. It seemed to Domenico that his father was constantly on another ship, sailing to his next prison.

Emidio, a persistent and resourceful man, could also be bull-headed in his convictions, leaving no room for compromise. Pasqua regularly shared Emidio's letters home with the boys. At first, they were a comfort that offered hope, but just like the war, the letters from Domenico's father began to take a darker tone. The messages allowed to come out of the prison and internment camps were usually short, fitting neatly on a postcard.

Domenico knew his mother had begun leaving parts out until she finally hid some letters altogether. A string of defeats for Italy, and his continued imprisonment was changing Emidio, the evidence clear in his letters. His father's words frightened Domenico at times. His mother told him all prisoner communication was monitored by the military before being allowed into Italy. Sometimes his father's letters arrived so heavily redacted, with thick black lines running through entire sentences and paragraphs that Domenico could barely make any sense of them. His mother seemed to have a special talent for reading between the lines, but Domenico could tell the spaces in between frightened her the most.

Only eight years old when his father had been captured, Domenico couldn't even begin to understand the long-term ramifications of this war. The destruction, the waiting, the fear, the hunger. Domenico always had an avalanche of questions for his mother after receiving his father's letters. The questions started out fairly innocent, curious, and proud even. However, the older and more aware he became, the more fearful and resentful he felt toward the war and his father for choosing the military over his family. The longer Emidio was away, the less enthusiastic Domenico became about donning his own uniform. He didn't really want his father to suffer, but somehow it made Domenico more resentful when the letters found him well and in good spirits.

Domenico suspected that his father's letters made his mother nervous; she seemed relieved when they went long stretches without communication from Emidio. It was easier to keep the peace. The last letter they received from his father four months earlier had made Domenico especially irate. The prisoners at some of the camps were permitted to learn a new trade or find some employment with skills they already possessed. Emidio worked as a tailor, sometimes even outside of the camps. As Pasqua read Emidio's words out loud, Domenico became visibly agitated.

"He didn't have to go all the way to Africa to be a tailor; that was his job here! He could have done it here and come home to his family every night! I hope he's happy sewing in prison on the other side of the world, while Italy is still *un pezzo di merda*!" Although Domenico's mother said nothing in response—she'd never admit it—he had a feeling she felt the same.

5

STELLA

QUEENS, NEW YORK
JANUARY 2020

"Stella, I heard someone speaking Italian from across the room," my Zia Leonarda said as she made her way over to me with her frail outstretched arms ready to deliver a hug. Her wrinkled hands were clutching a large mass card. She seemed to have shrunk more every time I saw her–I swore I could feel every one of her bones as we hugged.

"Nothing gets past you, Zia!" I said.

"I can hear Italian being spoken five miles away! There aren't that many of us 'off the boats' left anymore–a dying breed," Zia Leonarda said proudly.

Zio Donato watched Zia Leonarda, listening to her speak and seemingly perplexed.

"But, what language is she speaking?" he asked.

I wanted to laugh, but I just leaned down and gently reminded Zio that my mother's side of the family came from Sicily.

"And you can understand her? It's as if she's speaking another language," he said, still bewildered.

"*Si,* Zio. Sicilian *is* another language completely."

My uncle crossed his legs, like an elegant old Roman man, with a look on his face that read, *What do I know?*

"Wait, I recognize you. Domenico's brother. Dante?" Zia Leonarda's face lit up as she switched to Italian.

"Donato," he said as he reached out to shake Leonarda's hand.

"It's probably been thirty years, right? I never forget a face!" Leonarda asserted, in her best Tuscan dialect.

"Zio Donato just arrived this morning from Rome. I've been chewing his ear off and making him tell me stories of the war."

"The war? Why would you want to talk about such terrible things right now?" Zia Leonarda quickly dismissed the idea.

"What do you mean Zia, what especially bad things happened during the war in Sicily?" I asked.

"Ahh, what didn't happen! The things we saw that summer–1943." She shook her head.

"I was only seven years old, but I remember it like yesterday." Leonarda then grew silent for the first time since she arrived as I watched a child out of the corner of my eye. He stuffed one of each prayer card variation into his pockets as if they were trading cards.

"But Zia, didn't you grow up in Rocca Leone with my mother?"

"Of course! We lived on the same street, right across from our school. Everybody spent such terrifying nights in that school when the Allied invasion began. They had turned the giant cellar into a bomb shelter. We all thought we were going to die there or be trapped until the end of the war. What did we know? We were kids."

"Die? Sounds terrifying," I said, urging her to go on.

"On the first night, children were screaming, the women praying, and the men, well, you know men. They were all busy hatching crazy plans to save the day–as if they could take on a Nazi with their bare hands."

"My mother never mentioned the war, and I assumed it didn't affect her town." I was starting to understand how little I knew about my parents.

"Your mother, may she rest in peace. I can't believe she's been gone twenty years already. Maria actually wasn't in the school with us that night. Neither was Zio Salvatore." She shook her head.

"Where was she? She would have only been five years old in 1943 …"

Just then, a priest I recognized from my childhood parish, Father Tony, walked in.

"I forgot to tell them I didn't want a mass during the viewing."

"No mass? Eh, this generation. OK, we talk another time." Leonarda stood up and hurried back to her seat next to my cousins.

"Wait, come back! Zia!"

The whole room began droning in unison, "In the name of the Father, the Son, the Holy Spirit."

6

MARIA

ROCCA LEONE, SICILY
JULY 21, 1943

As Maria mindlessly bounced her leg against the tall wooden stool, loose flakes of the old pale green paint dropped off and collected below. Her head of dark bobbed curls barely reached the bottom edge of the kitchen window she sat beside. Outside Maria's little window, the landlocked hilltop town of Rocca Leone, right in the middle of the island of Sicily, basked in the hot sun. This represented the only world Maria had ever known. She'd never seen another town, let alone another country. She'd never learned any language other than Sicilian, other than the few words of Italian she'd picked up from her older brothers.

She craned her neck toward the window. She could just make out the tops of her older brothers' heads–Salvatore's coarse black hair and Alfonso's wavy brown hair–as they exited their building.

"*Hey! Wait for me!*" Maria yelled out the open window after her older brothers.

"*You're not allowed!*" exclaimed Alfonso, cupping his hands around his mouth.

Both dressed in tan shorts and leather ankle boots—Salvatore in a plaid short-sleeve buttoned-down shirt and Alfonso in a white one—they had just run down the stairs with their soccer ball, flaunting all the extra freedoms that boys enjoyed and were afforded.

"*Who says?*" Maria shouted back.

Rumpling the hem of the old brown chore dress she had outgrown, she knelt on the stool to see out the window.

"*It's not safe for you outside. The Nazis are coming. I hear they love to kidnap little girls!*" shouted her oldest brother, Salvatore, trying to get a rise out of his little sister.

At only ten years old, Salvatore always tried to act so much older than his five-year-old sister. Wise beyond her years, she seemed to understand, and it made Maria furious.

She huffed, anxiously adjusting the loose silver thimble that constantly spun around on her petite middle finger, the tiniest thimble her mother could find. Maria let out a deep sigh and got back to work, piercing the coarse fabric and carefully pulling the gray thread through in a backstitch to join the two sides of the torn seam in her brother Alfonso's shorts.

"Why don't you make yourself useful? I have some holes in my socks you can fix," teased her brother Alfonso, giggling as he lifted his socks out of his scuffed and ragged boots.

She yanked the needle free from the gray thread and jammed it into the thread spool that rested on the windowsill. Her brothers were separated by only two years in age, and they acted as a united front against their little sister. Maria constantly begged to join them, and every time she'd be denied, and then ridiculed.

"Everyone here tells me what I can and can't do, who I am, and who I'm going to be. Well, I'm going to be something they've never seen!" she muttered to herself.

She tossed the small pile of easy repairs meant to keep her busy onto the tiled floor. Her father Carmelo's missing shirt buttons and the torn pocket on her baby brother Rosario's overalls would have to wait. It wasn't just her brothers who were stifling Maria's spirit. She had begun to notice some strange things about her mother, Nina, short for Antonina, recently. Her mother had changed since the war began. She seemed more reactive, on edge. She had begun acting like some of the old Sicilian women Maria saw in town, who were suspicious of everyone and always looked angry.

Her mother had begun to remind her of her Nonna Arcangela more and more, sad every day, dressed in dark clothing, and always looking over her shoulder. Maria could remember running her little hands through her mother's thick dark hair, but now it looked like a tangled pile of hurried pin curls most days. Even her mother's eyes seemed darker.

Now treating Maria differently, too, Nina's expectations of her only daughter had become simultaneously tougher and less relaxed. She imposed more domestic responsibilities on the five-year-old, while also taking away some of the freedoms that could prepare her for the life ahead.

"Mamma, the boys are going to play soccer, and they won't let me join them, again!" complained Maria.

"Enough! Every day with this nonsense! Stop concerning yourself with your brothers' games. You'll be a wife and mother someday; how are you going to learn to take care of your family if you're always out playing and giggling like a silly girl?" she snapped back at Maria. "If you don't want to finish your work, you can help me with mine. I sure have plenty for you to do!"

Maria swung her head around in response to her mother sitting across the room, and for a split second, she saw her Nonna Arcangela instead. She flinched.

"La catena!" Maria whispered under her breath.

Maria didn't know exactly what *la catena* meant; her mother told her it was some sort of ancient curse that women could inherit from their mothers, grandmothers, and great-grandmothers. She remembered her mother told her if she wasn't careful, *la catena* could catch her, trap her, and force her to repeat the lives of the women that came before her.

"They can pass their pain down the bloodline as if it were the eye color you inherited from a grandmother or a mole you shared with your mother," she remembered her mother telling her.

Maria had been frightened when her mother explained how it could reach back through generations to find her. She never understood what any of it meant. It all sounded like a scary story until that moment. Maria began to think more and more each day that *la catena* was really just the curse of being born a girl.

She watched her brothers through the open shutter in the kitchen, bursting with envy as she witnessed them escape their little second-floor apartment, free to do as they pleased. Nobody questioned them, nobody tried to stop them. She felt her cheeks turn red-hot, her teeth clench, and her lips purse, pushing against her loose bottom tooth. She wanted to cry and scream. Her deep brown, wide-set eyes filled with tears. She'd been stuck in the apartment like a peasant princess locked in a tower, or like the story her mother told her of Persephone trapped in the underworld, solely for the crime of being a girl. Barely five years old, Maria already grappled with the effects of *la catena*.

"I'll prove that I'm braver and smarter than them, maybe that will cure this curse!" Maria muttered under her breath.

Watching her brothers go outside again on a scorching summer day, unsupervised and unquestioned while she suffocated inside, working with her mother, filled Maria with more jealousy than she could contain in her little body. She'd never been allowed out by herself, but today she was determined to 'see the world.'

Maria carefully and quietly snuck past her mother, preoccupied preparing lunch in the kitchen. She ran into the bedroom she shared with her little brother and dressed herself in a rose-colored linen smock dress with a white Peter Pan collar, expertly sewn by her mother. She slid her little brown sandals out from under her bed and clumsily buckled them over her white ankle socks.

"Shhh!" she said to her curious little brother, Rosario. She crept softly past him, trying not to let her heels touch the cold tiled floor, while holding one finger up to her lips.

As Maria trod slowly down the stairs from her second-floor apartment, she came across her neighbor, Paolina, on the first-floor landing. At seven years old, Paolina acted as if in charge of everything and everybody. She was barely taller than Maria, but Paolina's bouncy auburn curls and large almond-shaped eyes always commanded attention.

"And where do you think you're going?" demanded Paolina.

"*Fatti li fatti tuoi*, mind your own business!" snapped Maria in her little whispered voice, repeating something she'd heard Nonna tell a nosy neighbor.

Maria approached the ground floor and thought, "I'm free!" She paused, half expecting to hear a siren, an alarm of some sort signaling, "the princess has escaped the tower!" But nobody even seemed to notice, except nosy Paolina, of course.

She pulled open the green front door and descended out onto the Corso Umberto I, the main road that ran through the whole town of Rocca Leone. She looked south down the road, still able to make out two small figures in the distance playfully kicking a black and white ball back and forth to each other.

"There they are, my stupid brothers."

Determined to have her long-awaited adventure today, Maria skipped along the Corso Umberto until close enough to tail her brothers, but far enough that they wouldn't suspect they were being followed. Maria would experience the life of an "uncursed" boy and see what it felt like, even if just for one day.

As she passed the farmer's market at Piazza IV Novembre, she hid among the hustle and bustle of strangers and the skirts of women. She still had her eye on her brothers Salvatore and Alfonso, obliviously horsing around ahead of her. As they approached Piazza Margherita, Maria hung back, watching to see if they would stop.

Piazza Margherita was a large, round piazza made up of four curved buildings.

Maria's mother had told her about an even bigger and fancier piazza just like it in Palermo, called the *Quattro Canti*. Piazza Margherita remained particularly popular with the kids in town for its very unique zigzag labyrinth-like staircase. The staircase scaled the whole side of one building, and at its top, it gifted you with a view of the whole town. Kids had been inventing games to play on that staircase for decades.

Maria watched as her brothers walked into the piazza and headed for the zigzag staircase with their battered soccer ball. She continued to follow them to the edge of the piazza. Salvatore and Alfonso joined some friends in kicking the ball skillfully up and down the staircase, narrowly avoiding breaking the windows of the houses positioned along the staircase's route. Maria waited for the right time and ran into the piazza, announcing herself right at the bottom of the staircase.

"Surprise!" yelled Maria. But before she could even get the whole word out, Alfonso, who was indeed surprised, turned and accidentally kicked the soccer ball squarely toward Maria. With a resounding thump, the ball made contact with Maria's head, knocking her to the ground. Stunned, and with Salvatore and Alfonso leading the way, all the boys stomped down the stairs toward her. A dazed Maria sat up and was met with a deluge of emotionally charged questions ranging from panic to anger.

"What the hell are you doing here? Did something happen

at home; is everyone alright?" asked a shaken Salvatore, shifting between anger and concern.

"Mariuccia! Did I hurt you?" asked Alfonso, looking terrified at the possibility of injuring his little sister–more so at what his mother would do to him.

"I'm fine! Get off me!" demanded Maria as she stood up defiantly. "I followed you. I wanted to go out and see how the boys lived, and here I am. That's it. Nothing's wrong. Nothing happened!" yelled an exasperated Maria as she brushed dust off her dress.

"Good, so now you can go home, where you belong!" Salvatore snapped, fuming now since she wasn't hurt.

"Oh, I'm staying with you and Alfonso all day! Unless you want me to tell Mamma that you hit me on the head with a soccer ball?" asked Maria as she shifted her weight to one side with her arms folded smugly in front of her. Maria had outsmarted her big brothers, even if it earned her a gnarly bump on the head.

NINA HEARD A GROWING commotion outside the Sanfilippos' apartment. The voices below their second-floor balcony were getting louder and more frenzied. Turi, the fruit vendor, excitedly told everyone who passed him and his tired donkey, "The Germans are at the south entrance of the town! They have giant machine guns!"

"They have tanks on the main road!" yelled Ciro, hobbling quickly up the road, supported on his left side with his cane. All the gray-haired, black-clad nonnas were scowling and peeking out of their shutters and balconies to see what the commotion was about.

The townspeople were starting to gather up their family members, pacing about, whispering, and proselytizing about what was to come. Even the most fatalist of Sicilians, who left everything in God's hands, were now predicting the Axis and Allies' chosen battle towns as if they were teams on a soccer scoresheet. The men who were left in town—those unfit, too young, or too old to serve—seemed eager to get a taste of war. They were buzzing around with excitement.

However, to the elders who had known war and lived through the First World War, the news coming from the edge of town offered a grave warning. Nina remembered the stories the men told when she was growing up. She knew that everything was fair game in war. She knew both sides would have only one goal: to win. She also knew the battling soldiers would use their homes, their town, and their people as shields. The civilians in Rocca Leone would be the losers no matter who won.

Back at the apartment, Nina slammed her hands over her ears and let out a shriek as the first of four thunderous explosions rang out from south of town. They came one after the other, thirty seconds apart, as if perfectly timed. Nina stood in her kitchen, paralyzed with fear, until sure they'd stopped. As she snapped out of her fright, she ran to little Rosario and scooped him into her arms. That's when she realized …

"Where's your sister? She's supposed to be watching you!" snapped Nina at the toddler.

Rosario simply raised a curled finger to his lips, said "Shhh," and then pointed through the door as he mumbled, "Outside."

"What do you mean outside?! Nina ran to the balcony to try and see Maria, but she was shocked by the scene down below. All the normal chattering on Corso Umberto had come to an alarming and abrupt stop. The silence on the street was ominous as it felt like the town held its breath, waiting for the next explosion, but it never came. The voices slowly began again, but the townspeople were no longer boasting of their breaking news; they were frantic, distressed, in chaos.

"*Calogero! What's happening?*" Nina yelled down to her neighbor on the street.

"*The damn Germans! They blew up the bridge in the valley. Now we're trapped here with those maniacs!*" replied Calogero as he stood under her balcony.

"Trapped? I thought the Americans had reached Sicily!" said Nina, beginning to panic.

"They did, but there's no way they're getting to us now, not without that bridge!" said Calogero, looking up.

Those with families were all busy trying to track down wives shopping at the market at Piazza IV Novembre, or children playing at Piazza Margherita. Those with markets and stalls were rushing to salvage their food and goods, hoping they wouldn't have to abandon them.

"*Mi figghi!* I need to find my children!" Nina howled as she stood alone on the balcony.

It was happening, their worst fears realized. The war had literally come to meet them on their doorsteps.

———

AT PIAZZA MARGHERITA, MARIA screamed and covered her ears as her brothers shielded her, all lowering to the ground. Everyone in the piazza scattered to the four corners, running for cover. Soldiers wearing red armbands embroidered with strange symbols stormed through the south side of the piazza, forcibly clearing everyone out and screaming in the harsh sounds of a language she couldn't understand. Salvatore had been knocked over in the stampede. Maria and Alfonso were separated by the crowds until Salvatore spotted Maria still near the zigzag staircase. They were now mostly alone in the square except for the Germans.

"Maria! Go hide in the bathroom. I'll come back for you, Mariuccia!" Salvatore instructed her in Sicilian. Maria was relieved; the soldiers didn't seem to understand what Salvatore said.

Just behind Maria stood a big door with *"BATHROOM"* painted by hand over it. She ran, heaved open the giant door, and locked herself inside.

All I wanted was to be free like the boys.

Maria's eyes began to well up with tears. She had tried to show she was a big girl, but only found herself stranded in a stinky bathroom, with soldiers and loud bangs everywhere.

———

SHE WISHED SHE KNEW what the soldiers were saying, what they would do if they discovered her. Mostly, she wished she'd just stayed home with her mother. Maria pictured the last places she saw her brothers. Alfonso was at the exit closest to home, but Salvatore was all the way at the end of the piazza–the exit on the way to Nonna Arcangela's house.

Nonna is all alone. I bet Salvatore went to find her. Maria only ever remembered her Nonna being alone. *I wonder if she's as scared as I am right now.*

She'd never met her grandfather Giuseppe–he died before Maria was born. Her mother had always told her he was a great man, that he'd saved Nonna Arcangela. Maria had no idea what she'd meant. She envisioned a grand gesture like carrying her out of a burning building or fighting off a wild boar for her.

Maria waited alone in the bathroom for what seemed like an unimaginable amount of time. The loud bangs and screaming had stopped. With her ear pressed against the door, she listened for voices. There weren't any. She struggled to open the heavy door a crack, to peek outside into the square.

"Thank God," she whispered. Nobody else was around.

Salvatore had told her to wait for him, but she couldn't just stay there all day, waiting for a boy to rescue her.

He doesn't think I can survive out here on my own. But I will.

Maria made her way out of the bathroom, careful not to make a sound. She waited to cross the square, very much aware of the possibility of German soldiers appearing, to decide which way to go. Corso Umberto was too big, not safe, and there was nowhere to hide.

Although Maria had never made it up to the top of the

zigzag staircase, Salvatore had told her the whole town was visible from up there.

If I climb to the top of the stairs, I can use all those little hidden streets to find my way down to Salvatore!

Maria impressed herself with her thinking and hoisted her tired feet up all nine flights of the zigzag steps, stopping at the top only to catch her breath. She looked down at the disorienting jumble of terraces below and began plotting her adventure.

NAVIGATING THE SKINNY DOWNHILL twists and turns, her toes gripped her sandals to keep her from tumbling. As she approached a large opening to Piazza Branciforti, Maria spotted a large group of soldiers moving in unison and then separating as if they were performing a dance routine. The soldiers were followed closely by a giant roaring machine. She had never seen anything so large and menacing. She retreated around the corner, trembling.

As she squashed herself into a doorway, so frightened she'd be seen, Maria was startled by three sharp popping sounds. Assuming it was gunfire, she couldn't stop herself from letting out a short, high-pitched scream, but quickly covered her mouth. Trails of smoke wafted around the corner toward her. She hesitantly poked her head out and realized there was no gunfire, just smoke. Enough thick white smoke to fill the piazza.

Hearing shouts and more screams, she saw she could use the chaos and smoke to her advantage. Maria ran along the sides of the buildings with the smoke providing cover. Still dazed, she made her way around the familiar square. Maria remembered shopping at the farmer's market here with her mother. A staircase led down to a large door; she and Alfonso had played there once while their mother was busy haggling. Maria flew down the dark, dank set of concrete stairs. She barely reached the doorknob, so she climbed back up two stairs, leaned forward to grab the knob, and used her weight to push and pull while holding her breath. It was unlocked.

She exhaled in relief but recoiled as she stepped through the door.
Why do all my hiding places have to be this dark?

She tried not to be afraid of the dark, but she'd already spent most of her day without light, and she prayed to God that she was alone in this cellar. She stepped inside with caution, leaving the door open a crack, hoping to let in a bit of light to illuminate her way. Walking straight to the back wall of the cellar, Maria held her right hand out in front of her, while her left pinched her nose. The musty smell of the long-abandoned cellar was getting stronger with every step Maria took.

She ran into something large that felt like wood and heard the chink of glass as her hand met the back wall. As her eyes adjusted to the darkness, they and her mouth opened in astonishment.

I bet not even Papà has ever seen this much wine!

Maria marveled at the abundance she was unaccustomed to, but this seemed like a good place to wait for the smoke to clear. The entire journey from Piazza Margherita had been a blur; she shouldn't have known the way or how to stay safe and go unnoticed but felt as if someone had guided her here. She slid down onto the dirty floor between the wine bottles and what she'd recognized as giant wooden wine barrels. She pulled her knees close to her chest.

"Mamma's gonna kill me when she sees the state of this dress."

"We can't stay here, you understand that, right? We're not safe here!"

Nina glared at her husband and declared, "I'm not going anywhere without my children."

Nina couldn't remember Carmelo ever leaving work early before; she knew things must have been catastrophic for him to shut down the orchard, but she had different priorities now. Alfonso had almost collided with his father as he arrived home from Piazza Margherita after frantically escaping earlier in the day, but Salvatore and Maria were still out there.

Carmelo, a man of short stature with prematurely graying hair and dark bushy eyebrows, a hard-working farmer in an old peach orchard just outside of town, had done his best to console his wife since Alfonso relayed the terrifying story of German soldiers causing a stampede, and getting separated from Maria and Salvatore. He told his parents of the screaming, the gunfire, and the desperate look in Maria's eyes as he was left with no choice but to run out of the piazza.

Nina couldn't bear the notion of her children's last thoughts being of fear.

"*Mi figghi!* They're dead!" Nina screamed.

"*Mizzica,* Nina! *Basta!* Nobody is dead!" said Carmelo.

Now it was nearing 7:00 pm. The summer sun had gotten very low in the sky, washing the whole apartment in a warm golden glow. Any other day, and it would have felt comforting, a signal of a welcome dip in temperature. Today it felt like a harbinger. Darkness approached, but Nina would not back down. She was adamant that the whole family stick together through this. Carmelo should have known that in a battle between her husband and her children, a Sicilian woman would always choose her offspring. So they continued to wait, despite Carmelo's suggestions that the Germans would be here soon.

"How do you think we'll fare in a fight with the Nazis?" he'd said, but Nina insisted they wait for Alfonso's brother and sister.

They sat in silence until they heard a commotion and agonized screams coming from the street down below. The Germans had made it to the Corso Umberto. The balconies all along the street operated like a game of telephone. The most recent news coming up through the town was that the German and Italian soldiers had started carrying out home invasions nearby. They were kicking in doors, removing residents, or forcing themselves inside and taking over. Robbery was the best they could hope for at this point.

She finally relented. Staying would put her other two children in imminent danger. Nina, still in her apron, and Carmelo in his dirty work clothes and sweat-drenched *copolla* hat, quickly gathered a shaken Alfonso and Rosario. They packed a cloth sack with whatever bread they had left and two blankets. As they all headed to the door, Nina ran back into her bedroom to grab the burgundy beads that she prayed the rosary with every night out of her nightstand drawer and shoved them in her apron pocket.

Outside, they stood huddled on the crowded sidewalk in front of the now shuttered pastry shop below their apartment. They hadn't planned anything further than this moment. It was after 9:00 pm, and the town was shrouded in darkness. The only illumination was the silvery soft light from the half-lit moon, high in the sky. Nina looked into her husband's hazel eyes, hoping he'd have the answers. She received only a blank look in return.

"Papà, we have nowhere to go, I'm scared," said Alfonso as he held Rosario's hand.

Just then, a thunderous onslaught of artillery fire could be heard coming from the southern edge of town. Seemingly synchronized, all in the crowd instinctively cupped their ears with their hands and ducked for cover. Hugging Rosario to her hip, Nina reached for the rosary beads in her apron, wrapped them around her right hand, and closed her eyes. Keeping her hand in her pocket, she ran her fingers over the facets of the beads to soothe her nerves.

Nina felt the familiar sensation between her eyes she got when someone was watching her. She opened them, and they were met with the kind and warm brown eyes of her friend Giuseppina, crouched in front of her, stroking Rosario's cheek to wipe away a tear.

"Come, come," motioned Giuseppina as she stood up.

They all followed Giuseppina without any words spoken and crossed the broad street in a tight cluster toward the wrought iron gates of the elementary school, attended by both Salvatore and Alfonso. Tonight, it seemed, the school's cellar would serve as a bomb shelter for the people of Rocca Leone. There was still no sign of Maria and Salvatore. It was as if they had vanished from the Piazza Margherita without a trace.

How could they have gone the whole day without anything to eat?

The thought preoccupied her as they all descended the stairs into the cellar. Having found a place to squat on the floor, there were at least thirty families there already, Nina turned to the townspeople around her for help.

"Has anyone seen my Salvatore and my Maria? They're missing! Nobody has seen them since this morning. Please!" she said desperately.

She was met with only collective grunts of, "No."

"What if the Nazis took them away? What if those beasts killed my children?!" she asked, but everyone simply shook their heads.

"Who organized all of this so quickly? Who's in charge of all of this planning?" asked Carmelo, his voice booming over the crowd. A few names were half-heartedly thrown out from the crowd.

"Whoever it is, they should be in charge of the labor unions. If labor had organized this quickly, the people would own this country. Maybe we wouldn't have been at war!" said Carmelo.

Nina watched in amazement as her normally restrained husband commanded the full attention of the townspeople. They cheered at Carmelo's words and mused on a world in which the Italian people were spared from the war and their leader. A world where they held some agency over their lives.

Nina took the blankets from her cloth sack and spread them

out on the cold concrete floor for everyone to sit on. Rosario could stay in her lap as she watched all the people trickling in, hoping for a miracle.

Nina felt both relief and shame as she spotted her sister Rosina and brother-in-law, Angelo. Relief that they were safe, but shame that in her panic, she hadn't even thought to check on her family just around the block. Rosina was Nina's younger sister, the sibling with whom she had the closest bond. Nina then thought of her mother. Arcangela, long widowed, living all alone right at the center of the fighting in the Granfonte district. Nina knew she had no way of reaching her or keeping her safe tonight.

In an instant, the volume in the school cellar went from a soft chatter to a cacophony of emotions. The trickle of people coming down the stairs had turned into a wave. The artillery fire, which had continued relentlessly for thirty minutes, was letting up, but not before a grand finale of mortar shelling that everyone in that basement could feel in their bellies. At 9:30 pm, Diego, the butcher, ran down the stairs in a frenzy, pushing past everyone else on the staircase.

"The Americans are here!"

Nobody knew for sure exactly which army had arrived, but everyone on the continent to the west was American to them.

"The Americans?" Nina said with hope in her voice.

"Yes, the Americans! They've set the Mother Church on fire!"

Just as Nina suspected. Everyone was out for their own victory. Nobody was there to save them, and she couldn't save her children while stuck in a cellar. As her hope faded, she gripped her rosary tighter in her clenched fist.

———

MARIA DIDN'T KNOW HOW long she'd been sitting on the damp cellar floor, but she remembered how orange the daylight looked as it hit the clouds of smoke earlier–it would be dark outside now. She thought that if she used the darkness to her advantage, she might reach Nonna Arcangela's house unnoticed.

Who'd be looking for a little girl? I might as well be invisible.

It was quiet, and the smell of smoke had disappeared. Maria dusted off her dress and tiptoed up the cellar steps, trying not to make a sound. It took all her strength to heave the door open a sliver–she saw no movement above ground–and slipped outside as she took a big breath.

She crept around the edge of Piazza Branciforti, hugging the wall in the dark. Passing the *Chiesa Madre,* Maria descended Via Garibaldi, hoping for a glimpse of the *Granfonte,* the large fountain that signaled they were close to Nonna's house. She heard whirring sounds in the distance, the same ones she'd heard right before she saw the giant roaring machine earlier in the day. Maria spun around in a circle, looking for an escape from the main road, a place to hide. She ran into the first alley she found. It smelled of sweat and cigarette smoke, but she thought it would lead her in the right direction.

Is this the right way?

Maria sat on the step of a crumbling house that seemed abandoned. She rested her head on her knees, waiting to safely continue her journey. She was just about to set off again when she heard footsteps scraping against the cobblestones.

"Who's there?" she asked.

"Maria?" said a voice from the darkness.

No! It can't be! Is he trying to get to Nonna's, too?

"Salvatore? Is that you?"

She stood up, and when her brother saw her, he looked like he'd seen a ghost. Salvatore grabbed Maria and pulled her in for a tight hug.

"*Maria!* I've never been happier to see you! But what are you doing here?" he asked.

"I thought maybe you'd gone to find Nonna. I tried to find you, but the explosions and all the smoke–I hid in a cellar ... Salvatore, I thought I'd never see you again!" said Maria.

"I did try to go to Nonna's, but I never made it past the church. I hid in the *Chiesa Madre* all day like a coward," said Salvatore.

There wasn't time to regale each other further with tales of their misadventures. Hands clasped tightly together, they hesitantly edged closer and closer to Via Garibaldi, but the giant roaring machines seemed to have disappeared. Breathing a sigh of relief, they stepped onto Via Garibaldi as a blinding flash of light illuminated the night sky. They watched in horror as *Chiesa Madre* nearby, the church that Salvatore had spent the day in, was pounded by artillery fire. They ran terrified downhill, away from the church.

"I know where we are! We're really close to Nonna's house now!" Maria said as they turned onto Via Granfonte.

They ran the rest of the way to the fountain. Maria rinsed her hands and face with the water racing out of one of the twenty-four spouts while Salvatore cupped his hands to drink. As Maria wiped her hands on her dress, beams of light approaching and the sound of boots on either side startled them both. She grabbed her brother's hand again.

"Who are you?" Salvatore yelled.

Surrounded, Maria's heart pounded so hard she worried it might explode. Salvatore pushed his sister behind him to shield her. The men were dressed in dark green uniforms with some red patches at the top of their sleeves and helmets that looked more like pasta strainers than hats. Also, the patches on their uniforms were different from the ones the soldiers in the Piazza Margherita wore.

One soldier pointed at Salvatore and asked, "I-taliano?"

"Si, Siciliano!" Salvatore responded smugly.

"Sicilian?" The soldier chuckled. "Isn't that the same thing?" he asked in Italian with a funny accent. "My name is Jim, I'm Canadian."

Salvatore confirmed to Maria what the soldier had said.

"What do you want from us?" he asked the soldiers.

The man asked Salvatore his name in Italian, which Maria thought sounded worse than her baby brother's. Salvatore paused for a moment.

"My name is Antonio," said Salvatore.

"And I'm his sister ... Francesca," said Maria.

She thought they were playing a game.

The Canadian soldier furrowed his brow for a moment, like he was thinking really hard. He grabbed a piece of paper from his pocket and began scribbling something.

"Antonio, I need you to take this note and give it to *any* Canadian you can find out there."

"You want me to go out there? And take this note to a Canadian? *Me?*" Salvatore asked incredulously, pointing at himself.

"Yes, *si!* exclaimed Jim.

"What do they want?" Maria asked, and her brother explained.

That sounded like a dangerous thing to Maria; she knew that working for the Allies would make him a traitor.

"We need to go that way–to our Nonna's house," said Salvatore, pointing to the lower village.

"I'm afraid nobody can get there tonight," said Jim.

Jim rummaged in his pocket again and found something to sweeten the deal, flashing a 1000 lire incentive at Salvatore. Maria's eyes went wide, lighting up at the large sum of money.

"OK, I'll go find a Canadian!" said Salvatore, snatching the money from Jim's hand. "Do you all wear helmets shaped like *sculapasta*?" His expression turned serious. "But my sister comes with me!" he said.

"I think it's safer if she waits here with us, Antonio," said Jim.

"No, I'm not abandoning my sister again today! Both or nothing!" said Salvatore, gesturing. "No deal."

Jim put the note in Salvatore's hand and gave him a pat on the back.

"OK, *grazie,* Antonio."

"Even if we don't make it past German lines to deliver this note, at least we've made 1000 lire today!" said Salvatore to his sister.

───

AS AT PIAZZA MARGHERITA earlier, Maria somehow *knew* how to navigate through parts of Rocca Leone she'd never been—as if using someone else's memories. She wasn't afraid. Something inside her had guided her to the safety of the wine cellar and then reunited her with Salvatore. She *needed* to listen this time as well. As quickly as the thoughts were coming to her, she relayed her instructions to Salvatore. They hurried through to the outskirts of the town and down to the valley. Climbing through dried sun-seared grass and over rocky terrain in the dark, Maria sensed where to hide, when to duck, and when to dodge.

As they trudged along winding dirt roads, they were met with the changing aromas of the Sicilian landscape. The crisp scent of the plump prickly pear fruit gave way to woody olive trees and sweet orange blossoms. Maria and Salvatore ventured further into the wild outskirts of Rocca Leone.

Maria stopped to catch her breath. She looked up as moonlight gleamed off the top of crumbling ruins protruding from nothingness. She leaned against a stone wall, letting her guard down. Maria felt the hairs on the back of her neck stand up.

She swung her head around as a man in uniform emerged from behind the wall.

"Don't worry," said the man in Italian, holding his hands in front of him.

"An Italian soldier?" asked Salvatore in the same language.

"Yes! I'm Italian. My name is Serafino," said the soldier. "I don't care what you're doing or where you're going. I'm trying to get out of here, too," Serafino assured him.

"Why are you hiding? I thought the Italians and Germans were fighting together," asked Salvatore.

"Yes, the Italians and Germans were fighting on the same side, but many of the Italian troops are done with this war. We never wanted this. Some are retreating, leaving the fighting to the Germans. Some are even abandoning their units to join the resistance," said Serafino.

Salvatore explained to Maria what the soldier had told him, then turned back to Serafino.

"We need to find the Canadians," Salvatore said, and told of their encounter.

"I can't help with that, but if you kids have made it this far, you're probably safe," said Serafino before departing.

The air had cleared of smoke, and the ringing in Maria's ears had stopped. Nobody yelled, and no giant scary machines lurked around the corners. They walked further along the shrinking dirt roads until they came face to face with the base of the ruin of Tavi Castle.

"It's an ancient fortress–the Byzantines and Arabs used it to protect themselves from invaders–but now just a giant pile of rocks overgrown with weeds," said Salvatore. "Did you know you were taking us here?"

Maria shrugged her shoulders. She had no idea what her brother was on about.

They continued around the base of the castle and spotted a group of tents set up in the distance. Had they made it past the Germans?

"Maria, look! Those soldiers are wearing the same funny *sculapasta* helmets as the men at the fountain," said Salvatore.

They tried to run to the men but were stopped by a soldier with a stunned look on his face. His dark features mirrored Salvatore's, and he began shouting at them and waving his arms wildly, but they couldn't understand a word he said.

"*Cana-da! Canadese?*" shouted a panicked Salvatore.

That was enough to reveal that the guy spoke some Italian, and Salvatore handed the Canadian soldier the note from his pocket. The soldier quickly took Maria and Salvatore to a tent about fifty yards away to meet a large, important-looking man with a huge strawberry-blond mustache.

The man looked angry and began yelling, as a vein bulged in the middle of the man's forehead. Salvatore grabbed the note from his pocket again and nervously handed it to the officer.

Maria held her breath, watching as the man mouthed the words of the note to himself. His face completely transformed as he read.

"*Grazie, grazie!*" the large man exclaimed as he reached down to hug them. "Wait right here," he motioned to Maria and Salvatore with his hands.

Maria gave him one of her best grins that always made her father smile. Since escaping the bathroom that morning, she had felt safe. It was the same feeling she had when she was with her mother or her Nonna–protected. She felt as if she was being guided.

La catena? Mamma never told me la catena could ever help me. Did I break the curse?

Maria decided that the women who came before her must have kept her safe today. They gave her the power she needed to stay alive, to help Salvatore. She couldn't wait to get back home to her mother and tell her the good news about *la catena*.

7

STELLA

BROOKLYN, NEW YORK
JANUARY 2020

"It's really just an act, isn't it?" I asked.

"What is? What do you mean?" said Michael.

"They pretend that they've come to console me, but really I'm there to console them. To pretend to absolve them of something–not calling, not visiting. I don't know. Anything. They all want to share little gems of information they've been holding onto, stories to demonstrate their special relationship to your loved one."

"That's kinda dark, Stella."

"I just buried my father. I'm feeling pretty dark."

I stretched out on our green velvet couch with my face scrubbed clean of makeup. I'd changed out of my funeral attire into sweatpants and my favorite worn-in This Mortal Coil T-shirt, one I'd stolen from Michael years ago.

Michael handed me a steaming cup of chamomile tea in my favorite old lady teacup we picked up at Tea and Sympathy close to two decades ago. He set his timer for four minutes.

"You really need to get some rest, Stella. Tomorrow, the crowds of people will be gone, and it could feel even harder than today," said Michael, looking sleepy as he ran his hands through his messy brown hair. We were both exhausted and zoned out as a movie, that neither of us paid any attention to, streamed in the background.

"So, did I do OK?" I asked, warming my hands around the teacup.

"Yeah, you did great. I never really considered how hard it is being an only child until I watched you deal with everything by yourself."

"By myself? Are you kidding me? You were the helpful one, as always, so calm and collected with him when I lost my patience with him."

The timer went off to the sound of cathedral bells, startling me.

"Your tea is done steeping," he announced. "I'm heading into bed; you really should as well."

"Yeah, in a minute."

I was alone for the first time in days. My mind started replaying and obsessing over every conversation I'd had, pausing every pivotal funeral moment for me to zoom in on and dissect. I fast-forwarded to the enormous mound of dirt next to the six-foot hole they cover with bright green astro turf so we can pretend that our loved one isn't really going into the hole. They don't actually lower the casket into the ground in front of you anymore; that only happens in the movies. I pinched the image to get a closer look at the burial plot. My mother's concealed casket, which had now seen the light of day for the first time in twenty years, sat just a few feet away from me, somewhere under the astro turf.

I couldn't help but replay my conversations with my Zio and Zia from the wake.

"I'm missing a big part, an important part of this story," I said to myself out loud.

"Stella, it's 2 am. Who are you talking to?" a very groggy Michael asked from the next room.

"Nobody that interesting."

"Come on, Stella; come to bed."

"Yeah, in a minute."

I needed time. I needed not to be needed. I needed not to gloss over my grief to make everyone else comfortable. I needed the freedom to mourn in big, sloppy ways. I needed not to rush to be on time for work like I did the afternoon my grandmother died. I needed not to pretend to be OK like I did when my mother died twenty years ago–it had only compounded the grief I felt for my father.

I came from a long line of women who mourned deep and long– some of them made grief their entire personality. I'd seen grief consume my Nonna and spit her out as a completely different person. I remembered the day my uncle died, her firstborn. I remembered the early morning phone call that shattered her heart irreparably, but mostly I remembered the scream that followed. It still haunted me. I vowed never to let grief consume me. I thought I could decide to grieve in some enlightened and modern way, but I was learning now just how wrong I'd been.

I felt sick at the thought of going about my life, of going to work, business as usual. I opened my calendar and stared at the upcoming week with a mix of anxiety and disgust. Was I really expected to pack my camera bag and go photograph a marketing event for a giant oil company or a beverage conglomerate with a smile on my face? Should I stand at the edge of a red carpet and vie for the attention of a billionaire, like everything's normal?

There used to be rigid rules and etiquette around mourning. Someone mourning a family member was expected to avoid all social engagements for one year, and wear black for six months—I had the wardrobe covered. Those etiquettes were practiced out of respect for the dead, but they were also an outward symbol that communicated to society, "Be gentle, I'm grieving."

I can make all these commitments disappear with the stroke of a button. It would be so easy. Completely insane and irresponsible, but so easy.

My pointer finger hovered over the delete button on my keyboard, threatening to press it.

When I finally found the nerve, I gave my finger a little nudge, and every job I had booked, every planned event, every Zoom call for the next week was canceled. Freedom.

―

I WOKE UP CRANKY and with a headache pulsing over my left eye after just three hours of sleep.

"I totally should have gone to sleep with you last night," I groaned.

"Espresso?" Michael asked as he packed his lunch. I sat perched on the edge of the bed, trying to convince my legs to stand.

"Double espresso, please."

"Hey, did you see that the first case of that virus was officially confirmed in the US today?" Michael said as he handed me my espresso topped with the perfect amount of crema.

"Hmm, that's crazy," I said without truly registering his words.

"OK, well gotta go! Text you later!" Michael said as he dashed out the door. I scooped up my giant black cat with one hand and my tiny espresso cup in the other.

"Anubis, I think I may have fucked up last night. Why didn't you stop me?" I asked the purring cat in my arms. We both waved groggily to Michael from the front door as he left for the day.

I PARKED MY LITTLE red Fiat down the street from my father's house while I sat and waited for two neighbors to disappear into their respective homes. I'd decided my week of freedom would begin by searching through the decades' worth of documents in the giant musty metal filing cabinet in my father's basement. But I was willing to wait there all day for the coast to be clear if it meant I'd be able to avoid all mindless small talk.

"Maybe if this virus ever makes it to New York City, I'll have a legitimate excuse to be antisocial," I muttered to myself selfishly.

Inside, I locked myself in the basement and started with the bottom drawer of the cabinet, hoping it was in some sort of chronological order. Oldest last perhaps. I quickly lost all hope of any rhyme or reason when I found his 2018 tax return filed next to a business ledger from 1965. That chaos must have been a consequence of my mother Maria's twenty-year absence. Maria and her immaculately kept house would have never allowed that to happen.

Thirty years of canceled checks.

Twenty years of tax returns.

Payroll ledgers of employees I was certain were all dead by now.

Mortgage loan applications.

Deeds and closing contracts.

Telephone bills for defunct landlines.

But not one document that told any stories from Italy. Not one single scrap of paper that held any surprises. My eyes were burning from the half-century of dust I'd just kicked up. I needed to go back upstairs. Everything about this house felt so haunted and eerie now.

I hadn't been able to bring myself to put away his things, clean up the last traces of his daily life. His television remote still rested on the kitchen table next to his pill organizer, notepad doodles, and scratched lotto tickets. The crumbs from his last meal, eaten at this table, still lay sprinkled on the faded placemat. It was Pompei. A scene preserved in amber. Evidence of exactly the moment before he left this house for the last time, unaware he would never be able to return.

I remembered my parents' nightstands that always seemed like magical doors to Narnia, a small glimpse of them as people instead of just my parents. My mother kept family photo albums in hers.

My father kept an old, sealed carton of Chesterfield cigarettes in his, as a comfort after he quit smoking cold turkey forty years ago.

I popped open my dad's nightstand door, and the little brass handles swung back and forth, jingling to create the same little melody I remembered from when I was a child. It mostly just stored a mess of medications now. I slid out a wooden box with "Bolla" and grapes painted on the cover from the top shelf. Wine? Nope, a tangle of half-empty pill bottles and inhalers, in a wine box.

Then, crushed behind a square cookie tin filled with mismatched buttons, I found an old manila envelope. I opened the cracked, flimsy clasp and pulled out a folded document, yellowed with age. My legs were going numb from squatting. I slid down and took a seat on the dusty hardwood floor.

"Fiorinelli Emidio- *Foglio Matricolare,*" was written at the top in perfect calligraphy.

"Grandpa?!" I quickly scanned through the chaotically handwritten Italian cursive all over the front page. "Teramo. Naples. Addis Ababa. British. Rhodesia." These were the only words that initially jumped off the page.

What the hell does any of this mean?

"Teramo to Naples, Naples to Addis Ababa ..." My lips moved as I read and re-read the document. "Captured by the British ..." I knew my grandfather had been captured and held somewhere in Africa ... Rhodesia? Wasn't that now Zimbabwe? I'd found my grandpa's military records.

Attempting to read these Italian documents, the only thing that seemed clear to me was the timeline. As I did the math, my heart broke for my father, the ten-year-old boy in Abruzzo. I felt a tightness in my chest, as though I'd located one tiny shard of the pain he struggled to convey throughout his whole life.

8

MARIA

ROCCA LEONE, SICILY
JULY 22, 1943

Groggy from long naps and munching some enormous chocolate bars, Maria and Salvatore were antsy to get back home from the Canadian army camp. The town was cleared and was now in Canadian hands. One of the Sherman tanks circling back up toward Corso Umberto was tasked with giving them, the day's MVPs, the ride of their lives.

Salvatore and Maria climbed atop the hulking Sherman tank and proudly propped themselves high up on the turret, flanking the enormous, mounted gun. The tank rolled at a snail's pace through Rocca Leone, a town devastated, as the siblings proudly waved to the stunned bystanders. Maria helped the Canadians distribute food by tossing bread and packaged snacks to anyone standing on the side of the road. She giggled as the children of Rocca Leone clamored for the rare opportunity to get their hands on some sweet treats.

Upon arriving at the Sanfilippos, Salvatore gave the crewmen the Canadian salute he had just learned. Maria and Salvatore climbed down from the enormous tank onto the rubble, debris, and belongings that were strewn everywhere. The terrifying sights on their street sobered them of the previous night's excitement. It looked as if an entire house had crumbled, leaving its contents to pour out around it. Maria tripped on an old shoe and narrowly missed stepping in a small pool of blood congealing just inches from her feet.

The pride she'd felt for the last twelve hours had lifted like a fog. She looked at Salvatore, standing frozen in the middle of the street. She'd seen that look on her brother's face before—he was scared.

"I can't do it, Mariuccia. I can't go up there," whispered Salvatore. "I'm afraid of what we may find," he said, his voice trembling.

"Salvatore! *Amuni!*" Maria tugged the hem of her brother's dusty shorts, leading him in the opposite direction from home. "C'mon, they're over here. This way!" Salvatore reluctantly grabbed Maria's tiny hand and started to follow her.

"It's OK, Salvatore, everyone is safe," Maria assured him.

She crossed the street and turned left at the corner of the school building. They stopped at the side door.

"My school, why?" asked Salvatore, confused.

Certain of the feelings she'd had, Maria nodded, "Just open it, dummy!" As he did, she descended the stairs, leading the way, unafraid, hearing gasps and nervous chatter from the basement.

―

NINA AWOKE TO THE cellar buzzing with fear and anxiety. Her head was leaning on Carmelo's shoulder, and Rosario was curled up to her thigh. She had fallen asleep for a few moments in the middle of reciting the rosary to *la Madonna Addolorata*, Our Lady of Sorrows. Nina swore she felt all seven of the swords plunged into *la Madonna's* heart as if they'd been plunged into her own.

Nobody had seemed to get any sleep until daybreak. Although Nina couldn't see the horrors from the safety of her underground position, she heard every terrifying moment.

Everyone cowered at the sound of approaching footsteps. But as the footsteps grew closer, Nina could inexplicably feel her children's presence. With her burgundy rosary beads still wrapped around her hand, she sat up and swung her arms up, yelling.

"Maria! Salvatore! *Figghi mi!*"

The relief she felt just seconds earlier suddenly disappeared. Nina gritted her teeth, and with fire in her black eyes, she let out a guttural roar, *"You two! I'll kill you!"*

Salvatore took a step back from his mother as Carmelo pulled Maria toward him.

"Stop! Stay calm," Carmelo urged them all.

"Mamma, I–I think we'll wait to tell you what happened. Not today," said Salvatore. Maria nodded in agreement.

Holding up her rosary wrapped right hand, the medallion and cross dangling at her forearm, Nina cried, "*La Madonna, Madonna Addolorata* saved you!"

Maria looked her mother square in the face and said, "No. Not *la Madonna!* An angel."

ALL THE CHURCH BELLS in town rang out simultaneously, out

of time with each other, throughout Rocca Leone. A dramatic echo signaling the town had been secured, and the sound drew the townspeople outside. They cautiously emerged from their makeshift shelters, basements, and hiding places, pouring out onto the street.

The reunited Sanfilippo family huddled in a tight cluster as they finally made the short walk home, slowly taking care to avoid any obstacles and debris. They held their breath as they ascended the two flights of stairs to their apartment. Having no idea what to expect, what her home looked like, or if she even still had a home, Nina knew they were all together again, and the rest could be fixed.

The apartment door was ajar. Carmelo waved everyone behind him and entered first. He immediately tripped over the base of a shattered lamp that blocked the doorway. The apartment had been ransacked. Whatever food scraps they had were now gone, but there wasn't much else to take, with barely anything of value.

"This is going to take me a week to clean up," complained Nina.

"*Anna!*" exclaimed Maria as she hugged her favorite toy, a homemade, hand-sewn felt doll named Anna, that she retrieved from the mess.

Nina stepped out onto the balcony and looked out onto her little hilltop town that abutted the mythical land of Persephone and Demeter. For the first time since the battle began, she felt grateful. Destruction and sorrow stretched as far as the eye could see, but her family was safe.

"We're together again; the rest can be fixed." It had become a mantra as they all gathered on their balcony with Nina's arms pulling everyone in tight.

Loud banging on the door snapped them out of their group hug.

"*Nina!*"

"*Rosina?!*" Nina yelled back, startled.

Nina ran to the door and swung it open. Rosina, with her short, wavy dark hair, stood on the other side. Her large, intense dark eyes were spilling over with tears.

"Nobody checked on Mamma! I heard people saying horrible things this morning. They said the Granfonte district is practically destroyed! We have to find her, Nina, please!"

Nina looked at Carmelo as if transmitting silent instructions. Carmelo quietly accepted his mission. He met his brother-in-law Angelo on the street outside, and together they made the perilous journey on foot to Granfonte.

NINA AND ROSINA WAITED for hours, cleaning up to distract themselves. It was nearing dark when her husband and brother-in-law walked in, limp from exhaustion.

Carmelo took a breath in, closed his eyes, and slowly nodded his head. Nina let out a low, almost inhuman howl before falling to her knees in the doorway.

"Mamma? Zia Rosina?" squeaked a scared Maria, emerging from behind her brothers.

"Maria. Nonna is dead!" Rosina said as she hurried to a stunned Maria, her arms swallowing the child into a giant hug.

"Nina, I'm sorry, there was nothing we could do. It happened overnight," said Carmelo.

"I should have saved her. I'm the oldest daughter. It was my job to take care of her!" cried Nina.

"I tried to get to Nonna's house; I tried to save her! I'm sorry, Mamma!" said Salvatore.

"Nina, Salvatore—I promise you nobody could have saved her. Her little house never stood a chance, positioned in a war zone, right at the heart of the battle," said Carmelo.

"Arcangela knew she had no way out, nowhere to go. Her neighbors told us they watched helplessly as she fixed her hair with an eerie calm, put on her best dress, the one she wore to mass every Sunday, and climbed into her bed. They were right there, and even they couldn't save her. In the dead of night, a large artillery shell missed its target and careened directly into her bedroom. She was buried under a small avalanche of limestone."

DAMAGED CHURCHES, BLOCKED ROADS, and increased civilian deaths had all played a part in the delay of funeral services. Prolonging and adding to the ever-mounting grief, all the funeral preparations, masses, and burials were halted in Rocca Leone for at least a week after the battle. Arcangela's body remained on view in the very same bed she died in for one full, unusually warm, and exceptionally distressing week.

One cobblestone, one hunk of limestone at a time, the men cleared rubble from inside and outside the house and created a safe path for visitors. Family and neighbors took the chores of cooking and cleaning off Nina and Rosina's hands.

Nina and Rosina washed and dressed their mother in preparation for the extended viewing. Nina, dressed in the requisite all-black, refused to leave Arcangela alone. She remained in the crumbling house, holding vigil for her deceased mother for the whole week, reminded of her life growing up in this very house. Friends and family all passed through to pay their respects, each new visitor reviving Nina's cries and laments. Her deep, mournful bellows resonated through the house and spilled out to the street below.

When Maria grew tired of consoling her family through each visit, she would ask a never-ending list of questions. Was Nonna sleeping? Is she going to heaven? Can I talk to her?

"Go, go talk to her. I'm sure she'll hear you from heaven," said Nina.

Nina and Rosina had been receiving visitors paying their respects every day. To a weary Nina, they may as well have all been the same person visiting over and over again. Small but stocky women, with gray hair, dressed in black with thick stockings and low black oxford heels.

When not asking questions, Maria occupied her time at her Nonna's wake by eavesdropping on the guests as they whispered in corners and reporting everything she'd heard back to her mother. Maria repeated their words back to Nina, but she couldn't have understood the motives behind their gossip or known that some of their words would hurt her mother's feelings.

"Apparently, Arcangela had a weak heart, and they left her to live all alone in here," said the pharmacist under his breath.

"I heard she chose to stay in that house. She knew she wouldn't make it out alive! I always knew she was crazy," gossiped two housewives.

"All those kids and not one of them could have checked on their mother, saved her? The apple doesn't fall far from the tree, I suppose," mused the town lace maker.

"The way this happened now, during this war? Somebody must have put the *malocchio* on her," proclaimed the midwife.

By the last day of the viewing, Maria had more questions than gossip to deliver to her mother.

"Mamma, why does everyone spend more time talking to each other than they do to you and Zia?" asked Maria.

"Eh, Maria, even in the middle of a war, funerals are still a social gathering here in Sicily," said Nina.

On the 30th of the month, they finally laid Arcangela to rest. The extended family of siblings, aunts, uncles, and cousins all met at Rosina and Angelo's apartment on Via Orlando and began walking in procession behind the six black-suited pallbearers carrying Arcangela's humble coffin. In perfect step, they turned the corner onto Corso Umberto and were met with a waving Maria. The whole Sanfilippo family joined Rosina at the front of the procession.

Maria ran to Rosina and wrapped her arms around her thigh, causing her aunt to stumble, but also smile for a brief moment. They all slowly and solemnly continued through a demoralized Rocca Leone, picking up a few more mourners on their way to the family parish, *Maria S.S. Annunziata* church. It couldn't get much bleaker than a sparse funeral procession amidst war rubble. Twice they passed Arcangela's death announcement, along with dozens of others, posted on the side of buildings.

Nina felt unsettled by the meager turnout for the procession; it was smaller than she had hoped. It seemed like the town had begrudgingly come out to show their support during the viewing, but now Rocca Leone had washed their hands of Arcangela Tamburella. Rather than joining, neighbors and acquaintances had begun turning their backs or averting their eyes as the procession passed.

"Mamma, why are those people turning away? Aren't they Nonna's friends?" asked Maria.

"Maria, you'll learn that sometimes people only pretend to be your friend. It's times like this that we're able to tell the difference." Nina pulled her daughter closer to her, away from the townspeople, to the side of the road. Bending to one knee, she brushed Maria's soft cheek with a thumb. "If people do not want to associate with you, then you want nothing from them."

Arcangela was accustomed to being marginalized in life; Nina saw no reason for that change in death. As Nina moved slowly through her mother's funeral procession, she remembered being Maria's age, and hearing the whispers, seeing mothers squeeze their children's hands just a little tighter whenever her mother walked past.

Nina understood now that although marriage and family had eventually made the townspeople pretend to forgive Arcangela's past and treat her as a respectable woman, they'd never forget. In truth, it was her father, Giuseppe, whom they respected. After Nina's father died, the social contract had been magically severed, and everyone went back to shunning her mother. Once again, Arcangela became the mysterious dark figure to avoid.

"She deserved better; we all deserve better," said Nina, a sudden bitter taste in her mouth, as they turned the corner, arriving at the church.

Carmelo leaned in closer to Nina, "I bet your brothers in America aren't hiding in cellars. They don't have to bury their dead in the middle of a war. No, they're living the good life."

"So, what can we do?" retorted a distraught Nina, brushing him off.

"We leave everything behind, get on a goddamn ship and depart for *l'Merica!*" responded Carmelo without pausing for another breath.

Nina paused for just a second, but waved her hand and swatted him away, like a fly.

9

DOMENICO

MONTESCIANO, ABRUZZO
SEPTEMBER 1943

The sky over the countryside glowed pink in anticipation of autumn. Resting on the damp stone wall of the 17th-century *Chiesa Madonna delle Grazie*, Domenico once again tested the limits of his curfew and bemoaned the inevitably earlier sunset. The shorter September days were making him anxious. They meant less time to be enjoyed in nature, and more time spent in his German-occupied town. The only thing scarier than being caught breaking curfew by his mother would be getting caught by a Nazi.

He felt an uneasy rumble in his stomach and looked up to see a Heinkel He 111 German bomber, a large swastika painted on its tail fin, roaring through the evening sky. It flew so low it looked as if it would collide with the gray, weathered bell tower of the tiny church.

"Eh vaffanculo!" yelled Domenico over the roar of the engine.

Standing on his tiptoes, he gestured with his right fist in the crook of his elbow and his left forearm raised to the sky in defiance.

"Figli di puttana!" he continued, muttering an imaginative string of profanities at the sky until all that was left to curse were the fading white streaks of the condensation trails.

"You bastards already have my town, you can't have this place too! I won't let you take everything!" Domenico slouched back against the stone wall, sulking, determined to stay out as long as he could.

When Domenico finally arrived home, under the cloak of darkness that the countryside provided, he attempted to sneak past his mother. However, Pasqua had stayed up waiting for him in their dark kitchen. She sat perfectly still with only a small envelope on the table in front of her. They hadn't heard from his father for a full six months, the longest Emidio had gone without writing to his family since he'd left home four years earlier. The last they had heard, he'd been held in Rhodesia, in Southern Africa. Pasqua's letters to Emidio went unanswered, and some even came back stamped "Return To Sender" in red. They hoped he'd just been transferred, again. The alternative was just too painful to bear. With the fall of the Fascist regime and Italy's surrender to the Allies, Domenico eagerly awaited news from Emidio. Every day, he would wake up trying to convince himself, "Today's the day Papà will be released!"

"Mamma?" Domenico asked in a low voice, "What's happened?"

"You want to be treated as an adult, right?" Pasqua slid the envelope toward Domenico.

Domenico reached for the creased and stained envelope, covered in various postage and rubber stamps he didn't recognize.

"Or-orange Free State?" he slowly read aloud, confused.

"Africa? Is it Papà?" Domenico asked, trying hard not to get excited.

"Well, open it. I really can't do it, Mimi," said Pasqua, shaking her head.

Domenico carefully opened the envelope and began to read his father's letter aloud.

Cara Pasqua & boys,

It's been so long since my last letter, please forgive me. I've been shipped back and forth all over this continent ▓▓▓▓▓ I've been here in the south a month now, ▓▓▓▓▓ ▓▓▓▓▓ I'm back at work. I'm in a factory, making clothing for the ▓▓▓ I hope to send you some help soon.

Is it true what I'm hearing? Did we really surrender so easily?

▓▓ I'm sorry I don't have better news for you.

Domenico-I enclosed something for you, son. Please keep it safe for me. I've been warned I can no longer keep it here.

Love,
Emidio (Papà)

Domenico stood holding the photo that Emidio had enclosed in his letter, especially for him. A small black and white photo with scalloped edges of Il Duce, commemorating his rise to power.

"28 October 1922," Domenico's eyes hardened with anger.

"*Porco Dio*, this is what he's worried about?! I don't know what he thinks is happening here, but it's not the goddamn Roman Empire!" Domenico threw the photo on the table in disgust.

AS DAWN BROKE OVER the Gran Sasso mountains the next morning, still restless and agitated from his father's letter, Domenico couldn't stay in bed any longer. He quickly got dressed in yesterday's clothes that still sat rumpled at the foot of his bed. Attempting to avoid his family, he quietly left the apartment and ventured out into the eerily silent town. Domenico walked through the piazza and under the bell tower until he reached the tiny cobblestoned street he'd been born on, Porta Penta. He liked to revisit his parents' first home, which still held memories of his father, Emidio.

"Mimi!" whispered an echoed voice.

Domenico spun around, searching for the source of the voice, to face a large, shaded staircase nestled between two houses along the tiny winding road. Concealed by shadows, he barely recognized a small figure sitting on the top step alone. The profile was unmistakable–loose, unkempt curls and a downturned, pointed nose.

"Pepino? What are you doing here?" asked Domenico.

"I could ask you the same thing," retorted a cranky Pepino.

"I can't stand being in that house anymore!" Domenico said, and Pepino nodded in agreement, his face solemn.

"My father ran off with the *partigiani,* and the Fascists captured him. They'll probably kill him, those animals!" Pepino's voice trembled with fear and anger. He seemed to direct this comment right at Domenico.

"Are you saying my father is an animal? He may have been fighting with the Fascists, but now he's being imprisoned by *your people!*" The pitch of Domenico's voice grew as he finished the accusation.

Since the Allies had liberated Sicily, more and more Italian partisans were going to fight in the Apennine mountains. Pepino's father joined the Communist Garibaldi Brigades as a *partigiano* in the civil war against the Fascists and Nazis.

"The *partigiani* are the good guys! They're trying to do what the Italian army couldn't: protect the people and end the war. *My father's a hero!*" Pepino exclaimed proudly as if forgetting how angry he'd previously said he was at his father.

"No, my father is the hero–" Domenico stopped himself, exasperated. He didn't really believe his father to be a hero. He was so angry at his father that he wished he could be in those mountains with the *partigiani.*

"Listen, Pepino, we shouldn't be fighting. Both of our fathers left their families in this hellhole to go be heroes somewhere else. We're just the ones left here to suffer. Remember, when we decided we'd be friends even if our fathers said we weren't allowed?" Domenico pleaded.

The people you associated with in fascist Italy were a direct reflection of you. Last year, Domenico had sheepishly admitted to Pepino that his father had forbidden him to be friends with him.

"His father is a Communist!" Emidio had declared, seeing Communists as bitter political opponents and the most egregious offense to Italy. Pepino chuckled and finally divulged that his father had also forbidden him to hang around with Domenico for the sins of his father.

"His father is a Fascist! We don't break bread with Fascists!" Pepino snarled, mocking his father's bravado.

The two boys chatted a little more before Pepino hurried away to complete an errand for his mother. Now, the rest of the forlorn town had woken to another misty, gray morning when Domenico began to trudge back home. Through the low-hanging clouds, he could see sheep grazing the countryside below him. He felt better after his chance meeting with Pepino. He now had at least one other person that he could talk to, and that would understand what he was going through.

Maybe I will write Papà back today.

Domenico reminded himself that his father probably had no idea of the depth of suffering his family and Italians as a whole were experiencing at home, and the anger he felt toward him eased.

Domenico's plan, as always, was to sneak back home without his mother noticing he'd been gone. But as always, his plan would be foiled. He assumed everyone would still be asleep, so he crept up the stairs, making dramatic, slow, and drawn-out movements. As he opened his front door into the kitchen, he heard a commotion but couldn't see anyone. He stepped inside and found two small wooden kitchen chairs pulled out from under the table, facing each other as if two people had been in conversation.

They were definitely not like that when I left earlier.

"Who's there? Whoever's there, come out now!" demanded Domenico, mustering up his courage.

"Mimi, calm down and just listen to me, OK?" A familiar voice emerged from the darkness.

"Mamma? Are you OK? Who's here?" asked a panicked Domenico. Pasqua came around the corner alone slowly to confirm that Domenico had come alone.

"Mimi, I have to tell you something, something that I've kept from you. I need you to stay calm and quiet. And most importantly, don't get angry, and do not say a word until I've finished," urged Pasqua.

Pasqua turned back and motioned behind her. Domenico took a step back as two men, strangers, moved into the light.

"Mamma?!"

"Mimi, what did I tell you? Let me explain," started Pasqua.

"This is Sabatino and Ri-chard?" She looked to the foreign stranger for approval. The man nodded, "Yes."

"They need our help."

"But Mamma!"

"I said shut up; you'll get us all in trouble! *Zitto!* Sabatino and Richard will need a place to stay for a little while until they can find a safe way out. You just have to pretend they're not here and tell no one!"

"Why? Mamma, who the hell are they, and why do they need to hide?" asked Domenico.

"Sabatino is fighting with the *partigiani;* he and Richard were separated from his brigade in the mountains, but they managed to lose them in the hills and reached the edge of town," said Pasqua nervously.

"*Partigiani?* But Papà?!" Domenico was shocked that his mother would bring a partisan into their home. His father's home.

"The Nazis are more hellbent on revenge than ever; they believe the Italians betrayed them. Unfortunately, the damn Germans know who he is now. He needs a place to hide until they move on and forget about him," Pasqua tried to reason with Domenico.

"And now that the Nazis have broken Mussolini out of prison, who knows what will happen," warned Sabatino.

"What do you mean, broken out? He escaped? Is that true?" asked Domenico.

"That's what we're hearing. The Italian government was holding him right here in Abruzzo, in the mountains. The Nazis freed him and flew him out of Italy yesterday," said Sabatino.

Yesterday?

Domenico realized the plane with the swastika on the tail fin he saw the night before, probably carried Mussolini.

Glad I told him to vaffanculo!

Richard spoke slowly in a careful and measured combination of broken Italian and English, to say he was afraid he had caused the situation.

"If I weren't traveling with the brigade, they'd have stayed under the radar, safe."

"Nonsense! You had just as much right to be with the brigades as I did," Sabatino assured Richard.

Pasqua went on to explain, "Sabatino had been in the Royal Italian Army, the 6th Alpine division before the armistice. The *Alpini* were the perfect choice to join the *partigiani* because they were already experts familiar with navigating the mountain ranges."

"Since when do you care about politics? I thought that was a problem for men to solve?" Domenico asked sarcastically.

"I *don't* care about politics. I care about helping people. And I also don't care if your father would agree. Your father isn't here. He hasn't been here for four years, so he doesn't get a say in this! *Basta*!" Pasqua said, more assertively than Domenico was used to.

"And who the hell is this guy? Do you even know who he's fighting for?" asked Domenico.

Sabatino interjected, hoping to calm Domenico, "Richard was a POW, like your Papà. He'd also been captured in Africa, in Libya, by the Germans. Domenico, Richard is a British soldier. He was a prisoner in a camp here in Abruzzo, in Avezzano. After the armistice, the Italian officers abandoned their posts; they just left the camp with all the prisoners locked inside to starve. Many prisoners escaped before the Germans came in to take over. Richard endured a very arduous journey in escaping the Nazis. Wouldn't you do everything you could to get home to your family if you were in Richard's situation? Your father's situation?"

"You want to help a British soldier who fought in Africa? He could have been the one who captured Papà for all we know! *This is insane!*" Domenico added, losing his temper again.

"Domenico, Africa is a very large continent, and Libya is nowhere near Ethiopia," Sabatino attempted to rationalize with Domenico.

"So what do I do now?" Domenico asked, defeated.

"Mimi, you don't have to do anything. They will be using my room to sleep during the day when everyone else is awake, so we don't raise suspicions with any extra beds. At night, they'll be awake when we're asleep. They won't use any lights or candles at night, and they will *never* leave this house until they leave for good. It's only temporary," Pasqua assured him.

"Well, at least tell me we can use their ration tickets for extra food?"

"Absolutely not! No extra food can be purchased or acquired in any way. That will only raise suspicions. Do we understand each other, Mimi?"

"Yeah, sure, whatever, we'll all just starve together, I guess."

"You don't know everything about me, Domenico. Maybe if you did, you'd understand why I need to do this. *Coraggio, Mimi.*"

What the hell is that supposed to mean? She's my mother, what else is there to know about her?

Sabatino, a tall thin man of around thirty years old with a complexion darkened by the long days spent exposed to the harsh summer sun, wore a dirty red handkerchief around his neck, but he still traveled with the iconic feathered hat of the Alpini in his rucksack.

"Domenico, I understand you're scared, but please don't be angry with your mother. She's been very brave. You should be proud of her," said Sabatino.

Richard had walked two days from Avezzano through treacherous terrain before meeting Sabatino and his fellow resistance fighters near the Gran Sasso mountains. The Alpini turned *partigiani* had collected some pieces of clothing to give Richard so he could finally get out of his old uniform pants and hide his very conspicuous blond hair with a black wool hat. Richard piped in softly, trying really hard to speak all his words in his limited Italian.

"I am very grateful for help, Domenico. We hiding for little while now, and I think we got good at it. We promise you not notice us."

Domenico realized more and more, every day, that absolutely nothing was under his control as long as this war raged. So, with this latest indignation, he simply sighed and said quietly once again, "OK, whatever you want, Mamma."

10

STELLA

BROOKLYN, NEW YORK
FEBRUARY 2020

The window shade made a sharp snapping sound as the morning light hit the burnt umber walls and bathed the whole living room in the richest of warm tones.

"Michael! Stop. That's too bright!"

"Stella, you haven't eaten in two days. And I can't even remember the last time you showered. You need to take a break from this; it's absolutely consuming you."

"Shhh. I know I'm on the verge of discovering some really important information, something big. If I take a break now, I'll lose my train of thought, all this momentum. I've just written to the Red Cross, but what I'm really hoping for is an answer from the Vatican. The secret archives."

I looked up from my laptop screen and squinted at Michael. "I was in this chat room yesterday, and they said the real information is kept at the Vatican. How long do you think I should wait until I write them again, a follow-up?"

"The Vatican. Seriously, Stella? Just, please promise me you won't uncover some huge Catholic plot to kill the Pope or hide Mary Magdalene's bloodline. Oh! Let me know if you come up with any leads on the Holy Grail, though."

"Hilarious. Yes, the Vatican. It might be the only way to find out what happened to my grandfather. I mean, why did he remain imprisoned for so long after the armistice and even after the war ended?

"Why don't you just call Zio Donato? You can chat with him some more about all that family stuff."

"I think Zio's already told me all he knows–the events he witnessed in Abruzzo and the vague details that my grandfather shared in letters home. He was so young, even younger than my dad. Anyway, he's an old man now, and I don't really want to keep dredging up all these bad memories for him."

"OK, well, I wish you luck then." He kissed my forehead and headed for the front door. "Oh, and Mary Magdalene's bloodline *was* the Holy Grail, Michael!" I yelled out after him, hearing the door close before I could finish my sentence.

As I languished on the couch, cross-legged, in the same sweatpants and Bauhaus T-shirt that I'd been wearing for three days, I realized I had exhausted all my resources in the search for answers about my grandfather, Emidio. I was distracted by the strand of greasy hair that insisted on falling out of the messy bun sitting at the top of my head.

"Ugh, maybe I do need a shower and a change of clothes today?"

I grabbed a small plastic tube from the coffee table and slowly began to spit whatever saliva my dehydrated mouth could produce into it as I checked my email for the tenth time that morning. I'd written countless emails, in two languages, that I knew would never be answered. I'd requested documents from foreign countries and organizations that would see me as the lowest of priorities. I'd endured the parts of social media I'd long abandoned to join POW groups and follow pages dedicated to a small town in the Gran Sasso mountains that I've never had the pleasure of visiting. And as soon as I got my saliva to reach that little line on the tube, I would also be waiting for a genealogy DNA test in hopes that the results could help to narrow my search for ancestral names and documents, or even long-lost ancestors.

The mystery photo had opened up a real yearning to understand my family history, something I'd never really cared about before, and neither of my parents was now around to help. Great timing, I knew, but my desire to establish as much context as I could for exploring both sides of my family during WWII was an itch that needed some serious scratching.

Unfortunately, I needed some answers before I could pose more questions–I had a great deal of waiting to do. Patience had never been a quality I possessed. I'd always been more of an instant gratification kind of person. Until I had some new information to work with, I had to occupy my time researching and building a family tree for both sides of my family. There was certainly no shortage of questions on my mother's side. I always thought that I had a pretty firm grasp on the people and places I came from. I realized that I had accepted their Cliff Notes versions, but probably never asked the right questions. I knew absolutely nothing about any of my great-grandparents, not even their names. I'd always assumed that my parents' belief systems were passed down to them like heirlooms, that they were identical to their ancestors.

"What if they adopted some of their beliefs despite their ancestors? Hadn't I done just that?"

I'd always considered myself the outsider, both in my family and in the conservative Italian American community as a whole. I was the baby of the family–the little cousin in art school–always trying to register them to vote or ruin their new favorite song by telling them it was actually an anti-fascist anthem. I was the weirdo. I'd struggled to see eye to eye with them on most everything. To my horror, some of them even pined for fascist times. My uncles goaded me–a self-righteous teenager–into fights about politics. But what if they were the outsiders? What if somewhere in my family tree there existed a long line of passionate *partigiani* and *brigante*– resistance fighters?

My email notification chimed.

Much to everyone's disappointment, I had taken considerably more time off than I had originally anticipated. I hesitated to check my email, hoping it wasn't my work attempting to intrude on my ancestral research.

"Zonderwater!" I shouted with excitement when I finally worked up the courage to glance at my inbox.

I'll bet that's the first time anyone has been that excited to hear from an internment camp.

Zonderwater had been the largest and most famous of the prisoner of war camps in South Africa during WWII. Almost every

Italian soldier who'd been captured anywhere in Africa passed through Zonderwater at some point in their imprisonment.

Of course, everyone except my grandpa!

> *Dear Ms. Stella Fiorinelli,*
>
> *Unfortunately, I could not find any evidence of your grandfather, Fiorinelli, Emidio anywhere in our records. I would advise you to inquire with the International Red Cross.*
>
> *They hold all the records concerning POW captures and movements.*
>
> *Best regards,*
> *Ignazio Testa*

"Does that mean he definitely wasn't at Zonderwater, or that they couldn't find a record of him there? Those seem like two different things," I muttered.

I immediately wrote back with a succession of questions I'd already prepared.

"Is there any possibility that his records are missing, but he did pass through Zonderwater?

What are other possible camps that he may have been in?

Why would an Italian POW be interned so long after Italy had joined the Allies in

WWII?"

Less than five minutes later, my inbox lit up again with a response email from Signore Testa. He had sent me a strange, long copy and paste of every movement my grandfather made during the years of his imprisonment. The name of every camp that interned him, every ship that carried him—the whole timeline, with the corresponding dates. A looping itinerary taking him from Addis Ababa to Berbera to Durban, South Africa, to Rhodesia, then back to South Africa–this time in Koffiefontein, and then to Rhodesia yet again, with a final layover in Beira, Mozambique, before departing for Naples. This was it, my grandpa's entire journey!

This was brilliant, and I had visions of it all mapped out on a giant wall board in my office, a web of red string connecting all the important places and moments. All my questions would be answered. I was over the moon and celebrated by dancing around my couch. Then I read the closing part of the email.

"I've given you all I can. This case needs to be dealt with through the Red Cross. Please do not contact us again."

Ignazio Testa

Something didn't feel right.

Why would he tell me he didn't have any further information when he clearly had the details of Emidio's journey all cued up? What the hell did he find in those records that would cause him to cut all communication with me, a POW's family member? All these questions inevitably raised new ones, but would I find the answers?

11

DOMENICO

MONTESCIANO, ABRUZZO
SEPTEMBER 1943

The new school year had started the week prior, and Domenico had just begun his last year of primary school. As he woke up on Tuesday morning, Domenico didn't see much point in following anybody's rules anymore. There were potentially dangerous strangers living in his home; meanwhile, Nazi boots were marching on Italian cobblestones. Allied bombs were landing on Italian cities, British tanks rolling up the Italian Adriatic coast, and Fascists hunting partisans, partisans hunting Fascists. It was becoming neighbor vs. neighbor–civil war.

"*Ma vaffanculo!*" grumbled Domenico as he balled up his school smock and dunked it into the wastebasket.

Pasqua, not missing a beat, as she walked past, said, "Oh, good. If you're not going to school, then you'll stand on the ration lines for me today. We haven't had any meat in a month."

"But Mamma–"

"Don't let him get away with selling you bones. That butcher must be a communist or something. Bones he sells! Make sure there's some meat on them," said Pasqua, stuffing their ration ticket into Domenico's shirt pocket with the hint of a smile.

Domenico gathered a tattered notebook, a pocket knife, and a pencil that had been whittled down to its last two inches. His belly hollow with hunger, he dragged himself through the piazza and around the corner to the butcher's shop on Via Milano as if walking to his own execution. It was already 8:00 am, practically closing time for rations, and the line was already twenty people long.

This is a waste of time, the Germans already ate everything.

Domenico wasn't far off. The Germans took all the edible food, leaving the townspeople with what amounted to pig slop. While families couldn't even get rations of black bread and the dreadful faux coffee made of ground barley, the Germans sat in Montesciano's coffee bars, enjoying real espresso and warm pastries. He surveyed the area around Via Milano, an instinct whenever he was in a public space. It was under heavy surveillance by the well-fed German Wehrmacht.

He joined the end of the line and, not so patiently, waited. He rolled his eyes as the women in front of him groaned and gossiped. They side-eyed every patron with anxiety and envy as they exited with wrapped bundles tied with string. Each bundle seemed to shrink smaller and smaller than the previous. The starvation-level rations that the Italians were subsisting on, some of the lowest in Europe, were making everyone a bit desperate.

Only those lucky enough to afford some extra provisions on

the black market were able to live without the fear of not knowing where their next meal would come from.

"Finalmente!" sighed Domenico when it was finally his turn. He stepped into the shop, feeling queasy as the combined smell of meat and blood hit his nostrils. Luigi, the butcher, almost looked relieved to see a young boy standing before him, last in line, rather than another *casalinga* at her wits' end. Domenico, with his frail frame and dejected expression, seemed to evoke just the right amount of pity in Luigi. He plunked down a small bag of meat scraps you might hesitate to feed to your dog, and a paltry little nub of prosciutto on the counter.

"That's it, kid. That's everything."

Domenico felt panicked. His mother definitely wasn't going to appreciate his efforts today.

"C'mon! How are we supposed to survive on this? You must have some more, a secret stash maybe!" begged Domenico.

"Shut up! Are you trying to get me killed? That's it! That's everything! *Get out*!" growled Luigi in a gruff whisper, desperate not to attract the unwanted attention of the Germans. But, even in silence, the impassioned hand gestures from both parties would be enough to give them away. A German began to approach the butcher shop. Domenico and the butcher both froze.

"Pretend everything is fine. We were simply having a spirited conversation, OK?!" Luigi desperately instructed Domenico.

"*Si, si.* Everything is fine." Domenico grabbed his bag of meat scraps and attempted to make his way to the exit. A Wehrmacht soldier wearing jackboots and a gray-green wool tunic jacket, carrying a Karabiner rifle, appeared before him, blocking his exit.

"What is going on here? What is this argument about?" asked the German sternly.

"Oh no, everything is OK. Nobody's arguing. The boy just purchased the last of my cuts for the day," said Luigi nervously.

"It's not enough!" said Domenico impulsively.

"And why on earth would you need more food, young man? You're lucky to get even that slop. You traitors are taking food out of the mouths of our troops. As we're the only ones working hard around here, we deserve all the food in this town," said the German, looking at Domenico with disgust.

"Right. I'll just take my bag and go home now. I don't need–I'll just go," Domenico rambled, shaking with fear. Domenico felt as if the German's cold eyes followed him all the way home.

―

As Pasqua made a meager broth from the meat scraps Domenico brought home, there was a thunderous rapping on the door. It was almost dinner time. Everyone was home, including their illicit guests. Pasqua swung open her bedroom door to warn Richard and Sabatino, huddled on the floor in a corner.

"Get under the bed. Now!" she hissed, wanting to make sure they were tucked away as much as possible.

She tried to keep her boys in their room, but Domenico, of course, refused and insisted on answering the door himself. He made a tight fist with his left hand as he opened the door with his right hand. His stomach dropped at the sight of the German from the butcher shop. The soldier had an annoyed scowl on his face, his fist suspended in mid-air, as if about to bang on their door once more. Domenico was stunned.

Is he here to take me away?

He hadn't thought the altercation earlier was that serious. Pasqua, standing at the stove with her dishcloth still slung over one shoulder, gave the German a worried look as he glanced at the dishes laid out on the table.

"Three?" he asked suspiciously, tracing a large chip in one of the plates with his finger.

Pasqua nodded.

"I only see two, *zwei*," he remarked, holding up two fingers and pointing them back and forth at Domenico and Pasqua as if making accusations.

"Yes, three. My son, Donato," answered Pasqua.

"Where is he?" the soldier asked in his heavily accented Italian.

Pasqua motioned into the dark, narrow hallway toward her boys' bedroom.

"Well? Bring me the boy! Oh, Donato!" taunted the German.

"He has nothing to do with this. Leave him–"

"Domenico!" roared Pasqua. "It's OK, Donato, come out."

Donato sheepishly stepped out of the shadow of the hallway and hid behind his mother.

"So this is the whole family, huh? Nobody else is staying here?"

"No," everyone nodded in unison.

"No? You're not hiding any of your filthy criminals or communists?" he asked, scanning the room for any possible clues.

"Don't you have a father, boy?"

"My papà is in the war, he's in Africa. I'm the man of the house!" Domenico said defiantly.

"Africa? There's no more war in Africa. You mean he's a loser, a prisoner."

Domenico stood up perfectly straight and clenched both fists at his sides. The German's arrogance was forcing Domenico's temper dangerously close to the surface.

"Ahh, yes," said the German as he sauntered over to the stove. "Dinner? Is this the slop you were fighting with the butcher about today?"

Pasqua gave Domenico another familiar side-eye glance as if asking, "What have you done now?"

Their uninvited guest picked up the metal ladle and stuck it into the pot, stirring the broth as if looking for something. Then he pushed the edge of the pot, sending the contents spilling all over the floor.

"Oops. Well, it was going to taste like trash anyway," he said smugly as the family stood helpless.

"Now, get out of my way. I'm going to have a good look around this poor excuse for a–"

As the ground shook, a cacophony of frenzied screams, explosions, and roaring airplane engines rang out all over town.

"Scheiße!" growled the German, aborting his civilian harassment to investigate the chaos outside. His curiosity, more like

maliciousness, had gotten the better of him, and he'd abandoned his post, leaving the road into the square vulnerable. Just before the door slammed behind him, Domenico saw that the townspeople were gathering together.

"How many people can say their lives were saved by a bombing?" said Domenico.

He knew they had all just narrowly escaped certain death, but that would only be temporary if those explosions came any closer. He ran out onto the balcony, quickly joined by Donato and Pasqua. The sun was so low in the sky, it appeared to be suspended at eye level as they huddled together. It was barely evening; the sky was a deep shade of blue without a single cloud in the sky. Domenico kept his little brother close as they watched giant aircraft, B-24 bombers, circling and flying back toward the south. The relentless whistles and explosions continued as plumes of smoke filled the skies to the south. It became clear that Montesciano wasn't their target today.

"What if they come back for us, Mimi? What if we're next?" Donato whispered to his big brother.

"It's OK. I'll protect you and Mamma," Domenico reassured him.

"Maybe it's Pippo!" said Donato excitedly.

"Pippo? What the hell is Pippo?" Domenico asked, brushing off his little brother.

"Pippo! The plane, or maybe the UFO that comes every night. It looks inside our windows or drops messages for us in the country–"

"Come on, stop. That's just a kid's story. That's not real. This is a war, Donato, a real war! Those bombs, wherever they landed, just killed real people!" snapped Domenico.

"Everyone at school has been talking about Pippo. If you would show up to school sometimes, maybe you'd know all about it," argued Donato. Domenico just rolled his eyes.

"Just wait, he'll get what's coming to him! They all will," Pasqua proclaimed prophetically. She hadn't taken her eyes off the German since he ran scared out of their apartment. Her gaze followed him as he scurried through the piazza like a chicken with its head cut off, satisfied that he was at least off their backs for tonight.

"Get inside! Under the table, now! Nobody leaves this house tonight. Nobody leaves my sight for the rest of the night!" Pasqua warned her sons, still squeezing them close to her.

"Trouble always seems to find you, huh? As soon as this is all over tonight, you're both helping me clean up this mess!" She looked at both of them, but Domenico knew her final words had been directed at him.

"Mimi! Pippo's here, outside!" whispered Donato, trying desperately to wake Domenico.

"I told you to stop that nonsense!" Domenico snapped back.

Donato was insistent. He grabbed Domenico by the shoulder and dragged him, groggy and grumpy, over to their bedroom window. Donato opened the left shutter, just a crack. There he was, Pippo was real. A low, slow-moving craft that made a strange staccato buzzing sound as it patrolled. Neither brother could find any distinguishable marks or emblems that could signify Pippo's allegiance. But the unsettling, eerie feeling they were experiencing was definitive.

As Pippo vanished into the night sky–in reality an Allied single-engine fighter-bomber, Domenico and Donato decided in unison, "Germans."

When Donato finally fell back asleep, Domenico took the opportunity to sneak into the kitchen to talk to Sabatino. He wanted to know more about him. Becoming a partigiano went against everything Domenico was taught and everything he thought he knew, but he liked Sabatino.

"*Scusi* Domenico, did we wake you?" Sabatino asked.

"No, no. I just couldn't sleep. Umm–but I wanted to ask you about something–umm–what do you do with the partigiani?"

"I'm not sure your mother would want me talking to you about this stuff."

"No, I can handle it. Look around, nothing here is appropriate for kids anymore," Domenico said with a sweeping motion of his hand.

"You're right. You shouldn't have to experience any of this tragedy. That's part of the reason I joined the partigiani and the resistance. I have a young daughter, and another child on the way. I never want them to grow up like I did, like you are now. I fight in the places that the military can't get to, and in ways that they are not permitted. We have to fight ruthlessly because brutality is all our enemies–these Nazis and Fascists–know. I fight with the Allies because my enemy's enemy is now my friend. Do you understand Domenico?"

"I think I do. You know, I think you're really brave. And–I'm sorry if I was mean to you when you arrived. It all scared me at first. I'm still scared," Domenico said.

"Friends?" asked Sabatino, holding out his hand.

"Yes, friends."

―

Domenico had a plan to avoid having to stand in any ration lines again today. That hadn't ended well for anyone yesterday. He was still shaken, both from the unwanted dinner guest and the bombings they had witnessed in broad daylight, but he wanted to share stories about Pippo. He had to go to school.

Domenico and Donato passed the tobacco shop on their way; a group of pensioner men were clamoring to get their hands on newspapers and whispering to each other. The Italian public wasn't presented with many choices when it came to journalism. After twenty years of Fascism and now German occupation, Italians hadn't enjoyed much freedom of the press.

Domenico got close enough to read one man's *Corriere del Giorno* headline: *Allies bomb Pescara. 1000 Dead!*

"Allies? The bombs, the planes. They were Americans?" Domenico's heart sank.

Sandwiched between the German Gustav Line and Gothic Line, the Abruzzese were sitting ducks for the enemy, but lately the line between enemy and ally felt a bit blurry.

"The Allies are more barbaric than the Germans!" proclaimed one white haired man propping himself up with a splintered cane.

"I served in the Great War. War isn't pretty. They did what they had to do to get those damn *Tedeschi*!" said a hunched farmer in rebuttal.

It seemed the only males left in town these days were old men or boys—no one in between. With nothing to do and nowhere left to go, the town elders could be found gathering at the newsstand to swap old war stories or just to complain.

The Italians had led his father into war. The British captured and imprisoned him. The Germans were occupying his country and terrorizing his town. The Americans felt like Domenico's final hope.

Is there anyone left to bring Papà home?

Domenico picked up a discarded early edition newspaper left on the bench, rolled it up, and put it under his arm.

"Donato, wait here. I forgot something, I'll be right back," he instructed his brother.

Domenico ran back up to his apartment and pulled a book out of his bundle of schoolbooks. He tied the book and the newspaper together with some twine. Then he carefully ripped the bottom corner of a page from the back of his book, taking care not to tear any words. He scrawled a note for Sabatino.

For when you get lonely.
Your friend,
Domenico

Time went by with no real news on land or from the skies. The first snow, already visible on the peaks of the Gran Sasso mountains, announced the cold season. The townspeople had learned to keep score on the war based on how sadistic the Nazis were toward the civilians on any given day. Even when the newspapers didn't print the latest news, you could always gauge the level of loss or humiliation the Nazis had suffered. The accounts of Germans exacting revenge for the deeds of Italian anti-Fascist and partisans by rounding up and executing random Italian civilians were what made Domenico the most nervous. They were still hiding Sabatino and Richard in their home.

The anxiety ate at Domenico, and he couldn't help but replay the terrifying memory of the sadistic Wehrmacht soldier terrorizing his home on a never-ending loop in his head: the dinner that he'd waited in line for hours to purchase, violently splashing all over the kitchen. He shuddered at the memory of that terrifying German slowly approaching his mother's bedroom door, the only thing standing between them and their crimes. He had come so dangerously close to discovering Sabatino and Richard. Or them having to kill the German outside Domenico's bedroom door.

If it weren't for the bombing striking at the perfect time to distract him, they'd most likely all be dead or imprisoned, or still have a major problem on their hands. He just couldn't understand why his mother was willing to take such a risk. He admittedly considered them friends now, which meant he'd be just as concerned about their fate as he was about that of his family if they were discovered, but he wished they'd never appeared at their door.

Domenico repeated to himself to stop it, slapping the side of his head to rid himself of such images, those intrusive thoughts of him and his family dead.

Pasqua called him inside, jarring Domenico out from his latest rumination, and with clenched fists for courage, he joined his mother in the kitchen.

"Mimi, I need to talk to you about something important."

"Is it Papà? Is–is he OK? Is he coming home?"

"No, nothing like that. I think the best way to keep everyone safe is if you and your brother go to Bisenti to live with your Nonna, be out in the countryside for a little while–"

"You're sending me away? To live with her? *No!*"

"Don't break my heart, Mimi. They have more food; they have land to grow crops. They have animals for meat."

"If the Germans haven't already taken those away. Again, no, Mamma. Absolutely not!"

"I'm doing this for you. It's the only way we can all survive this. We have no food, Mimi. Winter's almost here, and it'll only get worse. Be reasonable."

"Can't we sell something? Then we can buy food on the black market. There has to be a way!" begged Domenico.

"I have nothing to sell, Mimi! The only thing of value I ever owned was my wedding ring, and Mussolini took that already. If I had known he would take my husband, I would have at least kept my ring to remember him by," Pasqua said mournfully.

What once felt patriotic now felt shameful. Domenico remembered the stories of the big event in the town square, where all the wives in town donated their gold wedding bands to Mussolini to support Italy's invasion of Ethiopia. Events like this happened simultaneously all over the country. Everyone made a big deal about Queen Elena donating her wedding ring.

As Domenico pleaded his case to his mother, there was a knock on the door. They sat frozen, with their hearts in their mouths. This time, Pasqua wouldn't allow her son to deal with any intruders, and she signaled for him to stay put. She stood up slowly and quietly made her way to the door. As Pasqua peeled the door open a crack, Domenico felt a cool breeze slipping in.

"Hello," she said cautiously to the uniformed stranger standing at her door–but not that kind of uniform. He wasn't military. He stood holding a box.

"Fiorinelli, Pasqua?" asked the stranger.

"*Sì*, I'm Pasqua."

"Sign here, please," said the stranger, and he was gone.

"The postman? Who the hell would be sending me a package?" muttered Pasqua.

"It's Papà!" exclaimed Domenico

"Papà? How could it be Papà? He's a prisoner, he has nothing," his mother said dismissively.

Domenico ran around the table and grabbed the package, ripping it open.

"*I told you! It's from Papà!*" Domenico rejoiced, waving a postcard in his hand.

He read it aloud, and a perplexed expression clouded his still young face.

"Every cloud has a silver lining. That's all it says."

"Great, he's a poet now," Pasqua muttered as she rummaged through the box to discover a pristinely tailored men's navy blue wool sport jacket.

"What the hell does he expect me to do with this! Nobody in this house can wear this, what a waste!" Pasqua threw all the contents back into the box and tossed it aside.

As Pasqua tried desperately to fall asleep and relax her body, her mind went into overdrive. She couldn't shake the feeling that the jacket and postcard meant something–something much more than they'd been able to understand earlier.

"I didn't marry an idiot!" she thought excitedly as she sprung out of bed to go retrieve the box.

"Every cloud has a silver lining," she read to herself over and over. "The lining! *Oh God!*"

Pasqua hurried barefoot into the kitchen and grabbed a knife. Back in her bedroom, she carefully popped each stitch on the jacket's lining. She nearly passed out as, one by one, lira notes were revealed behind the silky lining. Large denominations she'd never even seen before. 100,000 Lira notes, a dizzying amount of them. She tore the rest of the lining away in one fell swoop and stood staring at her windfall.

I'll have to hide this away or use it to buy black market food and supplies. How could I explain this money to the local shopkeepers? They'd turn me in for sure.

Then Pasqua had an idea.

Early the next morning, as the sun made the frost on the olive leaves sparkle, Pasqua was already awake, finalizing her plan. She woke the boys and gathered her guests, Richard and Sabatino, in the kitchen.

"I've come to a decision that I think benefits everybody."

Sabatino and Richard shifted awkwardly in their seats, looking like they felt they may no longer be welcome.

"I just want to thank you for everything you've–" started Sabatino.

"Please, let me finish, Sabatino."

"Mimi, remember what we talked about yesterday?"

"Yes." Domenico nodded somberly.

"I have a better plan now. You don't have to worry about going away anymore."

"Sabatino. Richard. I want to continue to help you, but I think I have a better place for you–only 15 km south of here–in Bisenti. My husband's family still has an old house in a tucked-away district. You would be surrounded by our friends and family. They're good people–helpful people," Pasqua said with a wink. "They have land to grow food, raise animals. But most importantly, fewer Nazis."

"But we don't have anything, neither money for travel, nor anything to barter," said Sabatino, looking stunned by this offer. Pasqua held out her hand, which concealed four banknotes, two for each of her guests. "This should help."

Richard could tell by Sabatino's expression that it was very generous, and Sabatino stumbled on his words.

"But we couldn't–I mean–I want to work for this, how did you get this money?"

"From my husband." Pasqua chuckled. "Emidio sent a parcel, the money hidden inside. I know from his letters that he has been working. They let the prisoners work inside, sometimes even outside, the camps. My husband came through. I had almost stopped believing in him, and Him," Pasqua said as she pointed up toward the sky.

"Thank you, Pasqua. Thank you so much." Richard's Italian pronunciation had gotten much better over the last few weeks. Pasqua was happy that she'd been able to teach him something–also that he might be able to pass as Italian if they were stopped on their journey.

*****

Since the autumn equinox, on September 23rd that year, the days gifted their hours to the night. The extended darkness made planning and executing an escape by the end of the month that much easier. Domenico and Donato were getting ready for bed, but Pasqua busied herself with every last detail of the escape she'd planned for Sabatino and their new English friend. They had money, directions, a cover story if necessary, extra clothes plucked from hers and Emidio's closets, and of course, some of the black-market crusty bread and salami she'd finally plucked up courage to purchase.

After brushing his teeth, Domenico slipped into his bedroom and rummaged under the bed. He pulled out his old notebook he used for sketches, ripped out two pages, and neatly signed each of them, before handing one each to Sabatino and Richard.

"When I'm older, I'm going to study art in Paris. If we all make it out of this war, these sketches could be worth something someday!" Domenico beamed.

Sabatino and Richard looked down to see their own faces come to life from the thin pencil lines and rich shading staring back at them from Domenico's parting gifts. Portraits that he secretly had drawn of his brave friends. Now it was time.

Piazza Vittorio Emmanuele was much too big and heavily surveilled, so the front door was not an option. Pasqua quietly led them down the stairs, into a vacant ground-floor apartment. As they hurried through the empty kitchen toward the back door, Pasqua could already smell crisp autumn air mixed with the damp moss growing between each small cobblestone. She opened the door onto the much quieter back road before pausing to give her friends one last look. One at a time, she grabbed Sabatino and Richard's coat lapels, closing them tighter to keep them warm.

"In bocca al lupo!" Pasqua whispered her wishes of good luck to Sabatino and Richard before sending them on their way.

12

STELLA

**BROOKLYN, NEW YORK
MARCH 2020**

The lanky, floppy-haired barista placed a second espresso cup on my table and looked at the uneaten croissant he had left there two hours ago.

"Is everything OK, ma'am?"

"No, it's definitely not," I said.

I didn't mean to say that out loud. And ma'am. Seriously? When did I start looking my age? I never should have stopped dyeing my hair.

I looked up to find him still there, looking at me.

"Oh, uh, yeah. I'm fine. Sorry, I keep forgetting to eat," I said.

I had sent away my DNA test in case it could help me find any surprises that my grandfather had left behind. A secret war child or family that knew his side of the story. I knew how crazy a wish that was, but my search for family history had become, according to Michael, a full-fledged obsession.

Since I received my DNA results two days ago, I kept coming back to stare at all the little blocks of colors representing the different pieces that came together to create me, trying to decide what it could all possibly mean. Southern Italy and the Mediterranean dominated the mix, but my results also came back 10% Egyptian and 1% Icelandic. They were beginning to feel like wild guesses.

Greece, the Balkans were no surprise. Egypt shouldn't have been a surprise, Northern Africa had a large influence on the culture and people of Sicily. Iceland though, that seemed totally out of left field. In the time that it took to down my espresso shot, I discovered that my DNA could be traced back to a Vendel Viking from the 9th century. By some accounts, the Vikings may have sailed to Sicily at about that time, so that mystery was solved, I suppose. However, this Egyptian DNA on my mother's side seemed too substantial to be from a distant relative. I knew where I needed to start this investigation.

"Are you a writer?" asked the same concerned barista towering over my table as he picked up my empty cups.

"What? A writer? Uh, no," I responded with confusion. "Wait, why?"

"Oh, sorry. It's just that a lot of customers come here to write, and I've seen you here, totally engrossed in your work, for the last few days. I thought, maybe you were a writer. But never mind, none of my business. Sorry." He walked away, trying to hide his flushed face.

Engrossed. Is that another way to say I look like I'm losing my mind?

I pondered, trying to figure out why people felt the need to speak to me at all. Just yesterday, a woman sat down next to me and regaled me with tales of her co-op board for twenty minutes. I hate that I'll never get that time back. I shouldn't have snapped at the barista. I have been a bit paranoid lately. I suppose it's a symptom of shutting myself off from the rest of the world for the last two months.

Left without any new leads about my grandfather to look into, I'd spent the last couple of days building a family tree. I'd made some great progress. Following the Southern Italian convention of firstborn sons being named after their paternal grandfathers, I flew through about three centuries of great-grandparents. I easily connected parents and children, husbands and wives, and brothers and sisters. Then the information dried up a bit in the 17th century, sending me back to staring at DNA segments and chromosomes as if I actually understood them.

Stella, you haven't reviewed your DNA matches yet. Find others that share your DNA here …

The notification banner flashed at the top of my phone screen. The genealogy site had reminded me of this twice already, but I had purposely put it off. I suddenly didn't feel prepared to discover a long-lost relative. I needed to brace myself for that sort of life upheaval. But I had grown impatient for answers.

"Oh well, here goes," I mumbled.

At the top of the list, I spotted a few familiar faces, cousins, and second cousins that I grew up with, so no surprises there. As I scrolled through five pages of matches, I still couldn't believe how many others around the world shared tiny slivers of my ancestral lineages.

I now found myself somewhere in the 4th-6th cousins category. Most likely too distant to be relevant. I jumped back to the first page to take a closer look at my cousins' profiles to see if they had created any trees that could fill in any of the blanks for me. The fourth DNA match down the list was Sabrina Leonforte, my second cousin on my mother's side–my Nonna and her Nonna were sisters. I hadn't seen her since my wedding fifteen years ago, when she got completely wasted on limoncello shots and told everyone on the dance floor she loved them.

Half-second cousin! What the hell is a half-second cousin?

I looked through her family tree: she'd only added immediate family, her parents, siblings, and grandparents. Nothing that would help me.

If we were half-second cousins, then her mother and my mother were really half-first cousins, and our Nonnas were only half-sisters? I broke it all down in my mind, fully aware that it probably looked as if I was talking to myself. Then I was ...

"Holy shit!"

Everyone in the cafe turned to look at me, including the young, flushed-faced barista who was now convinced I was, in fact, not OK.

Juggling my laptop, notebooks, and tote bag, I yanked my phone charger from the wall and quickly headed for the door. Two people were practically falling over themselves to grab my table–after all, it was near an outlet, and it also came with a free croissant. I figured if I continued having outbursts, I should probably be in the privacy of my own home.

My phone chimed unrelentingly with notifications as I attempted to power walk home. They were all Michael sending me a series of links and posts. He caught my attention with a cute and ridiculous video of a cat's meow that sounded remarkably like *buongiorno*. He immediately followed with a video of an Italian American saying *gabagool* with exaggerated hand gestures, just to aggravate me. I guess you could say it's our love language, small gestures to let the other know we're thinking about them, even if we couldn't have an actual conversation at that moment.

I looked up from my phone to see two attractive twenty-year-olds dressed in outfits straight out of my 90s and Y2K reject piles walking toward me.

Shit! How do I always do this?

I was so distracted that I had walked in the wrong direction for ten minutes and ended up in one of the more avant-garde neighborhoods of Brooklyn. The neighborhood I would have absolutely loved to live in at twenty years old. However, now the whole neighborhood looked like a marketing campaign, with beautiful people making videos of themselves detailing their latest designer thrift store scores. I even stumbled upon a college student photographing social media content for her very clearly handmade facemasks constructed from vintage concert T-shirts.

I finally made it home, after my detour, to my geriatric and painfully uncool neighborhood, where my large love-starved cat greeted me at the door.

"Jesus, Anubis, I've only been gone for three hours!" He clumsily began to scale my body, demanding to be picked up and held like a baby, a twenty-pound fur baby. Looking out my back door at the thawing ground, I realized I was comfortable with being uncool as long as I had this garden where I could grow my tomatoes, zucchini, basil, and rosemary every summer. There were some traditions I just couldn't break.

"Anubis, I need to put you down now. I have work to do." He dug his claws deeper into my shoulder to hold on as I tried to place him on the top rung of his cat tree. "C'mon! I may have just found something really important—a family secret."

More like a family scandal in my frustratingly straight-laced family.

How could they have kept this a secret all this time? Or maybe nobody except my great-grandparents knew of the secret?

Still wrapped in my black trench coat, I fell onto the green velvet couch that had become an extension of me, with my laptop. I resembled some sort of modern Columbo crossed with The Matrix reboot, but it felt more like a mysterious teen drama.

If I could get the full names of all nine of Nonna's siblings, I could search for their birth certificates, hopefully confirming their parents' names. It had become clear that one of my Nonna's siblings had a different father than the rest, but who? Nervous energy surged through my body. I needed to calm down if I expected to get anywhere with the methodical and most likely boring research I would need to accomplish today. I needed to start with my great-grandmother, Arcangela Tamburella. If I could find all the birth certificates that listed her unique name as mother, I would be on my way to some answers.

Arcangela had such a striking name that it almost didn't sound real, but I realized that I hailed from lineages with absolutely stunning collections of unique and meaningful names. It was as if when the Southern Italians left their country to immigrate to North America, they only packed a handful of now commonplace names with which to cross the ocean. Names that had been passed down, used, and reused so often, they're now just simply American.

I'D WITNESSED THE SUN set, rise, and set again from this exact sunken spot on my couch. Five genealogy site subscriptions and twenty-four hours later, I had only been able to find records for eight of Arcangela's ten children. Notably, my Nonna Nina's birth record was among the missing. I found it ironic and irritating that I couldn't find any information on the child I'd been closest to, the one I thought I knew everything about. My Nonna was like a second mother to me—even a best friend during some of my awkward pre-teen years.

So, what am I missing? Why is she the ghost? And why is there nobody left to help answer these questions for me?

My phone pinging with a message from Michael dragged me from my reverie yet again:

I'm not sure I should be sending you further down this rabbit hole, but I want to help you find your answers, sooner rather than later. There's a new Italian ancestry site called Progenitore. We can research together tonight. I miss you. I hope the real Stella comes back soon.

Shit!

Another reminder I'd been completely absorbed in my parents' strange world, a world that didn't even exist anymore, that I'd ignored everything and everyone else around me.

I suppose it felt like the universe owed me some answers after all I'd lost. I certainly wasn't the first person to lose their parents, but it felt like I'd lost an entire identity. With Dad gone, it felt like I'd lost my direct connection to my ancestral lands, and my only outlet was to speak my first language, and those opportunities seemed to dwindle all the time since the funeral.

It felt as if I was forgetting my Italian a little more each day. My body forgot the gestures. I no longer used the word *amaro* when I meant bitter. I forgot that I'd once been convinced there was no English word that was a good equivalent to *mal impressione* to convey the feeling of getting a chill down your spine. I was grasping, trying to find something to hold on to.

Michael doesn't actually think I'm going to wait for him before I dive into this site, does he?

I started to type in the web address and gagged at the realization that the grease I felt on my keyboard was the remnants of last night's dinner. If you can call slices of dry sausage sandwiched between chunks of caciocavallo cheese dinner. The fact that this new site hadn't tried to connect me with my 6th cousin 3x removed or tell me how likely I was to have an aversion to cilantro was already promising. There were thousands and thousands of digitized documents, photographed directly from the original dusty, tattered books used to record them. I narrowed my search to Rocca Leone birth records from 1910, Nonna Nina's birth year.

There were hundreds of birth records from Rocca Leone in the 1910 era, pages upon pages of expressively and hurriedly handwritten cursive combined with smeared and bleeding ink, all offering a distinct readability challenge.

Three hours later, not only had I learned the pattern of the entries, which made them easier to read, but also that some families were very busy in 1910. I read about a young mother who gave birth to a stillborn baby boy in January and then delivered a girl, a live birth, in December of that same year. She'd just been a machine for procreation, no time to grieve, to heal physically or mentally. No permission to decide if she wanted another child. I bet if I had checked the birth records from 1911, I would have found that the same young mother had given birth again. I imagined her husband, in his ignorance, would not have forgiven her for the death of his boy and the life of his girl. She surely would have been forced to try again until 'she got it right'. I started to feel as if each batch of birth records told a story that no history book could even begin to convey. I felt the sadness, the joy, and the complexities that sprang up from each page.

An entry caught my eye, "Antonina Tamburella? Maybe a cousin? Born on the 13th of December 1910. OK, what the fuck? That was Nonna's birthday, but her name was La Porta." My nerves were making it hard to concentrate: I had now read through this three times, attempting to make sense of it all. *Da Tamburella, Arcangela è nata un bambino di sesso femminile cui da il nome di Antonina.* From Arcangela Tamburella, a female child was born, who she named Antonina. I was shaking from this discovery, but I still didn't quite understand.

So, my great-grandmother gave birth to a daughter and gave the child her own last name rather than her child's father's name. That could only mean … I kept reading, trying to unravel this mystery and translate it all at the same time. I squinted, trying to decipher the r's from the m's, the t's from the l's, and got to: "From her union with a single man, neither a relative, nor someone recognizable."

My heart broke for a woman I'd never met, whose name I didn't even know three months ago, but whose blood lived inside me. I read the document over and over again, filling in more blanks each time and attempting to translate antiquated words. My mind kept circling the concepts of choice and agency. I imagined an eighteen-year-old girl having to present herself at the town hall to inform some unsympathetic and judgmental old man behind a desk about the birth of her daughter and declare her 'illegitimate.' I couldn't even fathom the stigma that followed Arcangela from that day forward.

What were Arcangela's choices? Did she have a say in her pregnancy or in keeping her child? What did she lose as a result? Did Arcangela's parents disown her? Did my Nonna know? I might never know the answers to those questions, but they were all I could think about.

I heard Michael's key turning in the lock and the front door opening. The cats, my two little shadows, left their warm spots on the couch next to me, where they had been napping, to greet Michael as I was ripped from long ago Sicily back into present day Brooklyn.

Michael smiled as he spotted me on the couch, but as he approached me, I blurted out the realization that my mind had been protecting me from.

"My great-grandfather wasn't really my great-grandfather! My Nonna was born illegitimate!"

―

THERE WAS VIRTUALLY NOBODY left to provide any insight into the mystery of my Great-Grandmother Arcangela's life. My Uncle Ross, my mother's younger brother, Rosario, was the last surviving sibling. He'd sold his successful law firm in New York City and retired to Arizona long ago. He mostly kept to himself these days and often shied away from his Sicilian roots–going by Ross and choosing not to pass his native language on to his son. But I'd always believed he was lured to Arizona by its Sicilian-like climate.

There may be one person who knows just as much as, if not more than, my uncles about what happened in Rocca Leone–Zia Leonarda.

―

SHE WAS HAPPY TO meet the next morning over coffee in her boldly decorated French Provincial-style living room. It was as if I'd stepped into a Rococo time capsule. Everything was exactly as I remembered it from childhood.

"Sit, sit. I'll bring the biscotti I just made. The ones in the shape of an S, your favorites!" said Zia Leonarda.

I placed my gilded demitasse cup down on the ornate whitewashed coffee table and slid onto the plastic-covered armchair.

"Zia, like I told you on the phone yesterday, I found some surprising documents that I have questions about. What do you know about my bisnonna Arcangela?"

Zia paused just as her espresso was to touch her lips, conflicted about how to approach the answer.

"Judging from your reaction, I guess you know what I'm about to ask you," I said.

She fidgeted awkwardly in her chair.

"I grew up with your mother and your uncles, so of course I knew Arcangela. I didn't know her well. I was only a young girl when she died. Most of what I knew about her was from what my parents told me and the whispers around town," said Zia Leonarda.

"Did Nonna know her mother's story, or who her biological father was? Did my mother know about these secrets, the stories about Arcangela?"

"There were rumors and accusations, but these things were never discussed within the family. Your Zio Alfonso and I never spoke of those stories. This is really the first time I've spoken about it. Most everyone's gone now–nobody's feelings left to spare."

Her last observation felt like a gut punch. Almost everyone was gone, and I had limited time left with my remaining family. I hadn't visited Zia Leonarda in many years.

"What do you think happened, Zia?" I asked.

"I think Arcangela fell in love at a young age with someone of a higher social standing than her–a forbidden love. This man probably broke many promises. I guess rather than risk being disowned by his parents over his affair with a peasant, he found it easier to abandon Arcangela and their child," said Zia with a shrug of her shoulders.

"The times change, but the stories stay the same for women," I said, absorbing this possible version of events.

Zia sat elegantly on her red velvet couch, dressed in a knee-length skirt, a silky blouse, sheer stockings, and high-heeled house slippers just to drink coffee with me on a Wednesday morning. As I looked down at my wrinkled Nick Cave T-shirt and vintage jeans, the gap between our generations felt cavernous. "The thing I don't understand is how she could have married after giving birth out of wedlock in those days. It seems like it would have been an impossibility; wouldn't she have been marked for life? What kind of man would it have taken to agree to marry Arcangela?"

"Your great-grandfather–he *was* your great-grandfather, no matter what–loved Arcangela and didn't care about her past. He raised your Nonna as his own, and God help anyone who tried to say differently," said Zia.

"So, he was a good man?"

"They had nothing, dirt poor. His family turned their backs on them. They survived on their own, and in spite of everyone," she said.

Survived in spite of everyone. The quintessential Sicilian ethos.

13

MARIA

ROCCA LEONE, SICILY
APRIL 1945

It had been almost two years since Sicily had been liberated, and now everywhere was abuzz with the news that Mussolini had been executed in Milan.

"By order of the mayor of this great commune, all remaining symbols of the past Fascist regime are to be removed today!" The familiar drumbeat of the town crier broke the sacred peace of Sunday morning.

As always, he was dressed in his dusty suit, vest buttons begging to pop, and wearing a tie without a shirt collar to frame it. The large snare drum strapped to the front of his body, when struck, produced a boisterous series of sharp rat-a-tats that announced his arrival.

He performed his usual job, making his way up and down the Corso Umberto delivering his official message of the day. As was usually the case, the children took full advantage of the town crier's inability to stop and retaliate. They chased after him as he walked solemnly down the street, drumming and shouting his message, groups of kids hurling pebbles at him from the sidelines, or they stole coins from the small carved wooden box he wore around his neck to collect alms. They also felt protected by the notion that he wouldn't be able to identify them. As his name suggested, *Pippinu l'uorbu* was blind. What the children didn't know, that the adults had learned the hard way, was that Pippinu had the entire town memorized–every street, shop, name, and all the voices that went with the names.

"*Bastards!*" Pippinu growled through his toothless grin as he waved them away with an old cane he kept hooked onto his left forearm without breaking step.

Maria frowned from the balcony as she watched Alfonso tease Pippinu and put pebbles in his alms box, pretending they were coins.

"*Cretino*," she said, shaking her head.

"Mamma, Pippinu says Il Duce is dead!" Maria said to her mother, who was busy making pasta in the kitchen–a rarity as flour was still scarce.

"Well, he was already dead to me! *Disgraziato*. Just another *cafone* desperate to be famous!" She dismissed her daughter's news, but Nina's sad scowl persisted.

"Well, I'm pretty sure he's famous now," remarked Maria, with her recently fine-tuned sarcasm.

"Come on, let's go. Go get ready for mass," said Nina, wiping her hands on her apron before taking it off.

"What about Alfonso and Sal–"

"Go!"

In the last nearly two years since the end of the Battle of Rocca

Leone, Maria's own war against perceived injustice at home had only intensified.

"And Papà?"

"Go. *Now!*"

NINA HAD HOPED THAT since starting school last year, Maria would discontinue her campaign of female empowerment, that she would dislike school and long for a woman's life at home. Maria loved school, but mostly she loved the attention and recognition that her intelligence garnered from all her teachers, recognition she had never received at home.

"Wait! Maria! What's this letter? What did you do? And why didn't you give me this on Friday?" asked Nina, finding an envelope under the previous day's newspaper.

"Oh, that," Maria said smugly. "I can't help it if I'm just smarter than those illiterate idiots!"

Her teachers had sent her home with a letter addressed to her parents, pinned to her smock. The previous similarly delivered letters had always been full of praise for Maria as a student, and pleas for her parents to provide Maria with extra money to buy the advanced books that weren't in the regular curriculum. Those letters all went unanswered by her mother. The latest letter, however, turned out to be a reprimand for an incident that occurred during a second-grade math lesson.

Maria was exceptionally smart: arithmetic problems were her specialty. She would say a jumble of numbers would only need to bounce around her mind briefly–solved before the other kids even dipped their pen in the inkwell. In those post-war days, that type of talent in a girl was still treated as a parlor trick, and a threat–not as career potential. Maria seemed to find a particular joy in outsmarting the boys, which she of course did regularly. However, on the day in question, the humiliated boy had not handled it very well.

"Be careful, little one, men don't like to be humiliated. You have to make them feel strong and smart. I tell you this for your own good," said Nina.

"Even if I know the answer, and they're wrong? I should pretend they're right?" Maria asked, annoyed.

"There's a right way and a wrong way to correct a man. Ahh, you'll learn …"

"All I did was go up to the blackboard and show that cry-baby, Santo, exactly what he got wrong. I helped him."

"OK, c'mon, let's go. We can't be late for mass!"

Nina suppressed the subtle smile that cautiously curled the corners of her mouth upward. Although Nina didn't want Maria to receive too much academic encouragement, she would have been lying if she didn't admit that Maria's strength made her proud. But, how far could a girl actually go in academics? Nina was just being practical, at least that's what she told herself. The truth was that Nina needed Maria. She needed someone to help with the house and her little brother, and in a few years, she would need Maria to work, to contribute to the household. She felt occasional pangs of guilt for condemning her daughter to a life like hers, but she saw no other choice.

As Nina and Maria later walked back home from Sunday mass through their dispirited and fractured town, the only thing that had fundamentally changed since their liberation day two years ago was the seasons. The people were constantly divided between the new and old ideas about all things political, social, and economic. Whatever the topic, the outcome always seemed to bring about discord, unrest, and sometimes even violence. Ongoing poverty, coupled with the tremendous and sweeping uncertainty, seemed to be the perfect storm to rekindle a once-powerful, now dwindling organization, the so-called Men of Honor. The war had seemingly extinguished the Brotherhood's influence on the general population, but everyone could see that their power was back on the rise. Nina often worried about her three sons. Although they were still young, she despaired over how to keep them safe from criminal influences and the lure of luxuries amidst those otherwise harrowing times.

She had spent many sleepless nights thinking about what Carmelo had said to her at her mother's funeral. Nina agonized over the thought of joining her brothers in America.

"Had Carmelo been serious or just upset?" she wondered. She hadn't dared bring it up again for fear that he actually was serious.

Nina knew one thing for sure: she would not even consider emigration unless her whole family went together. She refused to separate her family. Nina still grappled with the trauma of her family being torn apart when her parents shipped her teenage brothers off to America alone.

Maria remembered riding up the crumbling Corso Umberto on a giant Canadian tank with her brother as if it were a strange fever dream. The Canadians had stuck around for a few weeks after the battle, handing out food and medicine, but two years later, still nothing had been rebuilt. Nothing had even been patched unless the townspeople did it themselves.

After the Battle of Rocca Leone, Maria's father and older brothers helped sift through and move the rubble from the streets, working to make way for wagons and pedestrians to navigate the town's unpaved roads again. Her mother brought them a home-cooked lunch every day at exactly noon. It had taken weeks in the desperately hot August sun.

The percussive symphony of hammers striking chisels to break up fallen concrete could be heard all over town. Maria watched as countless men on ladders, tools in hand, also worked diligently, chipping away any surviving reminders of Mussolini and Fascism. Ostentatious etched marble plaques were pried off buildings and smashed, while commemorative street signs were dismantled. The emblematic torch that had been carved onto the stone railway arch had been fractured into tiny shards littering the ground. *"The people who abandon the land are condemned to decadence,"* read the hand-painted quote that had been emblazoned on the side of a neighboring building since before Maria was born, an inescapable sight from the Sanfilippos balcony, which got buried under a thick layer of white paint.

"It wasn't enough that strangers destroyed our town, now they expect us to finish the job ourselves?" her mother had said one day, as they looked around at all the commotion after delivering the food.

Maria knew her mother hated change, whether good or bad. First, it was the jolly Canadians coming through, tossing canned food around–horrible stuff. She gladly accepted the chocolate bars, on the other hand, for the children, of course. Her mother was suspicious of the new medicine they distributed, called penicillin. But mostly she resented the jovial attitude they had during tragic times, especially on the most solemn holy days.

Maria still winced in embarrassment whenever she flashed back to a now infamous Rocca Leone incident in the early days after the liberation. It was the 16th of August, the day the town celebrated the feast day of *Madonna del Carmelo,* the patron saint of Rocca Leone, who saved the town from the plague three hundred years earlier. Every other year, the iconic Sicilian religious procession graced the winding streets and piazzas of Rocca Leone. But like everything else reminiscent of normal life, the procession had been canceled that year. Of all the changes Nina had to accommodate during the war, Maria thought her mother resented that one the most. That afternoon, the Canadians who were stationed along the Corso Umberto were in especially good spirits. They broke into song, serenading all the beautiful women who strolled past them.

Her mother had endured just about all she could. Maria watched her march into the kitchen to fill a wash basin with water. She made her way to the balcony facing the Corso Umberto as water sloshed from side to side, escaping in small waves that left a wet trail throughout the house. Nina looked distinctly relieved as she abruptly drenched the Medical Corps, mid chorus. They'd finally been silenced. Anyone with the misfortune of having been walking by or standing below her balcony was also unceremoniously baptized by her mother's wrath.

"*On the day of Our Lady of Mount Carmel? Vergogna! Shame on you! Get out of here, go!*" Nina yelled at the stunned and soggy Canadians below.

Maria had heard so many different versions of this story across the town, told and retold in the last two years, that it had evolved into legend. She could no longer separate the truth from the fiction, or remember which parts she had actually witnessed, and which were fabricated. In some versions, her mother was a jealous wife dousing beautiful women who dared to look at her husband; in others, she was a loyal Fascist exacting revenge on the Allies. Maria's personal favorite: Nina was a wild woman, possessed like a *strega*!

Because she was still only seven, Maria struggled to remember happier times before the war, before the occupation, before the food shortages. The earliest memories she could recall now were all war-related. Her mind instantly retrieved images of that night and the battle, and her Nonna Arcangela's death–or rather the jarring sound of her mother receiving the news of Arcangela's death. She hadn't even known that humans could howl before that day. That sound still haunted her.

As Maria and her mother continued their return from mass, a tall young woman approached with her head down. She wore dramatic, long, flowing black robes with a white collar. Her head was veiled in a translucent black fabric, and an exaggeratedly large wooden crucifix hung low around her neck.

"*Maria! Zia Nina! Happy Sunday!*" the young nun exclaimed, extending the traditional greeting.

"*Grazia!*" exclaimed Maria, lighting up at the sight of her cousin, Grazia, who had followed them out of church.

"I dreamt of you both last night! You were in a strange place with red azalea flowers around you, but you looked really happy," Grazia said.

"Dream talk again, Grazia?" asked Nina, dismissing her niece.

"My dreams always mean something, Zia," said Grazia.

They said their goodbyes, and Nina gently reached for her daughter's arm to walk the rest of the way back home.

"See Mamma, everything's going to be OK," Maria said as she waved energetically to Grazia now going in the other direction.

"Maria, nobody should know the future. It goes against God!" warned Nina.

"Mamma, Grazia is a nun. I think she knows God better than you. I believe her," said Maria, with the confidence of youth.

"You're really fresh! One of these days you're bound to say the wrong thing to the wrong person," warned her mother.

14

STELLA

BROOKLYN, NEW YORK
MAY 2020

As I picked up my phone to translate some early 17th-century Sicilian baptismal records from Latin into English, my photo app started playing a slideshow, set to corny music, of all the old family photos I scanned on my phone last year. The slideshow seemed randomly heavy on my father's side of the family. Over and over, I saw an almost cuddly old man with thick, wavy white hair and a big smile, Grandpa Emidio. I looked happy and at ease in all my photos with my grandfather. I called my father's parents Grandma and Grandpa, but my mother's parents Nonna and Nonno. I have no idea who made that decision or who believed that they'd won that contest of American vs. Italian.

I had spent the last few months so focused on investigating and discovering all the things I didn't know about my paternal grandfather, that I'd almost forgotten who he was to me growing up. I looked at that smile again and remembered his playfulness and the way his house smelled when he cooked dinner. His shock of white hair made him look like a mad scientist, but he performed his particular brand of alchemy in his imaginative vegetable garden. I had glimpsed my grandpa again, not the ornery soldier named Emidio Fiorinelli, and I found them at complete odds with each other. When did he become the man I knew, the man who guided me as I took my very first steps? Had he always been both of those men?

Since Signore Testa of Zonderwater had responded to my information requests with such rudeness, I'd been desperate to find out what revelation, what unsavory information he could have discovered in my grandfather's files that made him unwilling to help me. What made Emidio's case different from the others? Hitting one brick wall after another, I'd planned to switch back to Sicily for a while, but seeing those photos today had all those questions gnawing at me again.

Michael, now working from home because of the COVID-19 lockdown, came to tell me he had found something about another of the South African camps my grandfather was in.

"Apparently, Koffiefontein was one of the only camps to house Fascists during WWII. They were held together in a separate prison block," Michael started carefully as he joined me on the sofa.

"OK, but all the prisoners were Fascists, weren't they?"

"Well, I think they mean those who refused to renounce Fascism, even if it meant leniency or release. The ones who weren't just taking orders. The ones who actually believed in the ideology and wanted to continue to spread it."

"Oh fuck," I said, reminding myself I'd agreed to be prepared for any information I found. "Go ahead."

"Well, I'm not certain, but there's a chance that your grandfather was held there because of his loyalty to Mussolini and the regime."

"And they wouldn't want to send a loyal Fascist back home to Italy, a country in a very precarious condition, before the war had ended." I finally began to understand.

"Exactly," said Michael. He was doing that patronizing head tilt that people do when they're forced to deliver bad news. He was clearly proud that he'd helped, but apologetic that he may have confirmed theories I didn't want to be true.

I at least had this small lead to point me in the right direction. I didn't like it, but I'd told myself from the very beginning that I wouldn't shy away from the truth, no matter how disconcerting it felt. It figured that I had spent months looking for these answers, and Michael hit on something important in one morning. The Google gods had always been on his side.

"I know you're going to throw yourself into this research today," he said, "but why don't you bring your laptop to the park, get out of the house for the day? Actually interact with other people, socially distanced, of course."

"I read that it's probably best to stay away from people right now, even outdoors. Also, it never goes well when I do my research in public. I get lots of strange looks when I talk to myself!"

"Yeah, yeah. It's just that I think you've forgotten how to be around people. You've cut yourself off from everything and everyone. You have to see that this is affecting you."

"Michael, I'm fine."

"I still think you should speak to your Zio Donato again. Call him. Even if only to see how he's faring with the pandemic in Rome," said Michael.

"Since I've been speaking to Zia Leonarda about life in Rocca Leone, I've been fighting the urge to drag Zio Donato back into these fixations of mine. I suppose it wouldn't hurt to check in on him and my cousins."

"I think he'd love to hear from you. And, are you sure people have been staring at you and not that *very* interesting hairstyle you've been sporting?" asked Michael with a smirk.

"Fuck you, Michael," I said, giving him an unconvincing steely glare, which only made us both laugh. "Stop making fun of me!"

Michael's probably right about my uncle.

I calculated the time difference between New York and Rome, remembering Zio appeared to be fairly tech savvy for a man in his eighties when I saw him last, and he *did* leave me his WhatsApp number. It was four o'clock in the afternoon in Rome, and so I stepped out onto the back porch to make the call to my uncle.

―

I STOOD ON THE porch to calm my nerves and watched as the tall branches of my overgrown fig tree were splayed open by a warm breeze, revealing the fruit hidden in the middle. I worked up the courage and dialed his number.

"Stella, I'm very happy to hear from you. Like I told you at your father's funeral, I'll help with whatever stories I can remember. Can I ask you why you're still digging up all this ugly stuff, though?" asked Zio Donato.

I spoke to my uncle while circling my yard, pruning shears in hand, clipping sprigs of rosemary and oregano, plucking a couple of fig and tomato leaves, and snipping some marigold blooms.

"I'm trying to better understand my father, and your father, and I guess, in turn, to understand myself. I feel a visceral reaction to things that I've never lived through, and ideas I shouldn't feel such indignation over. Sometimes it feels as if the past–my parents' past–lives somewhere inside me," I said, pausing. "That must sound crazy to you."

"I may not understand, but it doesn't sound crazy. *Va bene.* I can see that this is really important for you. What exactly are you attempting to uncover?" he asked.

"I'm positive the key to understanding my father is to learn all I can about Grandpa's time in the war and his imprisonment. Whatever happened in the war and in Grandpa's internment camps, I think Papà spent the rest of his life traumatized by it," I said.

"His imprisonment." I heard Zio let out a deep sigh. "I can only remember my father speaking of the camps once. Even then, he only let some things slip while in a fit of anger over something else," said Zio Donato.

His words snapped me out of my calm feelings. Suddenly keenly aware of the sticky fig sap on my hands, I wiped them on my Dead Can Dance T-shirt.

"What did he say?"

"He was ranting and raving about being strung up, forced to stand for days with his arms up over his head. It was a brief outburst. He never spoke of it again. We were still kids; it terrified us."

"Why would they do that to him?"

"I never found out. He must have gotten himself into some nasty ordeal to be reprimanded in such a brutal way," said Zio Donato mournfully.

As we said our goodbyes for today, I carefully bundled the herbs and flowers I'd gathered and wrapped them tightly in red string. Upstairs in my office, I placed the bundle on a small table perpetually illuminated by faux white candles and crowded with photos of my parents and grandparents, keepsakes, and tokens. A place where I went to speak to them, listen to them, and place offerings for them–honor them. My ancestor altar. I spritzed my mother's signature Shalimar perfume into the air and adjusted my Nonna's burgundy rosary beads that were draped over her portrait.

I couldn't put the disturbing images of what my uncle described out of my mind.

"I won't dig any deeper if you feel these answers aren't mine to have," I said to the framed faces of my grandpa and dad staring back at me.

I swore sometimes I could see their lips curl in judgment when I spoke to them, but today I believe I glimpsed a smile or two.

15

EMIDIO

KOFFIEFONTEIN - SOUTH AFRICA
AUGUST 1945

Emidio was incensed just as much as he was humiliated. He kept his head down, doing his best to avoid eye contact with Giovanni, who marched beside him. Cosimo, carried by two Union Defense Force soldiers, and Valentino were behind them. The four prisoners were followed close behind by two more UDF soldiers.

"I never should have listened to you! They'll never let me out. I'll die here!" Giovanni hissed through clenched teeth, furious at Emidio.

The four Italian soldiers had been interned together in the Koffiefontein camp in the Orange Free State of South Africa for almost two years. It was the longest Emidio had been kept in one place since his capture over four years ago. Here he'd been fortunate enough to be placed in employment outside the camp at a textile factory, allowing him to use his skills as a tailor. Off-camp work was generally reserved only for those who signed collaborator declarations disavowing Fascism. But Emidio knew how to win favor over others.

Work made the lonely days, weeks, and months go by a bit quicker. The privilege of leaving the camp for work kept the depression at bay, but certainty didn't pacify him. Emidio wasn't built to stay in one place for very long; he grew restless. His loyalties were what led him to remain in the military long after his conscription had been satisfied. Those same loyalties got him dragged into a war. The Fascist government had made him promises, and in return, Emidio put his trust in Il Duce just as he had since he'd been a teenager. As a loyal Fascist, he trusted that the Italian East African colonies would be a utopian oasis for Italians if they won the war.

If they conquered more territories. If they successfully spread Fascism throughout those colonies.

Emidio had hoped that he could move his family away to East Africa to live a life in which they would want for nothing. A place where he could even build a business, be respected.

Instead, he had remained trapped in foreign lands for over five years now without the ability to help Italy's war effort or protect his family from the inside of the internment camps. He'd already been imprisoned longer than most POWs, and he'd been isolated from prisoners who had renounced Fascism. His beliefs were only reinforced by the like-minded prisoners he was exposed to in his Fascist block.

As Emidio reflected on all the decisions and circumstances that led him to his current situation, he decided he wasn't of any use to anyone locked away. He desperately wanted to get back to Italy. He'd heard rumblings that his beloved Italy had been steered in the wrong direction by the Allies. There was even talk of free elections and women's suffrage. He needed to devise a fool-proof plan. But he'd need a great deal of help.

Emidio was employed in a factory constructing British military uniform items from pre-cut fabric pieces. He was assigned to the coats and jackets station. Employees on loan from the camps were all assigned different elements of the uniforms. It was a security measure preventing prisoners from getting a hold of a full uniform for use in escape attempts. Emidio was resourceful, stubborn, and persistent. He was used to getting his way, although the past few years had tested his abilities. He methodically befriended the men working at the other various construction stations. Giovanni in shirts. Cosimo in pants. Valentino in accessories. Over the past couple of months, he had taken calculated steps, planting ideas in each of their heads. He played the long game.

"Hey Giovanni, I bet you wish you could just go home and see your son. What is he, four years old now?" Emidio tested him, seeing if he could play on his emotions.

"Cosimo! Hey, is that girl of yours back in Naples still waiting for you to come home and marry her? I heard there's gangs of partisans sweeping into towns and just stealing our women. Has she written to you recently?" Emidio knew this would infuriate Cosimo, but it was exactly the reaction he'd hoped for.

And then there was Valentino.

"Hey Val, how are your parents? They're getting pretty old now, huh? I bet it's hard on them to be separated from their only child for so long." Valentino, barely nineteen when he was captured in Abyssinia, had never left his tiny town before departing for East Africa. He still called his parents' house home and spent his days feeling painfully homesick.

Emidio had his new pals foaming at the mouth to get back home—easily manipulated into going in on an audacious scheme with him. Emidio had been secretly concocting an escape plan for months. If each man could manage to conceal and steal four articles of their respective category of clothing over a period of months, they could build four British uniforms. One full uniform for each of them, a way for each to go unnoticed in an elaborate escape from Koffiefontein.

By mid-August of 1945, Emidio had received confirmation that all three of his co-conspirators had obtained the necessary components for creating what they needed to execute their escape plan. The next thing he did was to write one last, purposely mundane, postcard back home to Pasqua and the boys. There'd be nothing for them this time, but he was sure they'd understand later. If his plan was going to work, he needed to keep all the money he had saved recently for his time on the run and to fund his long journey back home; he'd no doubt need to pay some hefty bribes. He hoped that the next time he spoke to them would be in person.

"GIOVANNI, HERE ARE THE directions, map, and meet-up time I put together for an appointment on Wednesday night."

Emidio handed Giovanni a small square of paper filled with all his instructions. It was time to put the plan into action.

Giovanni looked down at the paper in embarrassment, but all he could muster was, "Wednesday? *Ferragosto*, huh?"

It did not escape Emidio that he had planned his disappearing act on *Ferragosto*, the Italian holiday celebrating the Assumption of the Virgin Mary. However, more poignantly for Emidio, it also traditionally marked the start of the Italian summer vacation. Freedom.

Giovanni looked at Emidio sheepishly. "I guess I should have mentioned that I never learned to read?"

Emidio shot him a sideways glance.

"Give that back to me. I'll give the directions to Cosimo, and you'll work with him to get all the info memorized," Emidio instructed.

After dark on the agreed Wednesday, Emidio, Giovanni, Cosimo, and Valentino all went to bed half-dressed in their escape uniform. After everyone else was asleep and all of block no. 4 was quiet, the men snuck out of their beds, slipped out of their barracks, and met outside at the agreed-upon location.

"OK, now finish getting dressed. We still have a bit more to walk," whispered Emidio. The men all donned their khaki wool tunic jackets and hats compatible with the chilly winter evening in the southern hemisphere.

Emidio, of course, had not yet revealed the actual escape location for fear the others would scope it out beforehand, even attempt the escape without him. Slightly paranoid, but efficient. They walked another hundred yards, past the barbed wire-adorned main entrance where the prisoners' artwork was proudly displayed–two giant murals of their leaders immortalized in oil paint. The profile bust of Mussolini was inscribed with the Latin title "DUX" and that of King Victor Emmanuel was similarly inscribed with "REX." As they arrived at the unrepaired hole in the chain link fence that Emidio had discovered long ago, he gave his partners in crime a hurried pep talk.

"We only have one try. I know it's dark, but if we can all successfully get through that hole in the fence, we can be free. Nobody will bother a British soldier walking through the streets around here," Emidio said confidently.

Giovanni, the tallest, went first. If he could make it through, then the rest of them definitely could. As Giovanni set foot on the other side of the fence, Emidio, next in the lineup, took his wool hat off and slowly made his way through headfirst. No sooner had he gotten his head and left shoulder through than two UDF soldiers appeared out of nowhere.

"Freeze! We have orders to shoot to kill any prisoner who attempts to escape!" yelled one soldier.

Giovanni, watching from the other side, raised his hands above his head.

"Please don't shoot! This can't be the legacy I leave my family!" said Giovanni as he surrendered–again.

Emidio slowly put his hands up in surrender, one hand still in the camp, and the other already touching freedom. Two more soldiers arrived to assist in the recapture of all four men, who were to be escorted back to their barracks in shame. Just as the soldiers turned their backs to apprehend Emidio and Giovanni, Cosimo made a daring run for it.

A UDF soldier turned and realized he was one prisoner down. He spotted Cosimo running along the outside of the fence just twenty yards ahead and fired on the desperate prisoner. Cosimo was down before Emidio could register the sound of a gunshot. Cosimo's agonized screams cut through the otherwise silent night and echoed throughout the camp. He writhed in pain on the ground, yelling and clutching his leg; a bullet had lodged in the back of his knee.

Emidio watched in horror as his elaborate plan violently unraveled before him.

That could have been me. I would have run as well in Cosimo's position.

Emidio knew he'd been selfish. He manipulated those men who considered him a friend into helping him, and they'd paid dearly. He dreaded the punishment that awaited them and hoped his already unbearably long internment would not be prolonged. He thought of his boys back home. He wondered if they could even recognize each other anymore.

How many more years will I have to miss out on the joy of seeing my boys grow into men? How long will I have to wait before I can kiss my wife again?

He knew in his heart that it was always he who got in his own way.

16

DOMENICO

MONTESCIANO, ABRUZZO
SEPTEMBER 1945

From a balcony adjoining St. Michael's Bell Tower, up above Montesciano, Domenico now regularly spent his early mornings with his fingers smeared in charcoal dust, sketching his ever-changing surroundings. From that height, he could simultaneously experience the antiquity and modernity of his hometown.

Ancient ruins of the fortress walls that once surrounded Montesciano were now the backdrop for the automobiles and scooters encroaching on the town square. Montesciano was not the same town Domenico remembered as a small child. His collection of sketches was proof– a living record documenting the transformation.

Three days was all it took for twenty years of Mussolini's Fascism and over a decade of Nazi rule in Germany to all come to a violent and fiery end in 1945. Mussolini's public execution at the hands of Italians in Milan seemed to have been enough to scare Adolf Hitler into death by suicide. A complete German surrender came very soon after. Domenico remembered the front pages of newspapers splashed with photos of confetti-covered people celebrating in the streets all over Europe—even as far away as America. He never witnessed any Victory Day parties in Montesciano. No bands had marched through Piazza Vittorio Emmanuele. Montesciano was a village unwilling to admit any part they had played in their own misfortune. They seemed all too eager to put war, Fascism, and their sordid history behind them. The townspeople had already begun to claim they were all against it from the start, mere victims of it all.

Domenico had jealously witnessed countless family reunions over the last two years, but Emidio was still no closer to setting foot in his homeland. Europe had been occupied and liberated. Fascism fell. Mussolini, Hitler, and Roosevelt were all dead. The Allies had liberated millions in Europe but also made the news in horrific ways when US Air Force planes dropped atomic bombs on Nagasaki and Hiroshima.

Nazi concentration camps all over Europe had been liberated, and the horrors of the Holocaust revealed. A defeated Germany had been sliced up like a pie—split up among the Soviets, the US, Great Britain, and France, respectively. World maps had been drawn and redrawn again. However, based on his letters home, Domenico's father remained half a world away, clinging to an ideology that was not welcome anywhere. Imprisoned by a war that was no longer being fought.

Domenico was just beginning his second year of secondary school. His drawing had fortified him through the war and protected his mind from the horrors outside. Being creative was the only thing that seemed to put his mind at ease and calm his intrusive thoughts. He hoped his art skills would eventually rescue him from this war-torn town, delivering him to someplace exciting like Paris.

The more buildings he drew, he developed a love of drafting and dreamed of one day becoming an architect's draftsman. After all, most of Europe needed rebuilding, didn't it? Domenico kept tight-lipped about his lofty goals. His mother always told him that sharing too much of yourself was one of the ways the evil eye of some jealous person could catch you. Tradition had it that this covetous curse lurked around every corner in Southern Italy, but people couldn't hex what they didn't know.

Back at his apartment, as he dressed for school, he remembered what his teachers had spoken of in class the day before.

"Mamma, are you going to vote for the monarchy or a republic?" Domenico posed the question to his mother as casually as if he were asking for her favorite color, as he found her making bread.

"Vote? Me?" Pasqua answered blankly.

"Haven't you heard? Women are allowed to vote, now," said Domenico.

"Voting is your father's business," said his mother.

"But he's not here, and who knows when he's coming back. You can vote instead of him!"

"Well … But … Of course I can!" Pasqua stuttered back into lucidity. *"I am going to vote!"*

"Are you OK, Mamma?" Domenico asked, watching Pasqua seemingly short-circuit over a simple question.

"Yes, Mimi, just a lot on my mind. Everything's fine," Pasqua assured her son as he went to the front door, hearing a shout from the mailman.

"*Mamma! There's a postcard from Papà!*" Domenico yelled as he hurried back into the kitchen.

Pasqua snatched it from him with floury hands.

"Just a postcard this time? I guess he had no money to send," he said.

Pasqua seemed disappointed, but he assumed she was glad to hear from her husband regardless. Emidio had sent a couple more surprises hidden in impeccable tailoring in the last couple of years, but nothing like that first surprise jacket. That initial secret lining had saved multiple lives.

Emidio seemed to be growing impatient and restless. The world had changed. Italy was trying to rebuild, and he wanted to be a part of it. Domenico read the card with his mother peering over his shoulder.

Dear Pasqua,
　I apologize there's nothing to send this month. I'll make it up to you. You will apparently be able to vote in the upcoming elections, but it seems I will not be home in time. I'll need you to go vote in my place. We need to restore the king to power, and you must make sure that the Communist party does NOT win! I fear for the Italy that I will come home to if they do.

With love,
Emidio

"Restore the king? The king who ran scared when the Nazis terrorized our country? That king? Has he gone crazy?" Pasqua ranted, waving her hand in the air, as if she were looking someone in the eye, as if Emidio were standing in front of her.

"Mamma?" Domenico muttered, confused.

"Oh, I'll vote! But I'll vote for whoever the hell I want to vote for, not that cowardly king! Women ran this country for the last six years, and now the women are going to use their right to vote to rebuild it! The king, my ass!"

"*Mamma!!*" Donato and Domenico yelled in unison.

"What the hell's wrong with her?" Donato whispered to his brother.

Domenico just shrugged his shoulders and went into his bedroom to continue getting ready for school.

PASQUA HAD BECOME SO incensed by the audacity of Emidio's postcard that she made it her mission to ensure that any woman in town who wanted to vote could do so without fear. Illiteracy was still rampant in Italy, but Pasqua had been fortunate to be one of the first generations from her small farming town to learn to read and write. The women in town were looking to her for guidance. Her unrelenting determination and sharp tongue made her the perfect choice to lead these new suffragettes. The war and her husband's prolonged absence had already given Pasqua a glimpse into what a matriarchy could look and feel like. For Pasqua and her friends, the wives of the men still imprisoned, missing, or widowed by Fascism, the election had become a defining moment.

That evening, four women, all clutching their sewing bags, had joined Pasqua to huddle around her humble little kitchen table. Catarina, Erminia, Santa, and Paola had all left their homes for a clandestine meeting, arranged under the guise of working on a large table linen embroidery. Now, Pasqua let her rebellious side take control, preparing everyone to cast their ballots the next day. Each woman had a few others to pass the message on to.

"I suspect there'll be some troublemakers. There will typically be chauvinistic men who liked everything better the way it was, and who will feel threatened by us. They'll be waiting for us tomorrow, I'm sure. We can't let ourselves be intimidated!" Pasqua began the meeting with this warning for her guests.

"Here's a sample ballot, everyone. It's OK if you can't read very well. At the top, it will say: *Referendum on the Institutional Form of the State*. All you need to do is tick the box next to the symbol of your choosing. Tick the box next to the crown to vote for the Monarchy, or the box next to the laurel wreath to vote for a Republic. Pass it around and get familiar with it."

"Pasqua, are you sure we're not going to cause trouble with the men for all this voting business?" Catarina, Pepino's mother, was nervous. Pepino's father had been presumed dead since the Nazis captured his partisan brigade three years ago. He was never found or heard from again. Catarina still spent every day full of hope and also racked with fear. Hope that her husband would one day walk through the door, but fear of retribution for her family's part in the Italian civil war.

"Catarina, the war is over. Our vote is legal. Actually, it's our right. I do understand your concern, though. I worry often about the day that Emidio comes home to a country and a town he no longer recognizes and that no longer welcomes him. But this is why we have to make these important decisions now. Your Pepino and my Domenico may not realize it now, but we're doing all this for them. Whatever happens tomorrow decides their futures, too."

Pasqua knew that the agitator and disruptor inside of her, her subversive and revolutionary tendencies, were something that she would have to tuck away again somewhere deep down when Emidio came home. So for now, she wanted to help as many people as she could.

17

STELLA

BROOKLYN, NEW YORK
JUNE 2020

I swung open the front door, and the man on the other side of it began his scripted speech.

"Hi, are you Stella Fi-or, uh Foranella?"

I nodded, "Fiorinelli. Yes, yes, that's me."

"Can we count on your vote this November to re-elect Congressman Robert Cortez?"

Election year bullshit. Just what I needed.

"Yes, I'm voting for him. But only if you promise never to ring my doorbell ever again."

He quickly left my doorstep but looked back at me twice, no doubt wondering when I'd last brushed my hair. As he hurried down the sidewalk, it seemed that, as usual, my house was the only stop on this block whenever any left-wing candidate was campaigning. I'm not sure when this neighborhood became such a firmly red territory.

As with my hair, Michael seemed to have given up on me doing anything he might remotely view as normal. The past month had me feeling absolutely intolerant of anything that didn't further my research and investigations. He also thought I had been unusually suspicious and irritable lately, but in my defense, Michael wasn't home every day now to see all the weird shit our neighbors did. I could swear that one guy watched our house all day, every time I opened my front door to grab a package or go outside to put out the garbage, he came outside, or he'd just be sitting in his car for no apparent reason. What was his game? I guess being cooped up inside for months made everyone act a little strange.

My research had been slow and with very few rewards. My grandfather had been in some of the more obscure prison camps, making information harder to come by. That was when people were willing to speak to me at all.

Armed with some tidbits of information about Grandpa's imprisonment from Zio Donato, I hunkered back down in my cozy makeshift living room office (my actual office space felt too formal). On the green velvet couch once more, cross-legged, I wrapped my fuzzy blanket around me and dived back into Google. I needed to find the diehards, the ones obsessed with the more niche aspects of the war. The lesser-known battles and prison camps, the stories that didn't make it into the blockbuster movies. Where were all the weird war fanatics when I needed them? I scoured through site after site until I found the Browzit WWII forum.

Was I a fanatic now? Did I really have the same interests as a seventy-plus-year-old man? This was absolutely not the future I had envisioned for myself.

I'd spent days reading through entire threads touching upon an infinite number of topics such as the treatment of Italians in South and East African POW and civilian internment camps, Italian POWs' memoirs, and even the biography of Jan Smuts—the wartime South African Prime Minister. Now I learned the Browzit lingo: OP = Original Poster, AMA = Ask Me Anything, and TIL = Today I Learned.

I'd gone down and crawled back up through so many different rabbit holes, I was finding it difficult to have any linear thoughts anymore. I finally worked up the nerve to post a question under the handle *bandiera_rossa*. It was a call for information, specifically about Koffiefontein.

> *First-time poster. I'm the granddaughter of an Italian WWII soldier stationed in Addis Ababa who was captured and held by the British for six years, two of those years were post-war.*
>
> *Looking for information on Italian POWs, specifically those held in Koffiefontein or other camps in South Africa. Documents, photos, firsthand accounts, possible reasons for late repatriation, living conditions inside, etc., are all welcome.*

Two full days had gone by with no comments or even a single vote on my post. As I began to nod off, clutching a double shot of espresso, my laptop chimed, and a little red bell appeared over my notifications header. I opened it to find a long, rambling response from a man who had probably spent his entire miserable day crafting the ridiculous diatribe glowing from the page in front of me.

> *First of all, you clearly have no idea what you're talking about since Koffiefontein operated as a civilian camp. Why are you looking for POWs in a civilian camp? Second, Koffiefontein closed in 1946, so he couldn't have been there two years after the war.*
>
> *This is what happens when women try to mess around in fields they don't belong in. I shouldn't have to waste my precious time schooling you. This forum is for men; why don't you go and make me a sandwich!*

As I attempted to collect my thoughts to craft a response that eloquently expressed what an asshole he was, my notifications rose to six, ten, twelve, and counting. That first comment had emboldened a few more idiots to respond, which prompted others to comment in my defense, which resulted in a war of insults being fought between strangers in my comments section. I finally logged out when the disgusting, misogynistic physical threats against me started pouring in. I've never understood how men can go from smug confidence to depraved violence in just a few words. A few comments had even slipped into my private messages, making this whole experience extra special.

What had I gotten myself into? I thought I'd given up

fighting with strangers on the internet long ago, but I somehow found myself here again. Maybe if I just endured the disturbing parts of this process, I could finally get to the answers I was looking for.

The little red bell appeared again as a notification sound pinged from my laptop. Another private message, this one from someone named *infinite scorn,* popped up in my inbox. I took a deep breath, closed my eyes, and opened the message. I reluctantly opened one eye to assess the message's threat level. It began with an apology. I opened the other eye. *Infinite_scorn*, who signed his message as Benny, had seen the clusterfuck that my comments section had devolved into and decided to message me.

Benny and I spent a couple of messages back and forth commiserating over the downfall of the internet, before he invited me to join a private sub-Browzit forum that he said presented WWII discussions from a more Italian point of view. He promised it would not only be accurate and informative but also frequented by a more enlightened crowd.

Thinking I might actually find my answers with none of the threats to my life, I cautiously joined Benny's sub-Browzit. I knew the window of time for speaking to a surviving POW had closed long ago. If Benny had documents and first-hand accounts without the American slant pervading so much of recorded history, I might truly find what I was looking for.

No piece of paper could ever take the place of hearing their stories in their own words. No historical record could erase the guilt I felt over never trusting the few stories that my father shared or never asking the right questions in response. But maybe I could discover some of my grandfather's motivations or comprehend my father's suffering.

18

MARIA

ROCCA LEONE, SICILY
JUNE 1946

Maria watched as her father buttoned up his best Sunday shirt and donned his brown linen flat cap. A somber, guttural chorus bellowed from below her parents' bedroom window. A crowd of workers—her father said they were farmers—had taken to the streets of Rocca Leone in a spontaneous procession singing slow and somber versions of the popular old socialist songs—the songs of the partisans. Carmelo hummed along to the familiar tunes the farmers sang in the fields.

"Salvatore! Come and watch me as I vote! Experience the new world we live in. It'll be your turn in a few short years."

Salvatore seemed uninterested, but Maria, of course, desperately wanted to be included.

"My teacher, Signora Russo, said we could write a report on the election for extra points. I'm coming with you!" said Maria.

Father and son looked at each other with exasperation, but they knew better by now than to argue with Maria about it.

"Well, come on then, Maria," said Carmelo.

"Am I making this meal just for myself? You better all be back home before three o'clock for dinner. *Voting or no voting, it's still Sunday!*" Nina's voice rose to a crescendo from the kitchen. "*And Maria! I thought you were going to stay here and help me! Husband of mine, don't come looking for my help if your daughter comes home in trouble one day. You give her too much freedom!*"

Carmelo let out a shallow sigh, and with a defeated look, he shouted over his shoulder as he opened the front door. "*It's best you just let her tag along with us this time! We won't be late!*"

As they arrived at the Piazza Margherita, Maria felt a bit intimidated at first. The piazza was packed with people and buzzing with emotions she couldn't decipher. She couldn't remember having seen the whole town out like this, apart from days of tragedy or catastrophe. It took a few moments, but the crowd's energy eventually calmed her. She sensed joy, anticipation, excitement for the future. She would write an amazing report for school.

Maria grabbed her father's hand. "Papà, what country has a red flag?" She got Carmelo's attention long enough to ask about the small red flags many people were carrying and had tucked into jacket pockets.

"That's the flag of the workers, the laborers, Maria," Carmelo told his daughter.

"Like, Communists? Are you a Communist, Papà?" Maria asked.

Carmelo leaned down to look Maria in the eyes.

"If I give you an honest answer, will you promise to drop this conversation?" asked her father.

"Maybe," said Maria with a smile.

"You most likely wouldn't understand, Maria. *Socialista, Comunista*, these are the parties of the workers. I'm a worker, a farmer. I have to do what's best for me and my family, right?"

"Papà, can I have a red flag?" asked Maria.

"That's enough! No, that's not something for girls! Anyway, your mother would kill me!" Carmelo said sheepishly.

"Papà, I don't know if you've noticed, but half of the people here waiting to vote are women. I guess you'll just have to get used to sharing the new Italy with us girls," Maria said proudly, her hands resting firmly on her hips. She looked like a mini version of the actress Anna Magnani, who had risen to fame the year before.

Looking across the piazza, Maria's attention shifted to a petite brunette woman in a neatly pressed floral dress wearing polished brown shoes. The brunette reached down and removed her shoes, one at a time, taking great care to protect them. There was a tug on her forearm, followed by a violent heave. She was being dragged away from the crowd by a man. He shouted at her as sweat ran down his face in the late morning sun. She held onto her shoes and made her body a limp, dead weight for him to carry. She stared stoically back at the crowd with her head held high. Maria couldn't hear what the man, most likely her husband, shouted, but there was clearly some disagreement around her participation in the election.

"Papà?"

"*Sì*, Maria ..." Carmelo seemed exhausted from his daughter's constant questions.

"Why isn't Mamma here? Doesn't she want to vote?"

"She doesn't need to, I'm voting. I represent this household."

"But–but all these women are somebody's wife. I don't understand."

"Ah, damn it, Maria! When you're married, you can have this argument with your husband. *Enough!*"

"With my husband? I'm never getting married," Maria muttered, more to herself.

Carmelo appeared to be rethinking his decision to allow his daughter to come along but seemed disappointed at how completely disinterested Salvatore acted. Carmelo had hoped to instill a feeling of pride in his eldest son. Salvatore was thirteen years old now, and their parents were always talking about how he would start working soon. Carmelo always said that Salvatore would join him to work in the peach orchards.

Maria looked up at everything around her, the people, their clothing, the expressions on their faces, the campaign banners hanging in the piazza, signs that read *"Death To The Monarchy"* and *"Viva the Savoys!"* carried by the men and women who were free and unafraid to be there. She took it all in, all the details, and tucked them away safely in her mind to retrieve later when she could write her report.

I'm going to get an A for this!

Maria felt Nina's absence very strongly. She wished her mother shared her feelings of hope for Rocca Leone and the future, but Nina had always warned against putting your hope or trust in politicians and leaders.

As they slowly moved closer to the town hall, Maria could see the crowd begin to diverge, splitting open down the middle like the Red Sea. She looked to her father for guidance, but he didn't seem to know what was happening either. As Maria ambled further through the piazza, the singing, rambunctious conversations, and soapbox speeches began to sound discordant.

It seemed almost as though people were being divided into opposing groups by men standing on either side of the crowd. Maria tried to understand, and it seemed that the men on the left were gaining supporters with calls for equality and reform, while the men to the right were hoping to encourage people through fear of change, and especially to be worried about this free election.

It looked, though, like the people were tired of being scared, tired of being bullied. When their attempts to herd people to one side or the other failed, the two groups of men began pushing and fighting each other, starting in the piazza and then moving away onto the Corso Umberto. By the time Maria had reached the front of the line with her father and brother, the fighters were far in the distance, already forgotten.

The Sanfilippos' turn had finally come, and Carmelo proudly dropped his ballot in the giant box.

"Salvatore, remember this moment!" Carmelo turned and shouted toward his son, caught in the line behind him. "Your time will come soon, my son."

Maria, significantly smaller than everyone else, was completely trapped. She was surrounded; all she could see were skirts and trousers, none of which belonged to her father or brother. Just as she was about to panic, she spotted a pair of feet wearing the most beautiful and bold shoes she'd ever seen. They were red leather kitten heels trimmed with satin bows. Maria couldn't see whose feet were in these mesmerizing shoes, but she imagined her to be the most powerful and carefree woman she'd ever seen. She remained focused on the red shoes until she felt a tug on her dress. It was Salvatore squeezing back through the crush of people to find her.

As Maria was led away, she relished watching people celebrate in the streets, have discussions, even disagreements about politics, mostly without real anger or fear now. She could feel a shift happening. She knew things would be different for her soon, but she wasn't sure how. She hoped it meant that she could continue with her schooling and have a proper job, not one making bread and pasta, or washing stinky socks. She was already determined to grow up with more choices than her mother.

Now that women were allowed to vote, surely they would be expected to finish school. I want to be just like that lady with the red shoes.

She saw a sea of people–so many of them women–their little red flags shining like beacons. That scene, that whole day, moved her so much she began to notice little hints of red everywhere. The bold color became synonymous with happiness, freedom, and hope for Maria–little signs from the universe dotting the landscape.

Most of the eligible voters in Rocca Leone, men and women, turned out to make their voices heard on that historic Sunday in June of 1946. Rocca Leone threw their support strongly behind the Italian Socialist and Communist Parties, just like her father said they would.

"Papà! Papà! Did you see? You won!" said Maria, holding the morning newspaper.

"The people won, Maria," said her father.

19

STELLA

BROOKLYN, NEW YORK
JUNE 2020

A slender olive-tanned hand beat a large hand drum repeatedly in a hypnotic rhythm. The small cymbals crashed and echoed as the drumming grew to a fever pitch. Startled awake, my alarm clock blared, intermingling with the drum sounds from my dream. *Drum? Tamburello. Arcangela Tamburella? Was my dream telling me something about my great-grandmother?* The simple answer was I'd fallen asleep listening to Sicilian folk music again. I rolled off my laptop, on which my head had been resting.

I'd spent the last few days totally absorbed with reading through the WWII forum, posting questions, and interacting in the comments threads. Even though nobody had outright said anything alarming, some posts alluded to political leanings I wholeheartedly opposed. I suppose that was the risk of researching WWII and the fascist periods of history. People approached the topic from all viewpoints. Everyone had so far been respectful and courteous. Maybe too much so. I kept waiting for the other shoe to drop.

I'd come to understand that Benny was a moderator on the forum, and he privately messaged me again in reference to a question I'd posted. He mentioned he might be able to point me in the right direction, that he knew of someone with tons of musty old Italian military documents from WWII referencing Italians who were held as prisoners. Of specific interest were documents related to repatriation, such as debriefing transcripts, that disclosed participation in crimes while deployed, etc. All the documents were intentionally kept undisclosed and unpublished, so I didn't ask how he'd gained access. I assumed whatever his means might be, they reflected the reason why he only ever sent private messages, rather than commenting on my posts.

This situation began to make me uneasy, but it was probably fine. He didn't even know my real name, and I felt confident nobody would miss these eighty-year-old documents. I knew I would need to take some risks to get to the truth, so I wrote Benny back and let him know I was definitely interested in whatever information he had to offer.

Zia Leonarda called me just as I accepted Benny's offer. I tiptoed out of the bedroom, trying not to wake Michael.

"Are you still coming over today, Stella?" she asked.

I'd almost forgotten about our coffee date, but I looked forward to meeting with her in person again after the pandemic had kept us apart for the last couple of months.

"Yes, of course, but I might have some different topics to discuss today," I said.

As my red suede sneakers pushed through the tall grass in Zia's enormous backyard, a flood of childhood memories came rushing back. Eating watermelon slices down to the rind on a scorching summer night during large family barbecues that felt more like *al fresco* banquets. The kids were served a drop of red wine in their soda with dinner and sugary espresso with milk with dessert. No kids' menu or kiddie tables, we were included in everything. My Zio Alfonso's vegetable garden, edged with peach and fig trees, always gave me the feeling I was tucked away in a secluded forest that stretched for miles.

Zia had pared the garden down considerably since my uncle's passing ten years earlier; she was satisfied with a small herb garden for her cooking. Zio Alfonso, who had owned a construction company, built this dream home in Brooklyn for his family shortly before the birth of their second child, Lorenzo. The garden was his pride and joy.

Zia and I sat at a safe distance from each other outdoors, across a large patio table shaded by a carport. There was a batch of her homemade iced espresso waiting for us with a plate of jellied quince fruit and crackers and a mouthwatering spread of saffron cheese, dry sausage, cured black olives, and dried chickpeas.

"As you know, I've also been researching my father's side of the family. The thing that keeps coming up is political fanaticism. I wish I could say we left that back in 1945, but we obviously didn't,"

I said, as I wiped the sweat from my neck and twisted my frizzy mop of salt and pepper hair into a bun.

Zia Leonarda shifted back in her white plastic patio chair and took a deep breath.

"Ah, Stella, I don't know if the fanaticism came back around, or if it never left. Look at the situation with your cousin Lorenzo. I'm not sure how much you know about that," she said.

"I know some," I said.

In fact, I'd watched my cousin's slide into the US's far-right movement in real time on social media. The conspiracy theories, scapegoating, and cruelty he spouted and parroted had caused me to block him online.

I knew he believed anyone to the left of him politically was his enemy. Cable news had convinced him New York City was a crime-ridden war zone, and when he 'escaped' to Florida, he begged Zia Leonarda to join him. He felt he needed to save her from what he called 'the communist agenda and invasion of illegals.'

"I used to agree with him. We've always been very conservative. Your uncle always voted Republican. I never really involved myself in politics, but I even voted for Reagan once," said Zia.

"Reagan. He was the beginning of all this. You know, I cried when he was first elected in 1980," I said.

Zia laughed out loud.

"You cried? *Esagerata.*" She waved her hand at me dismissively. "You couldn't have been more than five years old. What did you understand about politics?"

"I was four years old, and I did cry. I said Mamma, I don't want the bad man to be president! I've had pretty good instincts about the bad men that came after him, too," I said.

"If only it were that simple. I go weeks at a time without any word from Lorenzo, and when I do hear from him, it's impossible to have a normal conversation with him. He says the craziest things." She shut her eyes tight and shook her head. "It's like he's joined one of those ... what do you call them ... cults."

"It *is* a cult, Zia. I'm really sorry you're dealing with that, and I hate that I've lost contact with my cousin," I said.

It was true, I hated that I barely recognized a member of my already shrinking family. Lorenzo seemed brainwashed. As the youngest in the family, I looked up to all my older cousins as if they were siblings. I mourned this loss as I would a death.

"His newest thing is that he refuses to speak Italian, his first language. That hurts. He says we all need to speak English around him because this is America," she said.

We're making some progress; maybe the Italian American community will finally start to see that this sort of rhetoric only hurts the country.

"I don't understand. I keep telling him the Italians came here the right way, legally. Speaking Italian is nothing to be ashamed of," she continued. "We don't try to make Americans speak Italian; we're never disrespectful."

We were so close to making a breakthrough ...

I wanted desperately to produce the documents I'd found

proving that not *everyone* in our family came here legally, but I refrained.

"I promise to *only* speak Italian to you, Zia. It'll be good for both of us," I said

The truth was, I craved to speak and hear not only the Italian language but also Sicilian. Hearing Sicilian spoken felt as if I were summoning my ancestors. I felt protected and loved.

"I suppose the thing I can't make sense of," I said, "is why anyone of your generation, any immigrant, especially someone who lived through Italian Fascism, could help propel the American far-right to power. It hurts me in ways I can't explain as if I'd lived through the war myself."

"That was all we knew," she replied. "My parents believed in Mussolini; they believed in Fascism until the day they died. Don't get me wrong, there were also many Communists and Socialists in Rocca Leone, like your Nonno Carmelo, but not in my family."

20

EMIDIO

REPATRIATION & HOMECOMING
1947

Emidio awoke to a cacophony of horns blaring and honking. His room was pitch black, but he could feel his cot swaying to the muffled sound of water sloshing. He grabbed the edges of the cot to brace himself. Perhaps it was just his tinnitus making him dizzy. When the horns continued, he understood they were outside.

Still disoriented, Emidio sprang up from his bed. Some of the horns were even creating a melody of sorts. He thought they may have even sounded celebratory.

I remember now; I'm on a ship.

He could remember boarding the ship just before Christmas–yet another one away from his family.

Is this Naples? Is it New Year's Eve?

Was he in *Italia* at last? That must be it, all the ships and boats heading in and out of the port of Naples were blowing their horns in celebration as the clock struck midnight. It was 1947.

Emidio had missed so much. He missed so many years with his family, he missed most of the war, he missed all the monumental changes in his country, and then he missed when they changed all over again. Emidio wasn't even sure who he was anymore, or who he could be to a family who had survived so many years without him. Regardless of all his many doubts, he remained confident that Italy needed him and his loyalty to the Fascist regime to restore order and bring glory to a deeply shamed nation.

Suddenly, he was blinking as light filled the cabin, and before him stood a man in a familiar uniform.

"Good morning, soldier." The man looked and sounded annoyed.

Emidio felt cold; he was being stared down by a tall, thin man with small, dark eyes. He was an intelligence officer—a military interrogator from Naples.

"Fiorinelli, Emidio?" the Italian intelligence officer asked sternly.

"Yes, sir!" answered Emidio.

The officer led Emidio to an office, where they sat on wooden chairs, each side of a battered gray metal desk.

"Today we will begin your debriefing," the man began coldly. "I see you led a rather colorful life while imprisoned."

"I believe I've lived according to my oath. My loyalty was repeatedly tested, but I believe I've proved myself," Emidio proclaimed proudly.

"Prove yourself? Prove yourself to whom, soldier? the mistrustful officer asked Emidio.

"This is a different world from when you left. The rules have changed."

"To my country, my king, and my family! I suffered every indignity for them! I was locked up, humiliated, punished, starved, and even forced to build my own barracks once. I was imprisoned for trying to build an empire for my *Italia*!"

"Is that why you refused the offer of early repatriation? Loyalty to Il Duce? I see here that a British soldier by the name of Richard Walker tried to work out a deal for your release on three separate occasions. You refused each time."

"Of course I did! That was just a test!"

"I don't know many men who would pass up the opportunity to be a free man, to return to their families," said the Italian interrogator.

"Tell me, why would this man care about my freedom? They wanted to see if I would betray Italy and Il Duce! The British would never offer that sort of deal to the enemy out of the goodness of their hearts," said Emidio.

"Fiorinelli, Il Duce is gone, and the British have not been our enemy for the last four years. This Richard Walker says he owes his life to your wife. He claims she kept him hidden and arranged for his escape. Your family kept him safe from the Fascists and Nazis. This was his way of thanking them. There was indeed a real deal already in place with the British for your release. They only needed you to sign a simple declaration, yet you refused."

"No. That would have been treason!" Emidio pounded his fist on the desk. "My wife would never harbor a British man in my home! She would never disgrace me that way!"

Could all the 'fake news' I'd heard really be true? Could it really be over? It's coming from the lips of a fellow Italian in uniform, do I have to believe it?

"OK, let's talk about that ugly business you orchestrated in South Africa, your escape attempt. You got a fellow Italian soldier shot that night; he'll be in a wheelchair for life. Is that your idea of patriotism?"

"I didn't shoot him! I was trying to get us all back to Italy, to fight, to rebuild!"

"Soldier, pull yourself together, or this will take much longer than necessary! We will have to resume this interview tomorrow."

"Tomorrow?" scoffed Emidio. "Tomorrow I'm going home," he said with a flippant toss of his hand. "Everyone has tried to brainwash me, but I've stayed strong. I have nothing left to say to you."

"Many people from both sides of this war will need to speak to you before you can get that stamp of approval on your record, before you can be released to go home."

Emidio didn't understand why he faced interrogation about the very things that the Italian government had sent him to do and given him a salary to accomplish.

―

EMIDIO CARRIED AT HIS hip a small, faded green cloth sack, containing all he had to show for his eight years abroad. His old leather boots, cracked and shrunken from rain and mud, blistered his feet as he walked from the bus stop. He wondered if the mile-and-a-half walk from the bus stop to Montesciano would have been less painful in his bare feet. He felt more exhausted than he thought humanly possible. Weeks of interrogations, sleep deprivation, and accusations had all made him weak and numb, finally battered into submission.

At first sight of St. Michael's Bell Tower, Emidio knew he was home, even if it was painted a different color than he remembered. He walked along the winding road leading toward the town square, pausing at the guardrail to look at the vast swaths of farmland in the distance. They seemed neglected and dry. He spun around, distracted by the state of the town. Montesciano had aged even more than he had in the years since he last laid eyes on it. Both had suffered through captivity in foreign hands. The buildings and homes all appeared weathered and dimpled. Former thriving businesses were now shuttered, and the seams of the townspeople's clothing looked as if they had been taken in a few too many times.

Emidio paused and pressed his face against the broken window of Luigi's old butcher shop. An empty meat case and broken furniture lay on the ground, covered in dust and debris. He took two small steps away from the window and was struck with a rumbling gust of air and the sharp sound of a horn blaring right behind him. Taken by surprise, he lost his balance and nearly toppled onto the cobblestones below.

"Eh vaffanculo! Since when are there automobiles joyriding through the damn piazza? You could have killed me! *Stronzo!"* Emidio screamed out at the driver, who was long gone by the time he got his bearings.

Emidio had imagined this moment, his homecoming, so many times over the years, but it looked very different in his daydreams. He had imagined he would step onto the Piazza Vittorio Emmanuele to receive a roaring hero's welcome. The town would be gathered in celebration. Streets would be named after him. His wife would be overcome with emotion, and his sons would run out to embrace him in the middle of the piazza. But there were no celebrations today, no giant billowing banners thanking him for his sacrifices. Nobody knew he'd arrived, nobody even recognized him. There wasn't a single trace of the group of men, once permanent fixtures, smoking and playing cards in front of the *tabaccheria*.

He paused at the tobacco shop. *"Buongiorno,"* he said as he waved meekly at the shopkeeper, who just went on smoking his cigar without giving Emidio so much as a second glance. He could feel his stomach twist and tighten with every step that brought him closer to his little faded yellow house at the end of the piazza. He was nervous to see his family, more so that they would have to see him. He knew they would be the only people who could truly see just how much he had changed, and not only physically. He had acted tough, principled, even defiant in all his interrogations and debriefings, but in truth, he was terrified.

His military career was over, but he'd gotten his stamp of approval. He'd been cleared of any wrongdoing related to his involvement in the failed war campaigns in East Africa, his capture and captivity–even his escape attempt. But the last eight years continued to haunt him. Haunted by his long list of indiscretions repeatedly detailed for him over and over again, each time a new interrogator had their turn with Emidio. He re-lived his escape attempt and

Cosimo's blood-curdling scream every night as he closed his eyes in an attempt to sleep.

Finally, Emidio climbed the familiar crooked staircase leading to his apartment; it smelled differently. His heavy boots made a hollow sound and echoed longer than he remembered as they landed like cinder blocks on each step. He approached his second-floor apartment door and tried the doorknob. It was jammed or locked.

"Do I really have to knock to be let into my own house?" he thought, exasperated. He tried the door again, a bit harder this time. Emidio tried the doorknob once more, this time giving the door a push with his shoulder. The door swung open and banged against the wall.

"COME ANY FURTHER AND *I'll kill you!*"

Domenico ran into the kitchen at the sound of his mother's screamed warning.

Pasqua looked menacing as she stood in the doorway, wielding a large knife at an apparent intruder. The man ducked and ran to the other side of the kitchen.

"Pasqua! Pasqualina? It's me, don't you recognize me?" the man said.

"Don't come any closer or I'll do it! Get out of my house!" Pasqua growled.

"Mamma! Wait no!" warned Domenico. He looked at the man cowering in the corner.

"Papà?" he asked, his voice cracking.

As she heard her son call for his father, Pasqua stopped yelling and lowered the knife.

"Emidio? No, *no! Emidio!*"

She dropped the knife on the floor and ran to a stunned Emidio before collapsing at his feet, crying. "*No, Emidio, no! Forgive me!*"

Domenico froze at the bizarre scene unfolding. His father was home. His father was actually finally home after eight years–and his mother had just tried to attack him with a knife.

"Papà? Are you really home? For good?" he asked as Emidio pulled his wife to her feet.

"*Sì*, Mimi. I'm home for good. Unless you know something I don't."

"Call me Domenico."

Emidio had left behind a scared little boy that cold morning in 1939 but had now come home to a teenager who must have seemed more like a man. Domenico was tall and thin, with a deep voice. Emidio wouldn't find any trace of the chubby six-year-old Mimi he last saw standing in his place.

"Pasqua, it's OK, it's OK. I should have knocked. I'm sorry, I'm sorry I scared you. I know I'm not as handsome as you remember," he said with a wink. "You didn't recognize me, it's OK. I tried to surprise everyone."

"Yeah, I think you definitely surprised everyone," said Domenico sarcastically. "Wow, you got–old," he then added.

"Yeah, *guaglione?* So did you!" Emidio retorted as he

self-consciously ran his fingers through his full head of prematurely grayed, thick, wavy hair.

Emidio and Domenico helped a distraught Pasqua into a chair and brought her a glass of water. After she had calmed down, she flashed her crooked smile at her husband.

Domenico sat at the kitchen table with *both* his parents. He'd almost believed that would never happen again.

"I wish I could just forget the last eight years, but I can't. Why were you away for so long?" his mother asked his father.

"Mamma! He just got home–"

"Why were you so stubborn? You have a family!" said Pasqua.

"I did what I thought I had to do, what I took an oath to do. But maybe–" Emidio said mournfully as Pasqua cut him off.

"I tried to tell you in my letters! I tried to tell you there's nothing left of the old Italy, but you refused to believe me. Your oath is to a ghost; he's gone. We're still here, and we were here for all of it. The hunger, the occupation, the violence, the arrests, the fear! At least you got fed three meals a day."

His father seemed lost in thought, still clutching his cloth bag, as Pasqua spoke. He seemed like a stranger. Domenico gnawed his fingernails as he recognized his mother's indignant expression. He knew she wouldn't back down from this fight.

"What happened here? Montesciano is like a ghost town now. There's nobody left that I recognize," Emidio asked

"What happened? Eh, your friends the Nazis happened!"

Emidio pounded his fist on the table and stood up.

"My friends?! *I am not a Nazi!*"

"Maybe not, but with your help, they invaded and held us here like prisoners, scared and starved. Those who weren't killed in the war or on the streets by the Nazis left this place. They went to America, they went to Canada. Anywhere but here. So, Nazis, Fascists, they all looked the same when they took away young Antonio from across the way. They all looked the same when they threatened to arrest our son for trying to get an extra scrap of meat for us to eat. They all looked the same when they were beating people in the street as retribution, and they all looked the same when we almost got dragged to our death for daring to help some people in need."

Emidio looked down at his hands sheepishly.

The doorknob began to jiggle again, and both Emidio and Pasqua leapt to their feet, rattled by the earlier incident. The door slowly opened to reveal Donato tiptoeing through the doorway. He'd missed his curfew by almost an hour. Nobody had actually realized how late it had gotten with all the emotion and commotion. However, if he'd planned to slip in unnoticed, he'd definitely chosen the wrong day. Emidio let out a small cough, hoping to get Donato's attention.

"Papà?!" Donato yelled out, ran to his father, and wrapped his arms as far around Emidio as they could reach.

"Well, third time's a charm, I suppose." After a very exhausting and dramatic day, at least one out of his three reunions had gone as he'd prayed for and imagined.

If Emidio thought that his homecoming would cure all of his and his family's suffering, he was sorely mistaken. He sometimes felt like a guest or a stranger in his own house. It had been a humbling experience to see that his family had made it through the eight hardest years of their lives without him. They had their own routines, responsibilities, and even their own way of speaking sometimes. They could bond over their shared experiences. The boys had grown up far too quickly, especially Domenico. He was left to *act* as man of the house before, and now he almost was one.

A month had passed since his homecoming, but he continued battling insomnia and painful flashbacks. Every night, he went to bed and pretended to sleep until Pasqua was in a deep sleep. Then he would make himself a snack of bread and olives and go for a walk around the piazza. Tonight, as he snuck back into his bed and gently pulled back the blankets on the bed, Pasqua woke up and instinctively reached out for him.

"Emidio?" she called and felt around his side of the bed, but all she found was his cold pillow.

"I'm right here. I just got up for a glass of water."

"A glass of water, yeah. I'm not stupid. I know you get up every night, and you go outside," Pasqua said with a raised eyebrow.

"I'm sorry. I didn't want to worry you. It's so hard for me to fall asleep. I lie awake thinking until the sun comes up most nights.

When I actually do fall asleep, I have the most terrible nightmares. It's my penance, I suppose," said Emidio.

"Penance for what?" asked Pasqua.

"War is miserable, Pasqua. It changes everybody."

Emidio thought about Cosimo again. He wondered if he should tell his wife about his botched escape attempt. Tell her everything he went through trying to get back home to her. *Maybe someday.*

"I don't know how you did it, just you and the boys alone for so long. You kept each other safe and somehow managed to put food on the table. You even risked your lives to keep strangers safe—not that I agreed with that! I've had a lot of time to think, too much time maybe. I feel like a coward when I think of all my protesting, all the years I pontificated about oaths and principles while you were here suffering. You're an astonishingly strong woman, Pasqua. Why didn't I just sign that damn declaration and come home to you sooner?"

"You tell me. Maybe you had something, or someone, keeping you there?" responded Pasqua.

"How could you even think that!" asked Emidio.

Pasqua turned to face her husband, propping her chin up with her hand.

"When men go to war, they all come home with secrets. Tell me, what are you keeping hidden, Emidio?"

21

MARIA

ROCCA LEONE, SICILY
APRIL 1949

"Maria, come on, let's go! We're gonna be late for the test!" Concetta, her closest friend, ran past her with her oversized leather backpack bouncing behind her.

Maria caught up to Concetta and pulled her aside.

"I can't take the test. My parents won't let me continue with school," Maria muttered, trying not to make eye contact. She was embarrassed.

"What do you mean you're not continuing school?" Concetta stopped and looked Maria right in the eyes and said, "You're the smartest one in the class!"

"No, I'm not. Santo is the smartest," Maria said quietly.

Concetta rolled her eyes.

"No, Santo's just a kiss ass. You're the smartest, and you know it! C'mon, you can sneak in and take it with me."

"No, I can't! I don't have the money to pay for the test. It's done.

It's fine." Maria hugged her friend briefly before she walked home in the opposite direction, doing her best to keep her head held high.

At eleven years old, after only five years of elementary school, Maria's compulsory education was complete. Any student wishing to continue to middle school had to take a test called *licenza di scuola elementare* to qualify for advancement. Maria's parents were crushing their ambitious young daughter's dreams. As their three other children were boys, the responsibility of taking care of the home and her younger brother fell on Maria. Her parents felt she needed to prepare for her eventual outside employment that could contribute to the household. The Sanfilippos could see no future in a girl's or a woman's education. Maria saw no future in sewing fine clothing she couldn't afford, or cleaning houses she would otherwise not even be invited into.

"You're late! I told you I needed your help this afternoon, Maria! It would be nice if you thought of someone besides yourself sometimes." Maria got berated before she had even set foot through the door of her apartment.

"Sorry, Mamma."

"Why this *fungia*?" asked Nina, as she stepped out of the kitchen, seeing the all too familiar pout on Maria's face as she approached.

Maria ignored her and continued toward her bedroom, ripping her school smock over her head, pausing long enough to use it to dry her now tear-streaked face. Children removing their smock at the end of elementary school to celebrate their advancement to secondary school was a tradition, a rite of passage, but today, for

Maria, it felt like a prison sentence. She would wear that silly smock and repeat her elementary classes if it meant she could stay in school.

Maria's face was hot with anger, and her nostrils flared. She marched right into her parents' room looking for something, anything useful. She rummaged around her mother's nightstand until she found the one thing of value she knew her mother had. The earrings Nina wore on her wedding day, the dangly ones with the gold bows on them. She helped herself to the earrings without a second thought. Maria loved those earrings, and she knew they were the fanciest jewelry that her mother owned. She grabbed her wrinkled smock again and ran down the stairs, out the door, and back across the street to the elementary school. She stood determined, banging on the locked front door of the school until the secretary came to answer.

"I need to see Signora Russo. I'm late for the test!" Maria blurted out, as if her life depended on it.

"*Signorina* Sanfilippo, you know that you're not on the list to take that test, and the test is halfway over anyway," responded the secretary curtly.

"I need to see Signora Russo! I can pay for the test!" Maria yelled back.

"Quiet! Wait right here. We'll clear this up right now."

Barely two minutes had passed when the secretary came back with Signora Russo.

"Signora, here I can pay for my test now. I am going to advance to *scuola secondaria*!" Maria opened her sweaty little palm to reveal her mother's gold earrings as she desperately attempted to barter the earrings as payment.

"Come on, let's go. Now!" Signora Russo grabbed Maria by the collar of her dress and dragged her out of the school, across the street, and upstairs to knock on the Sanfilippos' apartment door.

Maria had left home without telling her mother; she knew her mother would be furious. Nina swung the door open and looked surprised to find–not her apologetic daughter standing there–but Maria's teacher clutching the girl by the collar. Signora Russo opened her palm to show Nina the earrings. "Signora Sanfilippo, Maria tried to use these earrings as payment for the *licenza* test. I assume they belong to you."

Maria watched as her mother's neck and face turned red with anger. Nina raised her hand threateningly.

"Disgraziata!!" she screamed at a pitch sharper than Maria had ever heard come from her mother. She pulled her daughter through the doorway and slammed the door behind them.

"Aren't you ashamed of yourself? Aren't you ashamed to disgrace your family like this?" Nina yelled, while landing a half-hearted smack across Maria's cheek before the sulky girl even had a chance to explain herself.

"You won't let me go to school! I had to do something or I'd end up just like you!" she lashed out at her mother.

Maria closed her eyes and cowered in the corner, knowing a line had been crossed. She expected another smack, but Nina didn't look angry anymore. She looked hurt. Maria didn't mind pushing boundaries and making her mother angry every once in a while, but today she'd acted cruel and hurtful. Maria watched her mother re-tie her flour-smeared apron, calmly walk back into the kitchen, and attempt to continue cooking as if everything were fine. She could see her mother wiping away tears when she thought nobody was watching. Nina would never let on that her daughter's words had hit a nerve and cut deep enough that she could cry. Crying was reserved only for times of death; everything else could be overcome.

"*La catena*," Maria whispered to herself. She hadn't really thought about that generational thorn in her side since the war. She thought life both at home and in post-war Italy in general had been improving. She thought she'd lifted her curse years ago, but today *la catena* tightened around her, suffocating her.

22

STELLA

BROOKLYN, NEW YORK
JULY 2020

I read and re-read the handwritten note that accompanied the thick folder of documents from Benny's source. All the information had arrived at my PO Box last week. They'd tried to soften the blow of the revelations inside with a note.

> *bandiera_rossa,*
>
> *These are likely not the answers you were hoping for. But you did say you were prepared to accept whatever I found. Here they are– everything I've retrieved with mention of your family member's service number.*
>
> *– chasing history*

I gripped the note in my hands and rehearsed in my head what I'd tell Zio Donato as I readied myself for my call with him.

"*Grazie*, Stella! I just received your package, they're *bellisimo*!" Zia Donato's voice boomed from my phone speaker.

I'd sent my uncle prints of my favorite photos from my New York City street photography series, as a thank you for speaking to me about his and my father's life growing up in Abruzzo on our now weekly calls.

"Now you'll always have a little piece of New York City," I said.

"It's clear that you inherited the Fiorinelli artistic gene!" said Zio Donato.

"There were other artists in our family–you mean in Italy?" I asked excitedly.

"Of course, there was your father. But also my daughter, Luisa, your cousin, is a sculptor," he said.

My father? An artist?

I could remember him creating a detailed pencil drawing of a giant ship for my book report in grade school, and unearthing a box of his old film, Polaroid, and Super 8mm cameras when I began showing an interest in photography in high school. Although his technical drawing skills were mostly used for the stacks upon stacks of men's tailoring patterns he created by hand, he did sometimes surprise me. Like when I was eleven and we moved into a new house, a total fixer-upper. He drew elaborate floor plans to convince me, a very skeptical pre-teen, of how great that little old ugly house would be after a renovation. *How did I not realize before?*

"Zio, I don't understand. He was the one who tried everything possible to dissuade me from going to art school. He swore I'd be 'the poorest girl in the neighborhood.' My mother, somehow, finally managed to convince him otherwise. She was always the voice of reason in our house."

"Maybe he was trying to spare you the disillusionment that comes with the intermingling of one's heart with a chosen profession. I don't think he ever recovered from that disappointment. I'm surprised he never told you about it," he said.

"What do you mean, recovered?"

"Some days he would sleep all day; it made him very depressed. Between him and our mother, it was a very sullen household for a long time."

"Is that when Grandma Pasqua fell ill?" I asked.

My grandmother, Pasqua, had been ill ever since I could remember, although I was never privy to any particular illness or diagnosis. I'd recently flipped through family photos and realized she'd gone completely missing from family gatherings from the time I was about three years old. She was always home in bed, without much explanation. She could be easily upset, and at times she didn't remember things or people. She once chased me out of her house because she thought I was an intruder. She didn't recognize me.

"Looking back," said Zio Donato, "there were signs of her illness toward the end of the war—confusion, paranoia, talking to herself. That war and the fear caused by that regime had consequences we wouldn't discover for years."

"How long before she was as I remembered her?" I asked.

"Your father, and my father—they didn't always tell me everything. I was so far away, and I didn't always ask. That was my mistake. When you're young, you think you have unlimited time, and the universe owes you something. You're so busy creating your life that you take for granted those who gave you life."

I could remember my grandmother holding entire conversations on her couch with people only she could see. Sometimes these ghosts made her angry, and sometimes she'd smile and laugh with them. I often caught my father talking to himself, with his facial expressions morphing as his lips moved. He would say he was thinking out loud, but it seemed more like a conversation. Was Grandma's illness hereditary; did my father suffer from it as well? Will it happen to me? He always did have a vivid imagination, but was it creativity or paranoia? Did I ignore something I didn't want to face? I flashed to my father, grabbing my arm as he was admitted to the hospital. "Don't let them kill me!" he said. Maybe it wasn't side effects from medications.

I'd stalled on telling Zio what I'd discovered about Grandpa Emidio and his time imprisoned in South Africa from Benny's contact. Some of it had been hard to digest, and I'd told myself I'd wait for the right time. How could there ever be a right time to tell someone their father manipulated fellow prisoners to orchestrate a prison escape that resulted in one of the soldiers getting shot? Or that he had opportunities to come home to his family but turned them down out of loyalty to Mussolini?

"Speaking of discoveries and consequences," I nervously segued into the next topic. "Zio, I know what happened to Grandpa in South Africa. I finally found the information I'd been searching for, thanks to someone I met online. The information also shed some light on the photo of Mussolini that had me obsessed for so long.

I heard Zio take a deep breath. There was a long pause.

"Stella, I'm really glad you've gotten some closure, but I've been thinking. I don't want to know what happened or learn another side of my father at my age. Good or bad, I think anything that could force me to look at my life or him differently is more than I can handle. I hope you understand, Stellina," said Zio Donato.

"I understand, Zio. Case closed."

23

DOMENICO

MONTESCIANO, ABRUZZO
JUNE 1950

"I got in, I actually got in!!" Domenico ran to his apartment from the post office, clutching the envelope that contained his future. "Mamma, I got in. I did it! I'm going to Paris!"

"*Porco Dio,* Mimi. When were you planning to tell me about this nonsense?" Emidio startled him so much, he almost tripped. Domenico hadn't expected his father to be home.

He hadn't even told his father that he'd applied to the *Académie des Beaux-Arts* in Paris. Emidio had dismissed his son's dream of being an artist or architect–of anything that he hadn't planned for him–since he first arrived back home in Montesciano almost two and a half years ago.

"Well, I wasn't going to tell you unless I'd been accepted. But look, Papà, look how well I scored, better than almost all of the other applicants! I told you I could be really good at this!" Domenico hoped that this letter would be the sort of validation of his talent that could convince his father to let him go to Paris.

"Were you just going to abandon your family and your job? You're seventeen years old. The deal was that you would contribute to this family. You just started your apprenticeship with me! I don't know why you're still wasting your time in school like some rich baron's son. You wanna go be a gentleman now, a *signore*?"

"Papà, I've never wanted to be a tailor. You know that I'd only done that for you! Besides, I wouldn't be leaving for another year. There are still more requirements I need to fulfill before I receive my enrollment letter."

"A year? What good is a year? You expect me to waste my time teaching, training, and paying you for a year just for you to leave me and go live with the goddamn French?!"

"You didn't want to be a tailor either; it was chosen for you. So why are you trying to force me to follow in your footsteps now? Where's Mamma? She'll at least be happy for me!" "Your mother's in bed, leave her alone."

"In bed? Again? It's the middle of the day!"

"She's not feeling well; don't bother her. Probably some kind of women's troubles. I don't know. OK, enough now!"

Domenico stormed out of the kitchen and headed to his room, but he stopped at his parents' bedroom instead. He slowly cracked the door open, just to peek inside.

Is she really asleep?

He walked in slowly. "Mamma," he whispered until a groggy Pasqua opened her eyes.

"Mimi?"

"Mamma, I got in!" Pasqua stared at him blankly. "Paris! I got into the school in Paris!" Domenico's voice grew louder now.

"No, Paris? No! There's a war going on, Mimi! You can't leave me and go to Paris!" Pasqua began to cry softly.

"Mamma? What's wrong with you? Are you sick? Are you dreaming? The war has been over for years now, Mamma."

"What? Eh yeah, yeah, that's right. The school in Paris. Don't tell your father yet," Pasqua said, holding one finger to her lips.

Domenico was dressed in his best crisp white shirt and charcoal gray trousers. His shoes were, well, his shoes were always scuffed. Cobblestone streets kept shoemakers in business in Italy. He headed to the post office again. He'd been so nervous anticipating his next instructions from *Académie des Beaux-Arts* that he'd bitten all his fingernails down to the quick.

"Hey Mimi! Where are you going dressed like a movie star?" Pepino teased him from outside the tobacco shop where he smoked a cigarette as he flipped through the newspapers for horse races to bet on. Domenico and Pepino's lives had taken very different paths since the war ended. Pepino had no interest in school, nor did he really have any interest in working. He relied on the occasional gambling win to get him through.

"I'm going to Paris, Pepino! You wanna come?" Domenico chuckled as he waved at Pepino and picked up his pace, adding a few more scuffs to his black leather oxfords. Autumn had brought a chill to the mountain air, but Domenico didn't notice. He strutted through the piazza and onto Via Roma toward the post office, confident he had fulfilled every requirement, taken every test, and expertly completed every assignment necessary to be eligible for enrollment at *Académie des Beaux-Arts*. He'd been willing to work seven days a week, whatever it took, to earn enough money for tuition and living expenses in Paris. He was ready to be a student of architecture and drafting, and definitely ready to leave Montesciano.

"*Buongiorno* Mimi!" The post office clerk grabbed Domenico's mail and slipped it across the counter as soon as he saw his old school mate arrive.

"Thanks, Pasquale! Looks like I'll be leaving for Paris soon!"

Domenico continued his confident strut all the way back around the corner as he excitedly opened his envelope. He stopped in the middle of the piazza, too impatient to wait until he arrived back home. He was completely oblivious to the cars and scooters now forced to swerve around him. As he read the first line of the letter, the smile melted from his face. He heard someone calling his name in the distance, but he stood frozen, almost as if he'd forgotten how to move.

"Mimi!" It sounded like he was inside a tin can. "Mimi! What the hell's wrong with you? Get out of the way, you're gonna get hit by a Vespa!" It was Pepino yelling from the tobacco shop; everyone was looking at him. Domenico ran the rest of the way to his yellow house at the end of the piazza, but he couldn't even wait to get inside.

"Papà! Papà!! Come outside and face me!" He stood under his

balcony and called for his father until Emidio appeared, annoyed, in his white undershirt.

"What the hell is wrong with you? You're embarrassing yourself. Get inside!" barked Emidio, looking almost as angry as his son.

Domenico flew up the two flights of steps to the Fiorinelli home to confront his father.

"What did you do?! Are you the reason my sketches never made it to Paris? You've ruined my chances of ever getting into that school. You–you've ruined my life!" Domenico was so angry that he fought back tears.

"Me? Why would I concern myself with that nonsense? I told you they wouldn't let you in. The French." He waved his hand dismissively. "Those bastards! They don't want an Italian peasant!"

"A peasant? Yeah, thanks to you, peasants are all we'll ever be!" said Domenico, furious.

"We had a chance in East Africa! That land was supposed to be for Italy, for us! The Allies ruined everything! Now you want to go sit with the French and draw your silly pictures? *Vaffanculo!*" yelled Emidio.

"That land was never for us. They just used you and every other Italian soldier that was taken prisoner or killed to make themselves rich! You believed the lie–you believed that maniac, and it almost got us all killed!"

There was no doubt where Domenico inherited his hot-tempered disposition and flair for the dramatic. Left without a clever rebuttal, Emidio resorted to self-pity, "Well, maybe they should have just killed me!"

Domenico stormed into his parents' bedroom and ripped apart his father's dresser drawers. A blur of undershirts and socks flew all around him. He furiously rummaged until a stack of papers cascaded out from underneath a drawer. Domenico sat on the floor in his now rumpled white shirt, the drawings and sketches he'd included in the package to *Académie des Beaux-Arts* fanned out around him on the floor. All the art he'd assumed had made its way to Paris along with the rest of his submission had been stashed away in his father's dresser.

"*Cornuto e mazziato!* It just keeps getting worse! My own father sabotaged my life. *I'm going to be a tailor, a miserable tailor for the rest of my life!*"

24

STELLA

BROOKLYN, NEW YORK
AUGUST 2020

"Sometimes I think Italian American culture is secretly a matriarchy. We just let the men believe they're in charge," I said to Zia Leonarda, who looked at me with confusion.

"Is that the sound of my little cousin spewing her feminism and social justice?" echoed a voice from the hallway.

"Agata!" I yelled.

My cousin Agata, Zia Leonarda and Zio Alfonso's firstborn lived the first ten years of her life in Sicily before they finally emigrated. The large age gap between us placed her firmly in the Boomer generation. She found me insufferable most of the time, but I always loved being around her.

"Stella, I didn't know you'd be here today," said Agata, balancing armloads of Zia's weekly grocery shopping. "Ma, aren't you hot? I'm turning the AC on; it feels like a sauna in here."

I thought it was just me. Zia seemed perfectly comfortable. Her jet-black hair was flawlessly set in her signature style, not one bead of perspiration on her forehead. I, on the other hand, could feel my mascara fighting a losing battle with the sweat pooling around my eyes.

"Your mom was telling me stories about my mom from when they were kids together in Rocca Leone. Can you believe she's already been gone twenty years as of last month?" I said.

"I miss Zia Maria, everyday. You know, I had her all to myself before you came along," said Agata with her familiar smirk.

"Yes, you've reminded me many times, Agata," I retorted. "Did your mom ever tell you about the time my mother stole Nonna's earrings to pay for school? Or, the crazy story she told your mom about some adventure she and Zio Salvatore had during the war?"

"No, she never told me any stories. But why do they all sound so familiar? So, where have I heard them before?" asked Agata.

"Not from me. I never told anyone your mother's stories. They weren't mine to tell. But I think her stories should belong to you now, Stella," said Zia.

"I only knew one story about my mother's childhood–and it was a terrible one," I said. "She told it many times, so I knew it really affected her. Most likely the first of the many medical traumas she had to endure in her life."

"It was a tough life growing up where we did, when we did. Coming here to the United States made some things better, but tragedy still followed us," said Zia Leonarda.

"You don't really believe that you were targeted by fate, do you?" I asked. "Zia, you, my mother, Nonna, you decided to change your lives, you took chances, you learned to do things you didn't even know existed."

"I believe things happened the way they were supposed to happen. Good or bad, it was *il destino*," she said.

After thousands of years of invasions, occupations, and foreign rule, the Sicilian people remained steadfast in their fatalistic beliefs. Crossing an ocean couldn't change that.

THE NEXT EVENING, AS I prepared dinner, my doorbell rang with an urgent insistence. I'd almost missed it over the sound of the kitchen fan and the summer storm raging outside. I hurried to the living room and peered through the curtains. A drenched, bleach blonde woman impatiently rang the doorbell again.

"Agata! What's wrong?" I yelled as I swung open the door.

She saw the panic in my eyes. "Nobody died! Sorry, I should have said that first!"

I exhaled in relief. "What's going on? Why did you drive all this way in the midst of a crazy storm?"

She was clutching old books to her chest, shielding them from the rain.

"Come in, come in!" I said, pulling her into the house.

"I told you I recognized those stories about your mother! I'd read them as a child–in these books!" said Agata, speaking quickly.

"Books? Agata, you're not making any sense."

"I'm sorry." Agata took a deep breath, ran her fingers through her wet hair, and started over. "OK, when I was a kid, back in Sicily,

"I found these notebooks wedged behind the dresser I shared with my mother. I used to read them to myself; they were the only storybooks I owned. I read them over and over again and packed them when we emigrated to the US. I haven't thought about them in so many years, but they were still in my old bedroom," rambled Agata.

A migraine threatened over my left eye as I tried to keep up with her. "Agata, there's a puddle forming around you; get to the point!" I said.

"These are your mother's diaries! That's why I recognized the stories you and my mom were talking about the other day! Was that concise enough for you?"

Heat filled my cheeks, and I laughed inexplicably as my vision blurred from tears.

"My mother kept diaries, and these are her stories? From Sicily?" I squeaked.

"I had no idea the books were hers; otherwise, I promise Stella, I would have given them to you decades ago!" Agata said as she pulled me in for a wet hug.

I hung Agata's rain-soaked jacket and lent her some dry clothes. When she left the room to change, I opened the first notebook somewhere in the middle but snapped it closed as soon as I recognized my mother's handwriting. I wasn't ready. I'd wait to read these alone.

"Sorry, Stella, I didn't mean this to unfold so dramatically. Blame it on the rain, I guess," Agata said as she towel-dried her shoulder-length hair in my kitchen. "What smells so good? I didn't know you cooked. I didn't think feminism allowed for that." She always tried to get a rise out of me.

I gave her an audible eye roll. "You don't even know what feminism is; you treat it like a dirty word. I love to cook, but I don't cook out of fear of what will happen if dinner isn't ready and on a perfectly set table at 6 o'clock sharp like some creepy trad wife," I said.

"A creepy–what–wife?" Agata peered inside the oven and snapped it closed again. "Is that your mother's *pasta al forno*?"

"Yup."

"With the peas and the hard-boiled egg." I nodded in the affirmative. "Before you ask– yes, the sauce is homemade, and the cheese is freshly grated. Caciocavallo, not mozzarella. Would you like to stay for dinner, Agata?" I asked. "Michael should be home soon; we can eat whenever the *pasta al forno* is done."

Agata's kids were grown and out of the house, and she and her husband Gianni had separated four years ago–everyone was supposed to pretend we didn't know. Italians still acted like divorce was a malediction brought upon them instead of a life decision. I knew she'd most likely be going home to an empty house.

After dinner, Michael reached over and squeezed my hand. I nodded and smiled. No words were necessary. I knew he'd been right all along by suggesting I look to my family for answers, and he knew I was thankful for the nudges.

25

MARIA

ROCCA LEONE, SICILY
OCTOBER 1954

It was the first rainfall after a summer drought in Rocca Leone. The whole town, especially the farming families of which there were plenty, were singing, dancing, and celebrating as if channeling their distant pagan ancestors. The invigorating autumn air carried a sweet aroma so strong that Maria could almost follow it all the way home from work. Women all over town were gathered around makeshift tables outside, unbothered by the drizzle and busy canning the late harvest unique to Rocca Leone. *La Settembrina* are the sweet, bright yellow Rocca Leonese peaches harvested in September and October. Her home was always well stocked with peaches in autumn. Her father, Carmelo, had long managed one of Rocca Leone's peach orchards.

Maria had been working full-time as the in-house seamstress at Vincenza's, the popular local dress shop just off Piazza Carella. All the shops had already closed, but she stopped at Gino's cobbler and pressed her forehead against the store window. That's when she spotted the most perfect pair of shoes she'd ever seen. Satin pintucked peep-toe heels in the most gorgeous shade of vamp red. She'd saved up a small bit of *lire* to buy herself something special to wear on her sixteenth birthday, which was only two weeks away.

Mamma would faint or call me a slut if she saw me strutting around in those shoes. And they cost way more than I have saved up.

She tried, unsuccessfully, to convince herself to forget about them.

As she entered her apartment, she could already hear her mother mumbling annoyedly.

"Peaches, peaches everywhere! What the hell am I supposed to do with all these peaches that your father brings home?! I'm only one person. How am I going to cook and jar all this fruit before it spoils?"

"You could ask your sons to help you. I saw Salvatore and Alfonso smoking and whistling at girls on my way home tonight." Nina just huffed and dismissed Maria with a wave of her hand.

"You know, Mamma, I really don't like Alfonso's friends. You should do something about them. I think they're all trouble."

"What can I do? They're all grown now, you know how men are."

"Men? That's funny! They act tough, but they're all such mamma's boys. And where's Rosario?"

"Don't disturb him, he's studying!" Nina ordered her daughter, protecting her youngest.

"Oh, of course he is. I wouldn't dream of disturbing our little scholar," said Maria, sarcastically rolling her eyes as she grabbed a paring knife to begin peeling the peaches, and a large pot to boil and sterilize the jars.

Maria understood that underneath her mother's dramatics lay the hope that her daughter would help her with peaches. Her mother always said she shouldn't have to ask for help. Maria knew from the moment she set foot into the kitchen that she would throw on her apron and lend her mother a hand, but she wanted to be asked. She simply wanted to feel appreciated rather than obliged for once.

"Mamma?" Maria said quietly as she peeled a peach and sneakily ate a couple of slices before they made it into the hot jars. "My birthday is in two weeks."

"Yeah, I'll cook a nice dinner for the whole family. I'll make your brothers stay home that night. Oh, and I'll invite your Zia Rosina. You love your Zia!"

"OK, but I thought I could wear something special, something new?" Maria tested the waters with her mother before asking for what she really wanted for her birthday.

"Something new? I have so much good fabric in my closet. Now you know how to make your own dresses, you don't need to buy any new dresses."

Maria took a deep breath. "Well, actually, there was this beautiful pair of shoes that I saw in the window of Gino's. I was hoping to wear them to celebrate my birthday with Concetta and some other friends. Mamma, it's my sixteenth!"

Her mother muttered her favorite expletive under her breath as she accidentally grabbed the pot of boiled water and held her fingers under the cold water.

"You don't think I know how old you are? Birthdays are to be spent with family, not with strangers! But if you don't appreciate your family and everything I do for you, then go! Go with your friends!" Nina dipped her fingers in cold water, again wincing at the pain.

Her mother had been pushed to her limits; the topic was no longer up for discussion. Maria put her head down and continued peeling the last of the juicy, golden Rocca Leone peaches.

MARIA CAREFULLY RETRIEVED THE keepsake box tucked away in her nightstand drawer. She emptied it of all the lire coins she'd been stashing away and tossed them into her purse. She'd taken on some extra alteration jobs on the side for the last week. She, of course, kept this from her family. This money was to be her birthday money and hers alone. She hadn't been able to get those red shoes out of her head since spotting them in the store window. She was desperate for them, even if the only place she could show them off was her birthday dinner at home with her family. Maria had lost her battle for a special birthday celebration out with friends days ago. In fact, now she was almost relieved to be staying home for her birthday tomorrow night–she wasn't feeling very well.

"Mamma, can you take a look at my throat? It's been bothering me for a couple of days, but now I can barely swallow," Maria complained as she massaged her swollen neck.

Nina brought her daughter over to the kitchen window. Maria opened her mouth wide, her chin pointed toward the morning light.

"*Bedda Matri, Maria!* Your tonsils are infected and swollen; why didn't you tell me sooner?"

"I figured it was just a cold, and it would go away," Maria said, unfazed. Nina had already begun buzzing around the kitchen, making her special concoction for all throat-related ailments: Hot chamomile tea with a chaser of honey and lemon juice.

"Mamma, I need to leave for work."

"First, you drink this, all of it. Then you go to work. This lemon juice will take care of that infection," her mother assured her.

Maria tried to down the piping hot miracle herbal tea, squirming away from her mother who was clutching her forehead to evaluate if she had a fever.

"OK, no fever. Go, go to work now."

An hour later, Maria sat at her sewing machine in the stuffy back room of Vincenza's dress shop, feeling worse, not better, from the pain in her throat. It was relentless, and she dreaded having to swallow. She felt so miserable, worse than she could ever remember feeling. She didn't want to be labeled as difficult or sensitive, so she continued to push through the pain. For her boss, Vincenza, who'd noticed Maria wasn't herself today, the last straw was when she watched her star seamstress yell at a customer. In Maria's defense, the uncooperative and demanding woman insisted on moving and fidgeting while Maria attempted to pin her dress hemline for alterations.

"Maria, I think it would be best for everyone if you leave early today!" exclaimed Vincenza; she'd clearly seen enough.

Maria agreed that it was the right thing for both of them. Tomorrow she'd turn sixteen, and lucky for her, it was also her day off. She was certain that if she rested enough today, she would feel better for her special day tomorrow.

As she dragged herself home, she approached Gino's cobbler and realized that this was the first time she'd gotten off work before all the shops were closed for the day. The red peep-toe shoes she had spent weeks dreaming of owning were still displayed in the front window, taunting her. She adjusted the leather purse in the crook of her arm, the extra coins inside jingled.

I'll just be a few minutes. I'll rest as soon as I get home.

As soon as she slipped her feet into those red shoes, she could feel something surge through her. It felt like magic, or perhaps it was merely confidence. There was no turning back; she had to have them. She exited Gino's shop and turned back to glance at the empty spot in the front window.

I can't believe they're really mine!

Her purse considerably lighter after spending every last cent of her extra earnings, she continued her way back home, up the Corso Umberto.

"Maria!" Nina called out as soon as she heard the doorknob rattle and turn. "Why are you home so early; are you still sick?"

"No, Mamma, everything's fine. It was a slow afternoon, and Vincenza sent me home early." Maria figured it would be much easier if her mother didn't know the whole truth.

THE LAST THING MARIA remembered was sneaking the shoes, her first significant purchase, into her bedroom and under her bed. She passed out, still dressed in her work clothes, for a full ten hours. Still somewhat groggy, she was the first one in the family awake; she'd even beat her mother out of bed. The rest of the Sanfilippo household remained perfectly still. Maria washed her face, got herself dressed, and began to prepare the kitchen for breakfast, in anticipation of her birthday to officially begin.

It was Saturday, the only one in any rush to go anywhere was Carmelo, who worked six days a week, resting only on Sundays. After he'd left for work, and Salvatore and Alfonso had gone out to catch up with friends, Rosario went back into his room to read. That just left Maria and Nina cleaning up in the kitchen, as usual. When they were done, Nina put the moka pot back on the burner.

"Maria, sit down." Nina brought over two espresso cups and emptied the little dulled silver moka pot into them. Gentle swirls of steam floated from the dark, aromatic espresso. Maria sat down slowly, looking at her mother suspiciously. Nina reached into her apron pocket and revealed a small box wrapped in brown paper with red string.

"Happy Birthday, Maria," Nina said to her daughter with an uncharacteristically warm smile. Maria looked at the little package on the table and slowly slid it closer toward her.

"Eh, open it," said Nina impatiently.

Maria carefully unwrapped the little pearly blue plastic box. She recognized the logo stamped in gold on the lid, *Gioielleria Restivo*.

"Mamma, you bought me jewelry?" Maria asked as she opened the box.

"Mamma! They're gorgeous!" Inside the jewelry box were beautiful, timeless gold hoop earrings adorned with delicate ridges. Maria's eyes widened; this was the most extravagant gift she'd ever received. She quickly unclasped them and slipped them into her pierced earlobes. She flashed to the day she tried to trade her mother's prized earrings for an education.

Maria reflected on her younger self–how different that little girl thought her life would look at sixteen. Would she be in school now if her mother had sacrificed her earrings then?

"It's your sixteenth birthday. I wanted to get you something special. You're not the only one who knows how to put a little extra money aside." Nina looked at Maria with one eye raised.

"Thank you, I'll never take them off," Maria responded sheepishly.

Nina grasped her daughter's hand, looked into her chestnut brown eyes, and said, "A woman should own at least one thing of value that she can always carry with her, in case of an emergency. Happy Birthday, *figghia mia*."

Maria got dressed up in her best dress, a three-quarter sleeve, navy-blue A-line silhouette with dainty white polka dots. She nervously paired it with her gift to herself, the shoes of her dreams. She joined her mother in the kitchen, helping with the birthday preparations.

Her mother looked down at Maria's new shoes with disapproval and took a deep breath.

"You know, your father will probably have something to say about those shoes," warned Nina.

"They're just shoes. He wouldn't even notice them if they were black or brown," Maria said, a bit exasperated.

"That's the point, respectable women shouldn't beg to be noticed." Maria just turned, rolled her eyes, and slipped her apron on. She felt ill again and inexplicably warm, but she continued to set the table and help prepare the meal. They were cooking her favorites–eggplants stuffed with tomato, bread crumbs, and garlic, and her mother's fried potato croquettes that melted in your mouth.

Salvatore had just returned home. He raced into the kitchen, lured in by the intoxicating scent of fried comfort food. "Do I smell croquettes?"

"Don't touch, those are for–" Maria couldn't even finish her sentence before Salvatore scurried away with half a croquette hanging out of his mouth.

Maria gulped a glass of water and cracked open a window to

feel the autumn air on her face. She closed her eyes and took a deep breath in and out, trying to cool down before anyone noticed her flushed face and sweaty brow. Carmelo had finally arrived home from work, so the entire Sanfilippo family gathered around the dinner table to celebrate Maria's birthday.

"I have to leave right after dinner. Leonarda's waiting for me to pick her up. There's a band playing in Piazza Margherita tonight." Alfonso had been dating Leonarda, a neighborhood girl, with whom he'd grown up. His whole life seemed to revolve around her now.

As their family dinner came to an end, Maria could feel her whole body burning from the inside out; it felt like her blood was boiling. She tried to stand up to get some more air but was unsteady on her feet.

"It's just these new shoes, I guess," she mumbled and chuckled weakly. "It's–it's really hot in here."

She stumbled. Carmelo stood up to catch her just in time.

"Is she drunk? What the hell is wrong with her, Nina?!" demanded Carmelo.

Nina hurried over to her daughter and placed a hand on her forehead.

"*Madonna mia!* She has a high fever! We need to rush her to Dr. Cardaci, now!"

"Nina! Look at her: she can't even walk!" yelled Carmelo as he propped his daughter up.

"Stop wasting time, Carmelo! Her brothers will have to carry her; it's only a few streets away. Go!" Nina had seen fevers like this before; she knew they needed to be dealt with immediately.

Salvatore and Alfonso each wrapped one arm around their sister to carry her down the stairs and over to Dr. Cardaci's house. Maria was too weak to protest. As they arrived at the doctor's house, hidden in a small alley off the Corso Umberto, they pounded on his weather-beaten door.

"Doctor! Doctor Cardaci!!" An old man with a thin mustache answered, cranky and grimacing.

"Something's wrong with our sister. You have to help her!" yelled Salvatore.

Dr. Cardaci took one look at Maria, and his expression softened; he could see that this was a real emergency.

"Bring her inside. What are you waiting for?!" he said.

The brothers waited in the front room while Dr. Cardaci propped Maria up in a chair. After a quick and painful examination, he confidently announced, "They have to come out!"

"What the hell are you talking about? What has to come out?" Salvatore demanded.

"Her tonsils, you idiots! They're giant, red, and completely infected. You can see them from the moon! It has to be done tonight!"

Salvatore stayed with his delirious sister as Dr. Cardaci drove them to his surgery nearby, while a stunned Alfonso ran home to notify his parents. When Carmelo and Nina arrived at Dr. Cardaci's office, Maria looked terrified. Dr. Cardaci quickly gave the Sanfilippos a rundown of Maria's condition.

"As she's a minor, I'll need your consent to perform this surgery to remove her tonsils," said the doctor.

Carmelo gave his consent with a quick signature on the

handwritten form that the doctor had hastily drawn up. They laid Maria down on the cold examination table that tonight would double as a surgical table.

"What are those? What are you going to do to my daughter with those?" Nina said with panic in her voice. Dr. Cardaci had retrieved thick canvas straps from an old cupboard and tied Maria's hands and arms down to the table. Finally beginning to understand what was happening to her, Maria began to scream and flail her legs wildly.

"Why is that necessary?! Stop! You're hurting her!" Carmelo lunged forward but was blocked by the old doctor.

"Everyone out, wait outside! Can't you see how sick she is? There's no time to waste!"

When everyone had left the room, the doctor strapped her legs down.

"No! Mamma!" Maria screamed and cried out for her mother, but Nina had already been forced out of the room. She made one more futile attempt to free her legs from under the tight straps as one of her brand-new red shoes slipped off her foot and fell to the floor.

BOTH NINA AND CARMELO sat helplessly in the next room, their eyes burning with rage as they heard their daughter scream in pain.

"I don't want to live here anymore, Carmelo. They wouldn't even treat an animal this badly in America! I never thought our children would have to endure a life like ours. How can we just stand by and allow that man, that butcher, to cut our daughter open without any anesthesia?!"

26

DOMENICO

**MONTESCIANO, ABRUZZO
OCTOBER 1955**

"Hey, stop fooling around! Sit normally! You're gonna make me crash!" Domenico's silver Vespa GS 150 sputtered and shook as it maneuvered around the tight bends leading out of town and toward the rugged interior of Italy's greenest region.

"I can't, I'm wearing a skirt!" Gina yelled from the back of the scooter, over the loud pop-pop of the 2-stroke engine beneath her. The headstrong young woman with an hourglass figure sat side-saddle on the rear seat, holding on to Domenico's waist and causing the unbalanced scooter to sway erratically as it battled the winds and rocky terrain.

Domenico lit the cigarette dangling out of the corner of his mouth with one flick of his engraved silver lighter as they zoomed past Bar Agostino, his cousin's new coffee bar at the northern tip of the town. He took a long drag and exhaled the stream of smoke as he shouted back to Gina.

"I should just leave you here! You're crazy! You're gonna get us both killed!" said Domenico.

Gina seemed far too enchanted by the wind in her hair and sun on her face as the woody and fruity scents of Montesciano's olive groves wafted through the air to pay Domenico any mind.

"Don't take it out on me just because you're upset about your parents moving to America!" yelled Gina over the rumble of the engine. "I think it's great that they're making a fresh start!"

Emidio and Pasqua had recently sprung the big news on Domenico and Donato. They would be leaving Italy and emigrating to America, and they hoped their sons would join them. They'd had a hard time settling into post-war life in Italy. Emidio couldn't let go of his dreams of owning a business in Italian East Africa. The more that became an impossibility, his choices were either to move his family north to Milan or abroad to New York–the garment manufacturing capital of the world.

"They don't know anybody in New York City–they don't even know the language! They're going to be more miserable than ever, and they want to take me down with them!" said Domenico.

Domenico veered off the main road, onto a narrow *contrada* road, and picked up his speed.

"I'm not going anywhere! I'm finally gonna live my own life!" he shouted.

Domenico could feel Gina gripping on for dear life. At the high speeds the Vespa was now traveling, he knew she couldn't swing her leg around to ride astride even if she wanted to. She laughed, exhilarated by their adventure ride. Domenico knew he could and should slow down, but the louder Gina laughed, and the more she sided with his parents, the angrier he became. He twisted the throttle further for more speed.

He could just begin to make out the bell tower of *Madonna delle Grazia* on the horizon, the churchyard that had served as a quiet solace for him as a boy during the war. As Domenico took the sharp curve at the church, the Vespa skidded on a chunk of concrete retaining wall that had crumbled off into the road. The back of the scooter swung left, sending Gina tumbling down the grassy hill toward the olive grove while Domenico flew over the handlebars and to the right with his Vespa quickly following to land on his legs with thunderous scraping and clanking sounds.

Walking barefoot up the hill, a stunned Gina emerged, steadying herself with one hand and holding her shoes in the other. Her tan pencil skirt was smeared with grass stains, and leaves littered her once perfectly coiffed dark hair.

"Asshole!" she yelled angrily across the road at Domenico, but she got no response, no reaction at all. She reluctantly crossed the road, approaching the scooter. Domenico, still pinned underneath his Vespa, was bleeding with his half-smoked cigarette smoldering on the ground beside him.

"Oh my God, Domenico!" Gina attempted to free him from under the mangled Vespa.

Domenico screamed in pain as Gina managed to move the scooter sideways a little. The pointed hand control had embedded itself into Domenico's inner thigh. His trousers were already covered in blood.

The leg freed, the bleeding was soon stopped, thanks to Gina's quick thinking. She used the belt from Domenico's trench coat as a tourniquet, a trick she learned patching up her older brothers after fights. They slowly staggered back up the road, leaving the scooter behind. When they finally reached Bar Agostino, Domenico waited outside while Gina ran in to find Domenico's older cousin, Vincenzo. Vincenzo ran outside, still wearing his apron, to help his cousin. He took one look at the two of them and shook his head.

"Jesus, you two are in a sorry state. What the hell happened?"

"Eh, she insisted on sitting side-saddle on the back of my Vespa, then there was a giant rock in the middle of the road, and I lost control. That's it. Just my luck, I guess."

Gina folded her arms defiantly. "You're forgetting the part where you were speeding like a maniac, and then I had to save your life after you almost got me killed!"

"Mimi, what the hell is wrong with you? Are you gonna be able to take care of yourself after your parents leave next week, or am I going to have to look after you?" Vincenzo asked, concerned. "Come on, I'll take you both home, but don't get any blood in my new car!" Everyone carefully piled into Vincenzo's tiny two-door, blue Fiat 600.

Domenico had hoped the unfortunate events of the day could remain just between the three of them, but Vincenzo went on to vividly re-tell the whole story to Emidio and Pasqua as if he'd witnessed it personally, "... and then he just flew through the air! Then, as if he was moving in slow motion, *'BOOM'* he crashed on the ground with the Vespa on top of him!"

Pasqua listened and listened until she couldn't bear it any longer. She stood up, put the palms of her hands together, and closed her eyes tight in exasperation.

"Mimi, why are you torturing us? You've been acting crazy and reckless ever since we decided to leave Italy. Why are you punishing us? We're not abandoning you. We've begged you to join us!" Pasqua began to cry. "*My God*, I can't take it anymore! I need another chance at this life. I need to leave all the misery of this place behind."

"Mimi, you're not a kid anymore; your little brother acts more mature than you. He's settled down already. He and Valeria will be married soon. At least he has a valid reason to abandon his parents." Emidio groaned in frustration. "Listen, I know you work hard and can support yourself, but I don't know if you can take care of yourself. If you refuse to come to New York, then you need to find yourself a wife!"

"Jesus Christ, Papà, I don't want a wife! Why does everyone think I need to be taken care of?"

"You're twenty-two years old–you want to continue wasting your time with foolish girls like–what's her name?"

"Her name is Gina, Papà.

"Yeah, Gina. Whatever."

"And no, I don't think I ever want to see her again. In fact, I'm done with all of them. All these damn women in town are trouble!"

Emidio reached into his shirt's breast pocket and retrieved a long rectangular card. He handed it to Domenico.

"There'll always be a ticket to New York City for you. Keep this safe, in case you change your mind. I'd really like another chance at keeping this family together."

27

STELLA

BROOKLYN, NEW YORK
OCTOBER 2020

I didn't come from an Italian American family that took their kids back to Italy to spend carefree summers together at the beach. Neither did I grow up in a house resembling Tony Soprano's. We didn't get dressed to the nines every weekend to eat and dance the night away at elaborate galas thrown by Italian American organizations, and Christopher Columbus wasn't our hero.

The truth was that my parents changed the channel whenever a mob movie was on TV, they rejected extravagant displays of wealth or success, and the women in my family dressed in black mourning clothes for much of my childhood. Visiting departed loved ones at the cemetery with my mother and nonna was an ordinary part of my week, and I watched Nonna pray the rosary every night before bed.

I'd always sensed an underlying sadness in my parents. Perhaps regrets from a life unlived. My Nonna was less subtle in her dissatisfaction with life–anyone who dared to telephone her during her afternoon soap operas would fall from her good graces, the grocery store being sold out of her brand of coffee was treated as a personal affront, and her boiler breaking down, a punishment from God.

My mother's diaries were so vivid with imagery and attitude, I wished I'd known the young Maria. So full of life, she was filled with hope and fight, even during the darkest of times. What a gift to be given these little pieces of my mother from before her light had been dulled with a never-ending string of health crises. In the weeks since Agata appeared on my doorstep, I had already devoured the first two notebooks like an addict. With her words bouncing around my brain, I'd dream every night of the people and places my mother described. Every day, I'd wake to embark on an imaginary ride through Rocca Leone in Google Maps, re-tracing young Maria's steps.

So keen to share them, and convinced he'd be as fascinated as I was, stories about my mother, the war, and Rocca Leone dominated every conversation I had with Michael. He politely listened, asked questions, and reacted in all the right places, but I could see he wished for normal conversations again, to listen to music sung in a language he understood, made with instruments other than a *tamburello*, *zampogna*, or some quirky jaw harp. My mother's life became my new obsession. I couldn't get enough of her words and being able to visualize her movements through her village with all its hills and absurdly positioned staircases, but my only reference had been the internet.

One night, I woke from a dream, trying to scream. Michael, jarred from sleep, instinctively grabbed me. It wasn't a nightmare.

It was my father I was yelling for, not at, in my dream. We were walking along the edge of a lake, and he said, "As long as you had a good time," then he leaned over and dropped into the water like a rag doll. Those were the exact words he'd always say to me whenever I returned from a trip. He never cared for details or vacation photos, just the knowledge that I'd had a good time.

When I awoke from another dream, I was now certain my father, like Michael, had grown tired of this journey of historical tourism I was putting myself through in the virtual world. But my dad was also telling me to take the journey in the real world—to actually *go* to Italy, to *visit* Sicily, and explore the country of my ancestors in a way in which they'd never been able. It felt like the time he'd been angry at me for taking a sewing class as an adult. I wasn't supposed to sew. He'd sent me to college so I'd never need to sew.

Now, I *needed* to go to Italy.

—

"Michael, can I use your Bronco today? My Fiat won't be big enough," I said as we bumped into each other while making espresso and slicing bagels in our narrow galley kitchen.

"Big enough for what?"

"I had a very different dream last night."

Michael took a deep breath and looked at me suspiciously over the top of his smoke-gray eyeglasses. "Yes, you woke me up screaming."

"Not that one. I had another one after I went back to sleep. In this dream, my father and I were sitting across a table from each other, and he asked me to get his sewing machine from his house–he implored me. There must be a reason, so it shouldn't stay there. It needs to be here, with me," I said.

"Where are we going to store it? It's a giant relic of a machine. And how are you going to lift it into the Bronco on your own? Wait until the weekend, I'll help you," he said.

"Nope, I got this, but I appreciate you!" I said as I grabbed his car keys and gave him a rushed kiss goodbye, my mouth still full of bagel.

I actually had no idea how I would pull it off. Michael was right, it was a giant, heavy relic, but in my dream, it seemed so urgent. It had to be today. Dreams have always been important in my family; we've never dismissed them. They featured a lot in my mother's diaries.

After almost putting my back out, I finally loaded the black and gold Singer sewing machine with its attached wooden cabinet table into the Bronco by sheer stubbornness. Later, at home, I checked the serial number of the machine, as I had done with my other two large sewing machines when I inherited them from my mother, to find the production date. Much to my surprise, not only was it older than I'd estimated, but it was also a significantly rarer model. My father, and obviously, grandfather Emidio before him, had kept the machine in optimal condition for sixty years. However, it seemed they'd purchased it secondhand because I had dated it to the late 19th century. The same model had recently sold on eBay for over four thousand dollars, and on a more curated site for close to five. The pandemic had created niche markets for all varieties of hobbies and collectibles.

So, that's why the dream. That's what he was telling me. My father had just funded my trip to Italy—from the grave!

28

MARIA

EMIGRATION
DECEMBER 1956 – DECEMBER 1958

Maria sat up, propping her chin on one hugged knee, looking out the window as glimpses of towns, most of which she'd never heard of, flashed by. Enna, Caltanissetta, Lercara Friddi, Bagheria, all dotting their journey across the island. Her mother was seated facing Maria; the consequences of her sleepless night had left obvious marks on Nina. She sat in silence for the entire four-hour journey. The exaggerated dark circles bordering her deep-set eyes made her face seem haunted. Her hair was uncharacteristically undone. Maria had heard her mother up half the night crying, the other half pacing, packing, unpacking, and re-packing.

Rosario was in a trance, watching the rapid changes in the landscape. A rich blue expanse, twinkling in the sharp winter sunlight–a panorama he'd only ever seen in books– slowly came into view.

"Maria, look! The sea! It's the Mediterranean!"

"I'm pretty sure we'll be seeing plenty of the sea very soon, Rosario," Maria said, but still smiled at her brother's enthusiasm.

Carmelo adjusted the peak of his flat cap to get a better look. "That means we're almost there," he said somberly.

They exited the train and made their way to the Port of Palermo, walking along Via Francesco Crispi, each carrying one brown cardboard trunk stuffed with only the bare necessities and some keepsakes of home. Maria hung back a few steps with Carmelo.

"Papà? What if I never see you again?"

"Don't say crazy things like that, Maria."

"I'm scared. What if the same thing that happened to the Andrea Doria happens to our ship?" The ill-fated Italian passenger ship had sunk just six months earlier, striking fear into future passengers everywhere.

"Impossible! I made sure you were booked on the best, safest ship in Italy, *The Roma*!"

"You can't be certain! Oh Papà! Why can't you come with us?" she pleaded, knowing the answer already, but she wanted him to know how unhappy she was at the idea he'd stay behind.

"You know it's going to be a big adjustment for everybody. I need to keep working here until we know that you, your mother, and brother are settled over there. Your mother is going to take good care of you and Rosario. When you've begun to build a life there, and your mother has found us a place to live, then I'll join you. Don't worry, your older brothers will look after me," he said with an unconvincing wink.

As the enormous ships became visible against the backdrop of Mount Pellegrino in the distance, they discovered about twenty of their closest family members waiting for them. From the elders to the toddlers, they were all there to surprise Nina, Maria, and Rosario and see them safely off to America. Salvatore, the newlyweds Alfonso and Leonarda, Zia Rosina, and cousin Grazia, were all among the crowd greeting the emigrants with tears, goodbye kisses, and well wishes.

Maria approached her cousin. "Do you think I'll ever find those red azaleas, Grazia?"

"I'm positive you will," responded Grazia with a wink.

Leonarda approached Maria, whispered in her ear, and then placed her hands on her own belly.

"I'm going to be an aunt?!" Maria couldn't contain her excitement. "Wait, does Mamma know she's gonna be a Nonna?"

"Not yet, we were afraid she'd swim all the way back to Sicily if she knew!" said Leonarda, laughing.

Zia Rosina pulled Maria to the side and wrapped her jiggly arms around her in a giant hug so tight it made her gasp for air.

"How am I going to make it through my days without my sister and favorite niece?" asked Rosina, through her tears.

"You'll visit us in New York, won't you, Zia?" asked Maria.

"One day, one day," Zia Rosina said as she placed something in the palm of Maria's hand.

"Wear these to ward off *the eye*. Watch out for jealous people, especially those who give you too many compliments." Rosina cupped Maria's cheek in the palm of her hand and whispered, "And you're gonna need these because I'll bet they've never seen anyone as beautiful as you, *goia!*"

Maria opened her palm to reveal two tiny gold charms, a *cornicello* amulet, and the number thirteen.

———

THEY HAD BEEN AT sea for seven days, and six and a half of those days had been spent in bed, severely ill. They were all bedridden, taking turns running to the bathroom to vomit. None of the family had ever traveled by sea; they had no way of knowing that they all shared a tendency to suffer from seasickness. The transcontinental journey, which could have only taken those seven days in total, had been plagued with rough waters and inclement weather, and it was likely to take twice as long. They were now rocking around somewhere at the center of the Atlantic Ocean, suspended in a liminal space between worlds. They were nowhere, held in some sort of nauseous purgatory. Maria resented this extra time to think because how bad she felt darkened her thoughts.

What if America isn't as great as everyone says it is? What if I hate it there? What if they hate me? What if I regret leaving Sicily?

Not that she or Rosario had been given a choice in the matter: Carmelo and Nina had made all the decisions and laid out all the plans. She was trepidatious in the face of the unknown, yet she yearned to reinvent herself in New York. She knew that was the perfect place to wear her red shoes.

There was a knock on the door. Both Maria and Nina turned to look at Rosario.

"Fine, I'll answer it," Rosario said, opening the door to see Enzo again, a new Neapolitan friend that Rosario had made on the first day. Unaffected by the boat's motion, the other boy had continually, and unsuccessfully, been trying to lure them out of their room to take advantage of the ship's amenities.

"Hey, uh, Rosario. I thought maybe you or—or your sister—were well enough to eat with us in the dining hall tonight."

"Sorry, I don't think so, Enzo. I gotta go–" Rosario answered before he ran into the bathroom yet again.

He emerged from the bathroom looking greener and even weaker than before. "I think we really need to call the doctor now. This is why they have them onboard!"

"*No!* No doctors! I'll throw myself off this ship before I see another doctor!" Maria snapped back, still traumatized from her last brutal encounter with the medical profession.

Nina chimed in, "Leave it alone, Rosario, your sister's right. We'll be OK as soon as we stop moving."

"Right. At this rate, we'll arrive next year," muttered Rosario bitterly.

IT WAS EARLY MORNING on day fourteen at sea, but everyone had lost track of days. Without any windows, the line between day and night had completely blurred, leaving The Sanfilippos confused and delirious. Maria was awoken by a now annoyingly familiar knock on the door. She left it to Rosario to answer.

"The captain said we'll be entering the Port of New York today! It's almost over. We'll be in America today! Happy Christmas Eve!"

"Enzo? What time is it? What do you mean about Christmas?" Rosario answered the door groggy and still cranky.

"It's Christmas Eve, dummy!" Enzo was wired; he clearly hadn't slept yet. "Wake everybody up, Rosario! Tell them we'll be in New York for Christmas!"

"Mamma. Mamma, wake up!" Rosario couldn't just keep this news to himself. "We're finally arriving today–it's Christmas Eve!"

"Today?! Oh, thank the Lord! I can't take it anymore." Nina immediately reached for her burgundy rosary beads, her lips moving as she prayed for the safety of her whole family. The family, which would now somehow have to survive being split in two and stretched across an ocean.

As the *S/S Roma* stood docked at Pier 97 in the Port of New York that afternoon, Maria still felt queasy and wholly unprepared to emerge from the enormous vessel and face the world. Once all the legal and medical formalities of customs and immigration were over and done with, the Sanfilippos were finally cleared for release into the overwhelming, overcrowded, and wild city they would now call home. After two weeks of illness, poor sleep, and no appetite, carrying their large luggage trunks felt like an extraordinary burden.

"Give me your trunk, Mamma, I'll carry it for you," said Rosario as he took his mother's trunk from her weak grip and slowly wobbled along the labyrinth of exit ramps, clutching a cumbersome trunk in each hand. Nina tightened her hand-knit shawl around her shoulders and held her purse close in front of her.

The crushing bottleneck of eager passengers finally diverged off the ramps and onto the enormous dock that led into the terminal. Maria could hear Christmas carols being sung and handbells ringing in the distance. There was an intoxicatingly sweet smell of roasted chestnuts in the air, which changed direction with the wind. Maria then turned her attention to the convivial cheering coming from above. Loved ones of the disembarking passengers, keen to reunite for the holidays, were packed in like sardines on the balcony to welcome them home. The crowd waved enthusiastically, some still gripping the flasks of whiskey, keeping them warm. Maria even spotted a group of women wearing Santa hats constructed out of paper.

"Mamma, we're arriving a week late, and it's Christmas. Do you think Zio Antonio will still be here to meet us?" Maria asked, worried they might find themselves stranded in this chaos.

Two passengers hurrying past her from behind each clipped one of her shoulders, jolting her forward. The kitten heels of her modest black leather shoes were intermittently getting caught in the grooves of the splintered and decaying wood of the dock. She was so pleased she'd packed her red shoes.

"My brother wouldn't abandon us? That's nonsense! C'mon, keep walking. He'll be here," said her mother.

Rosario wasn't tall enough to carry the trunks without lifting them above the ground, and he was clearly struggling. As they walked through the terminal building, Rosario rested the trunks on the ground and paused beneath an archway at the 57th Street exit to catch his breath. Beyond the archway, Maria's gaze turned to the sea of giant, bright yellow cars lined up outside.

Is there some law that all cars have to be yellow?

There was a very tall, thin man in the crowd, a head taller than the rest, positioned under the train trestle across the cobblestone street. Standing at the best vantage point to spot each family as they materialized through the steel archways, his head bobbed, scouring the crowd. The tall man's face brightened as he got a glimpse of the family of three approaching, and he didn't hesitate. He ran through the crowd. There was no doubt in his mind that he'd found his family, but when he started speaking, they had no idea what he was saying. Maria, wide-eyed, looked at her uncle in total confusion.

"Aha! I'm sorry!" He let out a deep belly laugh over his mistake. Switching from English to Italian, he said, "I've been in America so long I forgot you probably have no idea what I'm saying! So, Maria! My beautiful niece, Maria! How could I miss you! You look just like your mother, the last time I saw her!"

Zio Antonio, or Uncle Tony as he preferred to be called now, was a barber-turned salon owner in Queens. Maria's mother had told her how he'd sailed through Ellis Island thirty years earlier as a teenager, accompanied only by his brothers Angelo and Filippo. Together, the brothers survived the Great Depression, making a meager living as fruit vendors on the streets of Manhattan.

"Nina! Come here!" He pulled his exhausted sister in for a long emotional hug. "Maria, Rosario, this is your Aunt Betty, and your cousins Jeanette and Sandra." Uncle Tony introduced them to their newfound family: a petite, well-dressed woman adorned with an elegant pearl necklace, a teenage girl, and a young girl—all in blonde curls. Sandra immediately gave her cousins a big hug. Jeanette, a teenager about Rosario's age, seemed utterly unimpressed with the entire inconvenient situation.

"C'mon let's go home, your new home. What an amazing Christmas! I got my sister back!" Uncle Tony exclaimed while effortlessly grabbing everyone's suitcases, one in each hand, and the third tucked under his right arm.

―

AFTER THEIR WHIRLWIND HOLIDAY week, the only leisure they had allowed themselves, they all began their new lives. Rosario was thrown right in the deep end and started a lonely and confusing first term at the local public high school in Flushing, Queens. As dressmakers in a wedding dress factory in NYC's famous garment district, Nina and Maria were thrust into a world of subway commuting and workers' unions. Working side by side at sewing machines every day, the mother and daughter's lives were increasingly interwoven. Between the three of them, they couldn't even string together one sentence of English. The language barrier made even the smallest task feel like an impossible feat, taxing their bodies and minds. The Sanfilippo family—on both sides of the ocean when they first exchanged letters—worried whether their colossal efforts would be sufficient to achieve their goal of reuniting the whole family in the US.

"Stop touching my stuff! Do. You. Un-der-stand?" Jeanette mocked Maria, pretending to use sign language. She often lashed out at her cousin, but she had been acting meaner recently. The living situation had become tense. Maria was accustomed to living in close quarters without much privacy, but Jeanette was not, and she could not bear sharing a bedroom with her cousin any longer.

"*Scusa cugina*, uh so-rry. I clean the *stanza*." Maria was flustered whenever she attempted to use the few English words she had learned. She felt really small, not being able to properly respond to a bully, and even worse, that her bully was her cousin. Jeanette stormed out of the cluttered room.

―

"This is perfect! But Maria and Rosario will have to share a room, because there's no way we can afford a three-bedroom. We still have all our furniture to buy; we have nothing," Nina said to her brother Tony as her voice echoed throughout the empty room of the apartment he'd found for them.

"One thing at a time. As long as you all have beds to sleep in, you can get the rest little by little," Tony reassured his sister.

"Look, you can almost see the High School from the front window. Rosario can walk to school, and Maria and I can catch the bus a couple of blocks away." Nina's heels clacked along the hardwood floors as she looped back around the apartment, making her one last assessment. "OK, we'll show Maria. I think this is the one."

With Uncle Tony's help in translating, dealing with brokers, and navigating viewings, The Sanfilippos moved into their first apartment. Nina and Maria had been working full-time at the wedding dress factory for months since they'd arrived, and all their earnings were pooled for this very purpose. They were ready to finally rent their first American apartment, ready to write again to Carmelo in Sicily, and this time tell him their great news. They were especially impatient for the day they could write that they were ready for him to join them in New York. Nina was a natural matriarch, but it was a job she never wanted. She longed to be reunited with her husband, so he could help take the weight of parenting and simply be an adult in this new and still confusing world.

THERE WASN'T MUCH TO move in at first, except for a few boxes and the brand-new beds they'd purchased. Maria opened a box of clothes at the foot of the bed and pulled out the red shoes. That birthday had evolved into the worst day of her life, strapped to a table, having her tonsils cut out. The day that became the last straw for her parents, the day they decided to leave Sicily. She ran her fingers over the thin folds of red satin. That day seemed like a lifetime ago now.

She sat on the edge of her new twin bed, the mattress still encased in plastic, and dropped the shoes back into the box. She looked at the identical twin bed on the other side of the room and sighed. Maria wasn't thrilled about having to share a room with her little brother.

"It's only temporary," she told herself.

She reached for her purse and pulled out a flyer. She had been carrying it around for a couple of weeks, afraid to act on it.

"What am I waiting for," she said to herself as she dialed the number on the flyer.

She remembered that Georgios, a fabric cutter who worked on the same floor as Maria, had stopped her in the hallway one day and presented her with the flyer.

"You live in Queens. You said you want better to learn English, yes?" he said.

"Yes, you remember?" said Maria as she took the flyer, relieved that it was written in multiple languages, including Italian.

She and Georgios, a recent Greek immigrant, had briefly stumbled through a conversation months ago in their broken English about how difficult everything was as soon as they stepped outside of their homes, and into a world where they could barely read street signs or understand any social cues. Maria often felt like a baby learning to take her first steps and speak her first syllables.

"You not easy to forget," Georgios said with a sweet smile, trying to charm Maria.

It was a flyer to enroll in an adult elementary school program–night school–at a Flushing high school that was conveniently on the way home for Maria.

"I go here too, at night," Georgios said proudly, hoping that would help convince Maria to enroll. "I start class level two already, but I still need better English. You come maybe?"

Maria was so focused on surviving all the overwhelming aspects of her new life here that she'd left her school girl dreams behind long ago. Higher education was clearly Rosario's destiny, not hers. Going to school was the one thing she'd truly yearned for since she was a young girl. She felt nervous about the prospect of being a student again, about being judged and graded on her English skills, but mostly about how to tell her mother that she was enrolled in school. Nina was never exactly a cheerleader for Maria's continued education, but her mother knew they must learn the language.

"It's once a week; she can survive without me one night a week!" Maria was absolutely energized at the thought of improving her English and how that could make her and her family's life easier. But also, she was looking forward to actually having her own identity away from family, particularly her mother, for a mere two hours a week. She lived with her mother, worked with her mother, and commuted every day to Manhattan with her mother. This would be hers, exclusively.

FOR TWO YEARS, MARIA shared her evenings with an eclectic group of adults. Immigrants from all over the globe, speaking a plethora of different languages. They came together every Wednesday night at PS 20 in Flushing with the common goals of learning English and obtaining an American elementary education. For some, it was also their only real opportunity to socialize outside of their homes and cultures. Rosario had always been the scholar in the family, the one galloping toward his dream of becoming a valedictorian and university student. Maria, on the other hand, had only gotten a small glimpse into the 1950s American high school experience, minus the sock hops and homecoming games.

Georgios made every attempt to get to know Maria better over the first year; he even changed his night school class from Monday to Wednesday just to be able to run into her for a few minutes after class.

"Maria, can I ride the bus with you tonight?" he asked nervously, in English, one evening, before she'd even gathered her things.

Maria was one of the last students to exit her classroom. Dressed in a dark pencil skirt and a buttoned-up baby blue cardigan, Maria calmly gathered up her workbooks and notebooks. She removed her black cat eye glasses, trimmed with rhinestones, and slipped them delicately back into their purple velvet pouch.

"Georgios, you don't even live in Flushing. Why would you ride the bus in the opposite direction with me?" Maria asked, completely oblivious to Georgios' flirting, as usual. "Besides, I won't be taking the bus tonight, my brother's meeting me. We have so many preparations to make before my father gets here. He's finally joining us from Sicily!" Maria said excitedly.

It was autumn of 1958, and it had been two years since the Sanfilippo family had been separated. Two years since they began to create their place in this new world, this modern and bounteous, yet confusing and sometimes infuriatingly lonely new world. The postman had finally delivered the exciting green and red-trimmed air mail envelope they had been anticipating. Carmelo had booked his solo voyage from Sicily to New York to join his family. The Sanfilippo home was beginning to feel whole again. All that was missing now was Salvatore and Alfonso.

29

DOMENICO

NEW YORK CITY
SEPTEMBER 1958

"I told you! I told you this place is nothing like you thought it would be," Emidio yelled back to Domenico, who lagged behind, seemingly overwhelmed by the gritty, filthy, loud, unhinged neighborhood they were strolling through. The buildings were so tall they appeared to be distorted–as if they could bend and land on top of him at any moment. There were rivers of cars and pedestrians flowing in every direction. People could simply walk out into the middle of traffic, whistle or wave a finger, and a yellow checker taxicab would cross three lanes to meet and pick them up.

"Where is all that music coming from? Are there bands playing?" Domenico heard music everywhere, music that would change each time they traversed a new pedestrian crossing. Music from above, from below, from behind secret doors that required payment to gain entry.

From the moment Domenico had stepped off the *S/S Guilio*

Cesare in the Port of New York, he had been begging his father to take him to see the famous Broadway theatre district. Emidio tried his best to discourage his son, or at the very least manage his expectations about this notorious part of Manhattan. Domenico expected to see giant glamorous billboards and marquees lit by thousands of sparkling bright lights, high society folks dressed in their best black tie evening wear on their way to the opera, and bellhops guarding fancy hotel entryways as if it were Buckingham Palace.

Manhattan definitely delivered on the billboards, so many giant billboards that it felt claustrophobic. However, he did not expect the invitations to peep shows, the topless entertainment, the bounty of scantily clad prostitutes strutting around in broad daylight, and all the men sleeping on layers of cardboard in their own filth out on the sidewalk.

"Is this even legal? Anyone can just walk into one of these places?" Domenico's cheeks were turning red with embarrassment as he stood staring incredulously at a storefront window featuring a large photo of a woman barely clothed and seated in a suggestive pose.

"He he! See something you like or have you had enough?" teased Emidio as they took turns lighting their cigarettes with Domenico's silver lighter. "Come on, let's go home now, Brooklyn looks nothing like this." Emidio had a good chuckle at his son's expense.

"Stay to the right!" Emidio directed his disoriented son as they maneuvered up the dank staircase after their long, cramped, and sweaty ride underground. As they walked along Fulton Street,

Emidio stopped mid-block and turned Domenico's attention to a three-story building with a barber shop on the ground floor.

"Well, this is it. What do you think?" Emidio asked proudly.

"That whole building is yours?" asked Domenico in awe.

"No! We live in the second-floor apartment. That one there with the stars on the facade. Whole building, yeah, sure. Who do you think I am, Rockefeller?"

"OK, OK. Let's go see Mamma," Domenico said as they began their ascent up the stairs. Like most buildings in New York City, there was at any given moment a combination of food aromas from all different cultures and ethnicities wafting and mingling through hallways and stairwells. Midway up the first flight of stairs, with senses as keen as a bloodhound, Domenico stopped in his tracks with a familiar nausea.

"Rice?! Please don't tell me she's cooking rice!" he begged his father.

"How the hell do I know what she's cooking? I've been with you all day! Hey, don't make her upset, she's having a good day!" Emidio snapped back.

As Domenico burst through the door to surprise Pasqua, he did his best not to gag at the now obvious smell of cooked rice.

"Mamma!" Domenico hugged Pasqua so hard, he practically lifted her off the floor.

"Mimi! Mimi, enough!" Pasqua broke free from Domenico's constricting hug, smiled, and then went in for another hug with her eldest son.

"Mamma? Why would you cook rice when you knew I'd be here tonight?"

"Why? You don't like rice? Since when?" Pasqua seemed completely unbothered.

Domenico couldn't understand how his mother could forget his disdain for rice and all the fights they had about it during the war. His father gave him a stern look.

"Let it go, Mimi. Come, I'll make you a drink."

Emidio grabbed an ice tray out of the freezer and walked Domenico into the quaint living room attached to the kitchen. He opened a small cabinet and grabbed a bottle of gin and a bottle of vermouth.

"I was going to talk to you about your mother, but now you've seen it for yourself. Her mind, it's not what it used to be; she forgets things, and she gets confused." He reached back into the cabinet for two martini glasses.

"Since when do you drink martinis? New York made you a fancy man?" Domenico tried to lighten the mood, but it earned him a side-eyed look from his father that he hadn't seen in years.

"What's wrong with her? Have you taken her to see a doctor?" asked Domenico.

"Eh, these doctors!" He dismissed the idea with a sharp wave of his hand. "The doctor charged me a fortune just to tell me that she missed her family, and that she was depressed." Now he began to whisper. "If that's true, well, then maybe she'll get better now that you're here. I was hoping you could help me find a good doctor, one that will finally actually help her." Emidio motioned by tapping one finger on the side of his head. "I think all she needs is some medicine, or a big injection of vitamins. But let's keep this just between us." He dropped two Spanish Manzanilla olives into Domenico's glass and then raised his own in a toast. "*Salute!*"

"*Cin, cin,*" added Domenico.

This was already more than Domenico bargained for.

I thought I made it clear I was coming for a visit to see New York and maybe decide if I would make the move in a few years. He's already got me immigrated. I should have known this would happen.

DOMENICO WOKE TO THE unfamiliar faint buzzing of a city full of life. His parents' apartment felt still for the first time since he'd arrived; he was alone. His parents were both out–Pasqua at the market, and Emidio across the river in the garment district of Manhattan, where he worked at a men's trouser factory. They had let their eldest son sleep in after his seven-day journey by sea. His disdain for carrying anything larger than a billfold led to a half-empty suitcase barely sufficient for those last seven days at sea. He found himself in desperate need of some basic toiletries like a razor, shaving cream, and, of course, cigarettes.

Domenico took this opportunity to choose what he wanted to do to familiarize himself with the neighborhood–with America–and run some errands. He bewilderedly followed the overwhelming alien sights, sounds, and aromas to nearby Fulton St. He walked until he reached the first intersection–the crowds growing considerably with every step he took. Domenico could hear the roar of bus engines and the rattle of the train approaching on the elevated tracks above him. He was lost in confusion, staring out onto an intersection so enormous, he couldn't see to the other side. It looked like a never-ending ocean that went out as far as the eye could see. He stood teetering on the edge of the curb at the aptly named Atlantic Ave., hesitant to cross the perilous thoroughfare. He followed some confident locals ahead of him but froze in the crosswalk halfway through the intersection when the light unexpectedly turned green again.

A leather-faced man in a red and white Coca-Cola truck yelled at him as he leaned on his horn, but Domenico had no idea what he'd said.

Domenico leapt out of the way, his long tweed coat whirling and billowing behind him. He found himself standing in the turn lane, facing oncoming traffic. He scrambled and stumbled the rest of the way across Atlantic Ave., struggling like a cartoon character slipping on a banana peel. His blundering miscalculations landed him directly in front of what looked like a pharmacy on the corner. He was embarrassed but relieved to take refuge indoors at last, safe from the traffic and angry drivers.

The drivers here are crazier than in Rome.

He wandered up and down the narrow aisles at the Clinton Pharmacy in a daze.

Why do Americans need ten different types of shaving cream? What the hell is the difference?

While he could work out some of the signs, he didn't recognize any products. He squinted at the labels as if that could help translate them. He didn't even know how much one dollar was worth.

It never occurred to him that he might need to speak English to run a simple errand.

Everyone seemed to be in a hurry. Customers pushed past him with impatience as if he were an inconvenience. He stood dumbfounded in the hectic store, where he realized he could get medicine, buy candy and cigarettes, sample cologne, have photos developed, and eat an ice cream sundae all in one visit.

"Parli Italiano?" A welcome voice came from behind the counter.

The pharmacist in the white lab coat must have taken pity on him. Domenico's ears perked up at the sound of his mother tongue being spoken in the middle of this foreign land.

"Tomorrow you'll come to work with me and meet the foreman. He'll find you a good job there. I told him all about you already!" Emidio had every aspect of Domenico's trip planned out. Most importantly, he was manipulating his visit into a permanent move.

"Papà, I don't want to come to work with you tomorrow. I don't want to work with you. How many times do I have to tell you I'm only visiting before you finally respect that?"

"Eh, you'll change your mind," said Emidio flippantly.

"I almost got killed trying to cross the damn street today. This place is insane!"

"Maybe, but what do you have to go back to in Abruzzo? Your brother's moving to Rome. Your family's here now."

After a full week of the same conversations, the same guilt trips, and scheming, Domenico had had enough. On a Monday afternoon, when he knew he was alone in the apartment, he gathered up the few belongings that he'd traveled with, grabbed his passport from the coffee table, and tucked it safely into his blazer's inside pocket. As he descended onto Fulton Street, he decided to try a trick he'd watched performed in Times Square on his very first day in New York City.

"Taxi!" Domenico put two fingers in his mouth and whistled, and just like that, an approaching yellow taxi hit the brakes to pick him up.

The taxi driver rattled off some words in a thick accent, which Domenico assumed were to ask where he wanted to go.

"Uh ... Ship. Ship 8 - 4." Domenico managed to stutter in broken English.

"Ship 84?" More unintelligible babbling, but Domenico managed to pick out the English word 'Pier' before the cab driver repeated, "Pier 84?"

"*Si, si,* 84!"

The driver pushed the cab out into the traffic with a blare of horns, and Domenico closed his eyes, offering a silent prayer that he'd end up in the right place.

—

As Emidio returned home from work that evening, a panicked Pasqua rushed to meet him at their front door.

"He's gone! Mimi's gone. He took his passport, all his

clothes—everything! You have to find him. Don't let him leave us!" she said, alarmed and frightened.

Pasqua saw Domenico as her glimmer of hope. She had been feeling more and more like her old self this week. She didn't want to lose that feeling, but she especially didn't want to lose her son again.

"Mary, the old Irish woman from the third floor, said she saw Mimi get into a taxi this afternoon. Emidio, where could he have gone? He doesn't know anybody here!"

"Wait, he took his passport?! I know where he's going. I'll find him. I hope I'm not too late!" Emidio was already down one flight of stairs before he finished his sentence.

Pasqua, dressed in a sleeveless summer floral house dress layered over a navy-blue sweater, looked at her tiny kitchen where she was about to begin cooking dinner. She looked at the laundry pile by the front door that she was supposed to bring downstairs to the laundromat, and then she shuffled in her slippers toward the bedroom and cried until she fell asleep.

―

MEANWHILE, DOMENICO CONSULTED THE Trans-Atlantic Steamship Line schedule and pricing list that was posted at the ticket office. A third-class ticket on the *S/S Augustus* bound for Naples was the only Italian Line voyage he could afford. $195 US dollars, everything he had left. With a combination of his pidgin English and the booking clerk's rudimentary Italian, Domenico thought he'd got through and started pulling money from his wallet.

Emidio raced to make it to Pier 84, all the way over at 44th St., where the Italian Line of passenger ships docked and departed. He was forced to take three different modes of transport: the subway to a bus, and finally a taxi for the last stretch of the journey along the waterfront, to get from downtown Brooklyn to the west side of midtown Manhattan.

He threw a $10 bill into the front seat of the taxi as soon as the taxi driver tapped the brakes, and he sprinted toward the terminal building at the edge of the pier. Inside was a chaotic scene of aimless passengers and luggage strewn about the terminal. Lines of people stretched out in every direction, making it impossible to know if the lines led to the telephone booths, the ticket booths, or the restrooms. Emidio ran from line to line until he spotted the "Tickets" sign. He inspected every person in line, from the last person until he worked his way to the front of the line.

"*Mimi! No!*"

He spotted his son trying to hand money over to the ticket booth clerk.

"*Stop!*" Emidio slammed Domenico's hand down on the counter, still gripping his stack of $20 bills. The line of people behind them was in an uproar, with insults flying in Italian and English.

"You're never going to stop interfering in my life, are you? Not unless I do exactly what you want me to do, live where you want me to live. I'm twenty-five years old, I'm an adult, but I guess that doesn't matter. You're going to make me stay in New York." Domenico stormed away, back through the terminal building, with Emidio chasing after him.

30

STELLA

ABRUZZO, ITALY
DECEMBER 2020

I'd always joked that sewing machines had put me through college. Now they'd also sent me and Michael on the trip of a lifetime to visit my ancestral lands and other exciting and historic towns along the way.

I squeezed Michael's hand so hard I could see him wincing out of the corner of my eye, not that he'd ever dare to break free. "Bella Ciao" played on the crappy red corded earbuds that were plugged into the armrest. I always chose one meaningful song to play on repeat from the moment we began taxiing until we went completely horizontal, coasting through the clouds. Today's choice, obviously inspired by our NYC to Rome flight, had looped eight times before I could confidently press pause and release Michael from my death grip.

"Are you excited?" asked Michael.

"Yeah, I am. I'm just hoping to find a little magic," I said almost mischievously.

"I hope you haven't set your expectations too high. It won't play out like a film, Stella," said Michael with a familiar, concerned head tilt.

"That's not what I meant. I'm not on a mission to uncover anything. I'm looking forward to a wonderful Christmas and a beautiful couple of weeks with you in a place I consider magical.

WE'D BARELY DRIVEN AN hour from the airport, but the scenes outside my window didn't seem to exist in the same universe as Rome. Michael drove through tunnel after tunnel, all carved out of the snow-capped Gran Sasso mountain range of Abruzzo, while I translated the road signs. It looked more like Switzerland than Italy—more wilderness adventure than *la dolce vita*. This was the land of shepherds, nestled between the sea and the mountains. I felt ashamed I'd never visited Abruzzo before, always opting for the most popular or predictable beacons of tourism—Rome, Florence, Venice, and Milan—of the land of my ancestors. None of those places even offered a glimpse into my family's lived experiences, and now, as Michael liked to remind me, with my father's passing and the discovery of my mother's diaries, I'd gone from zero interest to obsession.

By the time we drove across to the eastern side of the Italian peninsula to our destination just outside Montesciano, we had already been awake a full twenty-four hours. With mutual sighs of relief, we drove up the long, winding driveway to our Airbnb rental house. I held my breath as we were greeted by the lulling sounds of the crystal clear river running through the land at the rear of the three-bedroom stone-built property with a terracotta tiled roof. I marveled at the beauty of our secluded temporary Italian home, running my fingers along the plants surrounding the patio and over the smooth internal stone walls. I felt as if I'd just landed on a new planet.

Michael tore open his suitcase in the living room and changed his clothes as I excitedly mapped out the short drive to Piazza Vittorio Emmanuele in Montesciano, where my father had grown up.

"You're not wearing your sweatpants out, are you?" I asked.

"Out?" Michael said, looking exhausted.

"Yes, out! We're only here for a couple of days, so we can't waste any time!"

Michael trudged back to his suitcase to change clothes again.

We approached Piazza Vittorio Emmanuele as the car stereo played one of my favorite Italian folk music playlists. It felt like we were starring in our own movie.

"There's St. Michael's bell tower!" I said with excitement. The pink tower, the tallest structure in town, stood at the head of the piazza. As we turned the corner, my father's little bright yellow house beckoned from the end of the piazza.

A quintessentially Italian coffee bar with a green marble wraparound counter now occupied the first floor of my father's old building. We sat outside enjoying our *caffè* and chocolate-dipped *cantucci,* a crunchy almond biscotti, while Montesciano's community cats weaved in and out of our legs, hoping for a crumb to drop. My gaze was fixated on the yellow house above the cafe, picturing my father as a little boy, running in and out of the second-floor front door. I imagined my grandmother standing on the little balcony, calling her boys home. I wished my father could have been here with us.

Why didn't we all just take this trip together when we could?

"Are you OK?" asked Michael, placing his hand on my arm.

"Yeah, just thinking about Dad, and what it would have been like if he'd been able to show us around his town—to see Montesciano through his eyes," I said, downing the cold remnants of my espresso.

As was our tradition whenever we visited any European city, we stopped into the *tabaccheria* to buy my father the craziest looking Lotto scratch-off ticket we could find. Even though he was gone, I wanted to keep the tradition alive. We wandered to the edge of the piazza, where we stumbled upon a shiny plaque adorned with red poppies, tucked away from the bustle of the piazza.

"*Partigiani?*" I read out loud.

It commemorated the Italian partisans and anti-fascists of Montesciano from WWII. *Partisans operating in Montesciano?*

"You know, I do remember my father proudly telling me my grandmother 'hid people' during the war," I told Michael, also thinking of the files Benny's source had found for me.

"My grandfather's debriefing transcripts mentioned my grandmother hosting 'guests' while he was away in South Africa. I never gave it much thought; it was vague. I'd always thought it was just a story my father had made up; he never gave me any details."

"You think your grandmother could have worked for the resistance?" asked Michael.

Last month, I found out my Nonno Carmelo was a socialist; now I may discover that my paternal grandmother worked for the resistance. Why did it have to be the two grandparents I never learned much about?

"Don't know, but it makes me grieve for the woman I never got to know, the stories I never heard, the role model I missed out on," I said.

I stood there in view of my father's old home, imagining my grandmother Pasqua shuffling people in and out of the piazza to safety under the cover of darkness. Maybe it was just a fantasy. I resisted the urge to delve deeper.

We meticulously examined the decorative cobblestone patterns and compared sight lines, attempting to match them to old family photos from the piazza. An elderly gentleman approached us in his mobility scooter and pulled his blue surgical mask down around his chin. Italy, much like the rest of the world, still reeled from the Covid pandemic.

"Are you looking for anybody in particular here?" he asked in Italian.

The man, who told us his name was Gianfranco, appeared to know every resident, the unofficial town mayor. "The house we're in front of used to be mine. I unfortunately had to leave after the terrible earthquake we had in 2009 made it uninhabitable."

"Oh, I'm so sorry to hear that," I replied.

"Oh no, it's OK. We were luckier than most. And I still live nearby," said Gianfranco.

"I was planning to pose for a photo in the same spot as my father did in this photo from about seventy years ago." I showed him the photo on my phone, "His name was Fiorinelli, Domenico."

"Fiorinelli? Ahh, Emidio's boy! Emidio was a great tailor; he made me a beautiful coat once when I was a teenager. I brought him my older brother's old wool coat, and he took that whole thing apart. He reconstructed it into an even better coat with a satin lining. It fit me like a glove. That coat was a piece of art! He wouldn't even take any money for it."

Is this really happening?

"Emidio Fiorinelli was my nonno," I muttered, when he must have already worked that out. This was unreal.

"Yeah! They lived right over there, in the yellow house," the man said confidently.

I felt dizzy with joy.

"Did you know my father; did you know Domenico?" I asked.

"Yeah, of course, Domenico and Donato. They were a little older than me. They used to ride their Vespa all over the place!" Gianfranco said matter-of-factly, as if recalling a memory from last week, rather than seventy years ago.

"I don't know what to say, Gianfranco. I'm a bit in shock. My name is Stella. I can't believe I found you on my very first day in Abruzzo–or actually, you found me," I said nervously, suddenly stumbling on my Italian.

"It's a pleasure to meet you, Stella. Will you come join me at my house for coffee with my wife and me? Please, I would really love it if you would," said Gianfranco. I turned to look at Michael, who nodded. This was my decision.

"Yes, of course, Gianfranco! Thank you!"

The words came cheerfully flowing out of my mouth before I even realized what I'd said.

Michael winked at me and whispered, "The Stella Fiorinelli I know would never follow a stranger back to their house in some little mountain town, in a foreign country."

He wasn't wrong. As lifetime New Yorkers, this situation should have certainly raised a giant red flag for us both.

"Well, this place feels more like home to me than the country I was born in," I said, as we set off to keep up with the little scooter.

I could recognize the dialect spoken by the barista as my father's, the nose protruding from the face of the old woman shuffling along the narrow cobblestone alley as my own, and the divergent eyes of the man who sold me this lotto ticket at that tobacco shop as my grandmother's.

"I know this all feels very strange to you right now, but it feels oddly like I belong here. Don't forget, Michael, I'm a citizen of this little foreign mountain town!"

"OK, come on, you'll follow me up that hill!" Gianfranco called over his shoulder, motioning for us to follow.

As we walked to our rental car to follow Gianfranco's scooter back to his home, I turned to Michael, "See? Just a little bit of magic."

We slowly followed Gianfranco's scooter away from the piazza as all the townsfolk along the way stopped to chat with him. As we arrived at the inviting one-story house surrounded by colorful flower pots, we were greeted at the door by Gianfranco's wife.

Introduced to us as Giuliana, she was soon busy preparing a tray full of espressos and sweets. An elderly gentleman next door stood watching us with his hands clasped behind his back.

"They're from America! Her father was a Montescianese! Do you remember the Fiorinelli family?" said Gianfranco to the elderly man.

The man looked blank, shrugged bony shoulders, and went back inside.

We all sat around their kitchen table getting to know each other. As Gianfranco spoke proudly of his time with the *Alpini*, Italy's elite mountain infantry, I recognized the infantry's iconic green-gray felt hat with the black raven feather hanging on their coat rack, the *Cappello Alpino*. Gianfranco peppered in some English phrases throughout, excited to use the language skills he'd picked up in the army, and seemingly wanting to make sure Michael was comfortable.

They seemed genuinely eager to get to know us–how I learned to speak Italian, where I grew up, and how much of Abruzzo we'd visited. They were interested in my family's immigration story from both sides, and even the traditional foods my parents continued to prepare in their new home country. I did my best to keep Michael involved through my translations and summarizations. He held his end of the conversation through hand gestures, Gianfranco's snippets of English, and Google Translate.

Our encounters with the people of Abruzzo had proved the internet wrong. A few scrolls through social media would have you believe native Italians felt no connection to their vast diaspora and our stories as Italian Americans, that they rejected the notion of descendants of immigrants identifying as Italian. It sometimes felt like we were a dead weight, cut off decades ago, and there was no room for us now. Did they not understand how deeply connected we felt to this land? How out of place we felt at times, straddling two cultures, never fully finding our footing in either?

By the end of that first afternoon, both Michael and I left the welcoming homes of kind strangers, turned friends with full bellies and warmed hearts. Everyone we met showed the same warmth.

"Maybe my father did just show us around his town after all," I said to Michael.

"Maybe ..." said Michael, smiling. He even seemed to catch some of my longing to belong and to feel at home there.

Now I knew it was true what was said about the Abruzzese people–*forte e gentile,* strong and gentle. Through each serendipitous conversation with a stranger, each invitation to *caffè,* the people of Abruzzo claimed me as one of their own.

―

EARLY THE NEXT MORNING, after a long, much-needed sleep, I woke to the sight of snow-dusted olive trees outside our bedroom window and the tranquil white noise of the crystal-clear river running behind the house.

"So it wasn't a dream?" I said to myself.

I stepped out into the frosty mountain air alone, with only my coat and a steaming cup of espresso to watch the sunrise over the Gran Sasso. Never in a million years did I dream that I'd be able to step out my back door to see the majestic mountain range towering over me, standing guard. My first day in Abruzzo had felt like a wonderfully strange fever dream. The quaint town of Montesciano had already provided more magic than I could have hoped for, and we still had a couple of days left to explore.

That day, we were headed to a hamlet where the Fiorinelli lineage dated as far back as the 16th century. Ever since I'd stumbled across a real estate listing for a home among a community of dilapidated centuries-old houses in a hamlet bearing my name a few years ago, I'd wanted to visit *Villa Fiorinelli* in Montesciano. I'd now found documentation that evidenced members of my branch of the Fiorinelli family tree having lived and died on this land for hundreds of years.

We arrived to find one street sign propped on a bench covered in community cats, with another hung on a pole with an unreal blue and white backdrop of the mountains meeting the sky. Both bore my name, pointing us toward Villa Fiorinelli. As we made our way past modern houses at the top of the hill, on the way down the path, I struck up a conversation with a woman in her forties, wrangling three dogs–she turned out to be a Fiorinelli. The woman, Elisabetta, invited us to stop by on our way back up the hill for *caffè* with her and her mother.

We'd thought Gianfranco's invitation the day before had been the rare exception, a gregarious man eager to swap stories, but it seemed hospitality and geniality were a way of life for the Abruzzese.

As the path gave way to a wide-open terrain, the weeds reached our calves. All that was left standing were the empty stone skeletons of the houses that once filled the hamlet, wrapped in English Ivy and surrounded by Bay Laurel, the native plants that had reclaimed the land that was once farmed by Fiorinelli hands.

Our conversation with Elisabetta and her mother revealed that my grandfather Emidio was born in one of these houses, and his father died inside another, now all ravaged by earthquakes and the passing of time. Given the history of these lands, the soil was steeped in Fiorinelli blood.

As we made our way back to the car, I stood at the center of this all but forgotten place, my feet planted firmly on the ground, and took a moment to visualize the lives that once pulsed through here. The strong women who came before me walked these paths, delivering water in large copper *concas* they balanced expertly on their heads. They experienced the joys and the sorrows of home births and deaths, illness and epidemics, right here where I was standing. I pulled a small, thin glass vial from my jacket pocket and grabbed a stick from the ground to scrape some of the cold, sandy soil into the vial. As we took a small detour to check out the rest of what was left of the village, we were escorted along the way by stray dogs of all shapes, sizes, and temperaments, as well as a few nosy sheep, eagerly bleating and following as if we were their shepherds. Even the local animals seemed to want to welcome us and stop for conversation.

Later that evening, over a generous glass of Montepulciano, I used the edge of a 1 Euro coin to scratch the Lotto ticket I purchased for my father. The tiny bits of foil scratched away to reveal I was a winner, 10 Euro. I cried.

"We don't have to cash it in, you know, we can just take it back with us," said Michael.

Claiming my 10 Euro would have meant leaving my father's ticket behind. The thought of leaving his gift behind made me irrationally sad. I shoved the ticket deep into my duffel bag to add to my ancestor altar at home.

31

MARIA

FLUSHING, NEW YORK
JUNE 1965

Carmelo slowly stepped off the Q28 bus, still wearing his white canvas cook's apron, onto the sprawling boulevard that stretched across most of the borough of Queens. From where he stood on Francis Lewis Blvd, his quaint mid-century ranch house was already coming into focus. The intense heat from DiMaggio's kitchen and the clouds of cigarette smoke that filled the restaurant's dining room combined with the humidity of the sticky summer air had drained every last bit of energy that remained in Carmelo's body after his closing shift at the popular Italian restaurant.

It was a whirlwind year with so much excitement still in store for the Sanfilippos. Rosario had gone from a shy teenage boy who couldn't utter one word of English to a man who had earned a Law Degree and secured a position at a well-respected firm in Manhattan in less than nine years. However, the real event would be next week. Rosario was marrying his college sweetheart, Peggy. Nina and Maria were throwing her a bridal shower in the official Italian American party venue, the basement. Carmelo looked at all the extra parked cars on the block, a particularly garish one even occupying his driveway, and then his unusually brightly illuminated house. "Ah, damn it!" he muttered as his shoulders slumped forward.

He'd completely forgotten about the party. All he wanted to do was have himself one drink in silence and go straight to bed. He stepped onto the black and white checkerboard floor tiles as he entered the bottom floor of his house, dodging all the buoyant white balloons and pink streamers hanging overhead as the celebratory sounds got closer and louder.

"Eh, Carmelo!" the men called out in unison.

The husbands and boyfriends who had come to pick up their significant others had stayed to join the party. Carmelo looked around the room at the games of *scopa* and guests playing bartender with his bar cart. They summoned the exhausted Carmelo to join their game.

The men's side of the room swirled with cigarette smoke, mixed with the woody and sweet aromas of Scotch whiskey and Italian liqueurs. The plastic-covered dining table was strewn with sculptural ashtrays, crystal-cut tumbler glasses half-full of Strega or Cynar digestif, and stacks of dollar bills. Their combined spirited conversations created a wall of sound pierced only by the sporadic, sharp clinking of their ice cubes.

The young women huddled at the other end of the room, at the buffet table now covered with the remains of rum-soaked sheet cake and cream-filled works of art like dense doughy *sfingi* and delicately flaky *sfogliatelle*. They had carefully constructed a humongous bonnet made of paper plates and an entire array of bows and ribbons from Peggy's gifts. They delicately placed the comically large, colorfully crafted hat on Peggy's head as she laughed.

"Smile!" Maria gleefully prompted, as she snapped a series of photos with her Kodak Brownie camera.

As Carmelo passed through the basement kitchen, the origin of every family meal and banquet-worthy platter, he heard the comforting sound of his wife's roaring laugh. Nina entertained and held court for the women of her generation. She had surrounded herself with her sister Angela, who had finally made the voyage over to America, her sister-in-law Lina, and the various close friends she considered family, her *cumare*. The women didn't seem to notice Carmelo as they feasted on the ever-flowing pots of espresso and trays of homemade biscotti. They were all riveted as his wife regaled them with an old tale from when her brother Gennaro's dim-witted donkey escaped and kicked off a full-scale chase through the streets of Rocca Leone.

"It was like the Sicilian Running of the Bull, except with hundreds of farmers and a stupid donkey!" said Nina as he moved past the kitchen.

She was the raucous storyteller to Carmelo's strong silence. Nina seemed to find wisdom or levity in even the painful stories, transforming them into moments of hilarity. Her delivery was always impeccable, and her infectious laughter brought people to tears of happiness. Even the newest, most American family members who could barely understand Italian, let alone Nina's Sicilian, craved to be around her.

Carmelo looked around the room at everyone he loved, the dreams they were fulfilling, the accomplishments that would not have been possible in their old life back in Sicily. He'd only received a third-grade education, but his son was a college graduate with a Master's and a Law Degree. He'd spent most of his life on a farm, but his daughter had a great job in New York City and became a homeowner at the age of twenty-two.

Carmelo, Nina, and Maria had consolidated their savings and purchased their first house in Flushing in 1960. It was a beautiful modern hi-ranch with a large front lawn trimmed with azalea bushes, bedecked with red and pink blooms every spring. They created a home not only for themselves, but their entire extended family. It was a place where they found community and felt at home.

They welcomed family and friends new to the US, just as Tony and Betty had done for their family when they arrived. Alfonso was still adamant about remaining in Rocca Leone with Leonarda and their little family. Salvatore had married the year prior, and Rosario was set to leave the nest in a few short days. Carmelo prepared to be a family of three, as Maria remained resolutely single.

NINA WAS IMPECCABLY DRESSED in a new sage green silk dupioni dress of her own creation, paired with a luxurious tan fur stole. An inconspicuous pill box hat trimmed in a short mesh veil sat atop her sculpted jet-black hair–Nina went to great lengths to ensure that not even one strand of gray hair would ever be revealed.

"Carmelo, what's going on up there? What's taking you so long? They're all waiting for us to take family photos!"

"I can't get this stupid tie right!" He had tied and re-tied his sleek, pale silver tie so many times that it had become wrinkled and damp. Carmelo looked frustrated, as sweat trickled down from his temples.

"Come here; let me fix it. Men, they can't do anything for themselves," Nina muttered under her breath as she effortlessly and expertly tied Carmelo's tie.

Nina's entire family waited in the Sanfilippos' backyard for her and Carmelo. Any annoyance Nina felt melted away as soon as she saw her son Rosario in his white suit.

"*Il professore*! Congratulations! Come here, you! I'm so proud of you, Rosario!" Uncle Tony, still towering over him, wrapped Rosario in a joyful embrace on his wedding day.

"You know, I think I'll start going by Ross from now on, Uncle Tony," said Rosario, trying on his new American persona.

"Ross? I don't like that," said Nina, eavesdropping.

The family had formed a perfect semi-circle around the fiery red azalea bush that encircled their prized cherub bird bath. Flash bulbs instantly began to pop as Nina and Carmelo, parents of the groom, took their rightful places up front, flanking Rosario.

"Eh, smile a little! C'mon, your son is getting married today, look how handsome he is!" Nina and Carmelo, not yet accustomed to the modern trend of cheerful and light-hearted photographs, had to repeatedly be reminded by the very animated photographer to drop their stoic expressions. Maria, dressed in a simple but elegant pale-yellow shantung bridesmaid dress, came up behind her parents, wrapped one arm around each of them, and pulled them in closer to her.

"Ahh, that's what I'm talking about, what a beautiful family!" exclaimed the relieved photographer as he shot Maria a sly wink to thank her for the assist. Nina's smile soured as she noticed the flirtatious looks exchanged between her daughter and the photographer. She wanted Maria to be married and become a mother, but they had to find the right man still.

"Nina, hey Nina," Carmelo called out breathlessly, waking his wife. They all had a late night out celebrating Rosario and Peggy's wedding until the early morning hours. "Nina, I don't feel so good."

"Well, I told you not to eat and drink so much last night. It's just some indigestion. I'll go get your pills."

Nina slunk out of bed. Her perfectly coiffed hair was wrapped up like a mummy's in pink toilet paper to preserve her hairstyle for an extra day. She gingerly walked barefoot down the hall to the kitchen. She climbed back into bed with the pills and water for Carmelo. Nina gently nudged her husband.

"Carmelo, you're asleep already?" Nina shook his shoulder a bit harder. He didn't move. She wailed in agony, screaming for Carmelo to wake up. When he still didn't respond, she cried out for her daughter.

"Maria! *Maria*!!"

Nina could hear Maria scrambling out of her bedroom and

across the hall. When Maria appeared in the doorway, Nina shook her unresponsive husband, begging him not to leave her.

"I swear I was only gone for two minutes, and now he won't wake up!" said Nina.

For the first time in her life, Nina had no idea what to do. Her mind would not let her take charge of the situation. She looked up at her daughter, stunned and helpless.

The silence in the house now frightened Nina. She shook him again; she pressed her ear to his chest. Nothing. Maria stood equally frozen in the doorway in her nightgown; she seemed afraid to enter her parents' bedroom.

"This isn't really happening. It can't be happening. We just danced at Rosario's wedding. I must be dreaming," Maria repeated.

"Don't just stand there, help me! Help me wake him up, Maria!" screamed Nina.

Maria walked into her parents' bedroom, leaned down and touched her father's hand, and kissed his forehead.

Her daughter looked at her and shook her head, "No." He was gone.

Warm tears began to stream down Nina's face, stinging her cheeks. Maria's confirmation had made it real. Nina was forced to face the unimaginable tragedy, to feel the rug being pulled out from under her. Betrayed by the universe again, Nina erupted in the haunting howl that Maria remembered well.

NINA PLACED A BLACK and white portrait of Carmelo, framed

in silver, on her shiny cherry wood dresser. Carmelo's photo now stood somberly alongside those of her parents and her sister Giovanna. She honored all her departed loved ones with this growing shrine that was continuously bathed in the red light of her electric votive candle.

Nina dressed in a tailored black skirt and a rigid, boxy black jacket with three-quarter sleeves. She picked her gloves up from the nightstand on her way out of the room when an inexplicable surge of grief angrily shot through her entire body. She tossed the track door of her closet open so hard it made a loud crashing sound against the opposite wall. She looked at the sage silk dress she wore to her son's wedding just days prior. She had laughed and danced in that dress—the last time she would ever dance with her husband. Nina swore it would also be the last time she laughed. She hastily grabbed anything in her closet bearing any resemblance to a color or exuding any amount of youthfulness and cheer, but she couldn't bear to part with the sage silk dress.

I'll be buried in that dress ...

She raised her bedroom window with one hand and hoisted the entire pile with the other. Any glimmer of the carefree times she only recently became accustomed to burst out of the second-floor window like silk and woolen confetti, hangers and all, into the now neglected vegetable garden.

I'm a widow—at fifty-four years old. My life is over now. I have no use for any of this anymore. There will be no more parties, no more celebrations for me.

She slammed the window shut.

As she left her bedroom, she saw Maria waiting for her in the hallway.

Had Maria been there this whole time?

If she had, she didn't let on; she hooked her gloved arm around Nina's and guided her down the long corridor. The household had gone from four to two overnight. It was just them now, mother and daughter left alone in this eerily quiet house that was once the beating heart of the family.

MARIA SAT STOICALLY IN the funeral home with her brother Salvatore, speaking just above a whisper, shortly before visiting hours began. Carmelo's casket was surrounded by a small fortune's worth of baskets, sprays, and bouquets draped in satin sashes that read "Beloved Husband," "Beloved Father," "Beloved Uncle." A large rosary made of fresh red roses hung inside the raised casket lid. The special arrangement, commissioned all the way from Sicily, simply read "Nonno." Yet she still felt disconcerted: American funeral customs were strange and sterile to her.

"I didn't feel comfortable leaving Papà in the hands of strangers to prepare for his wake. I don't like leaving him here, in this cold room overnight, alone, while we go home and sleep comfortably in our own beds. It's not right," she said to her brother. This new concept of funerals and rules around mourning felt so foreign to Maria.

"Maybe it's for the best. Maybe it's better that Mamma doesn't have to deal with all-night vigils right now. You both need some rest, so you can be strong for each other. It's just the two of you now," replied Salvatore, taking her hand.

"Salvatore, I begged him. I begged him to get on that ship with us all those years ago. I was so scared that we would never see him again. Mamma could have had another two years with him. I could have had another two years with him."

"Maria, you can't fall apart now. She counts on you more than you think!" Salvatore urged his sister in a loud whisper.

"You weren't here to see Mamma take charge, be the head of this family before Papà arrived. And boy, was she hard on all of us, but look at everything we have here now. Look at everything that we've all accomplished. That's because of Mamma and all the risks she took! I know how strong she is. I just wish she didn't have to–I wish none of us had to always be this damn strong!"

Maria thought about how they called it a wake, but it in no way resembled the long emotional vigils of the wakes she remembered from Sicily. The few funerals she'd attended in the US all felt like catered events for strangers. She didn't understand how Americans could forego the mourning rituals and emotional vulnerability in favor of decorum. Maria missed the death announcements plastered to the walls of Rocca Leone. She felt the more people who knew, the more people could pray for them. She longed for the funeral processions on foot that invited the whole community to mourn along with you. She disliked the scheduled viewings at funeral homes with short, convenient time slots, like a pit stop where everyone fulfills an obligation and offers the same clichéd condolences before heading to their next appointment.

"Carmelo! Aye aye! Carmelo, no!" Nina wailed and lamented for her husband as she took her first steps toward him, guided by Rosario. Maria watched, heartbroken for her mother, as the nightmare unfolded for them both. Her father was displayed in a gray suit and a gold tie clip. He was lying with his hands folded across his chest amidst the white quilted interior of his bronze-colored casket.

"*Oh Dio*! Carmelo, why did you bring me here just to leave me alone?" cried out Nina as she hovered over Carmelo. Maria's brothers stood beside their mother as if they were her bodyguards.

Maria knew her mother didn't care much for decorum in the face of tragedy. She was prepared to witness every single one of her mother's emotions. They expected emotion from their guests as well, as a show of respect.

"Oh, Marie, I'm so sorry. But he's in a better place now." Her cousin Donna gave her an insincere hug as she delivered her canned condolences. Maria was startled by her cousin's cold sentiment.

A better place?

"Marie, is Aunt Nina OK?" Donna asked while turning away from Nina in embarrassment.

"I don't understand what you mean," said Maria. "How could she be OK? Her husband, my father, just died. He didn't get his Last Rites, and she didn't even get to say goodbye."

"Oh, I'm sorry, Marie, I didn't mean anything by that. It's just that she's crying so loud. She's kind of causing a scene, don't ya think? Maybe you should take her outside," said Donna.

"My mother should leave her husband's wake to make *you* more comfortable?" asked Maria, fuming.

Maria had kept her head down, worked hard, and brushed off the small stuff since immigrating. She had learned it was much harder to express herself and speak up for herself without the comfort of her native language, so she shied away from conflict.

"And my name is Maria, not Marie!" She finally blurted out what she'd been too polite to say for almost a decade.

"Ah, well, it's the same thing. I just think Marie sounds better, more American," said Donna.

32

DOMENICO

CORONA, NEW YORK
NOVEMBER 1965

"What the hell is going on in there?!" Domenico sat in a dimly lit, depressing waiting room that looked as if it hadn't been updated since before the war, when he heard a series of short, muffled screams. He jumped up out of his seat and bolted straight past the alarmed receptionist, who chased after him.

"Sir, you can't go in there! Sir!" Domenico burst through the door of the doctor's examination room to find his mother reclined on an exam table with a bite block in her mouth.

"Get away from her right now!" he ordered the frightened nurse at Pasqua's feet.

"Mr. Fiorinelli, please calm down. I really think these treatments have been helping your mother." The doctor stood over Pasqua, holding a device resembling a headset.

"What the hell are you saying? You've been giving her these treatments without our knowledge?"

"Mimi, what are you doing here? Go away!" yelled Pasqua, saliva running down her chin after removing the bite block.

"Pasqua has agreed to these treatments." The doctor tried to reason with Domenico while still backing away from him.

"Agreed? She can't agree to something like this! Can't you see the state she's in for Christ's sake?!"

"Mr. Fiorinelli, I can assure you–"

"You take one more step toward her, and I swear I'll have you arrested!" Domenico helped his mother from the exam table, ripped off his long tweed coat, and swung it around Pasqua's shoulders as he quickly forced her out of the doctor's office.

"You're making a mistake! You're cruelly sentencing her to a lifetime of suffering!" yelled the doctor, in vain as they stormed out of the office.

He rushed them out to his silver Buick Skylark parked around the corner on Nicholls Avenue. Pasqua, distraught, began to cry.

"Mimi, no! He helped me! That was my last chance. Why do you want to hurt me? This is why I didn't tell you. You and your father, with your hot tempers, you ruin everything!" said Pasqua through tears.

Pasqua had been dragged all over New York City to every recommended doctor and specialist since the Fiorinellis made the move to the Italian enclave of Corona, Queens, five years ago. Each visit proved less productive and seemed to have left Pasqua feeling more demeaned than the last. They were given a wide spectrum of dodgy diagnoses and advice, from "It's the change of life," to "It's a shame she didn't have more babies before it was too late, babies always make women happy," to "I think it's all in her head, take her on a vacation."

Pasqua seemed desperate for her son to understand, and it made Domenico feel even more helpless. She cried in the car all the way home.

"No, no, please! Don't say that! No, please! I don't want to hear that," she sporadically spoke, begging and crying out to somebody it seemed only she could see.

"Mamma! Who are you talking to now?" yelled Domenico.

Domenico gripped the steering wheel until his knuckles went white. It terrified Domenico when his mother talked to herself, or whoever she thought she was talking to, but his fear always seemed to come out as anger instead.

I don't know if I'm doing the right thing, but nothing I saw in that doctor's office looked right to me.

They entered their first-floor apartment to the subtly sweet aroma of a roasted pork loin pierced with the sharp fragrance of freshly minced garlic.

"Dinner's almost ready," Emidio said without even turning around as he continued cooking, laser focused on the instructions scrawled on the scrap of paper in his hand. Emidio had been slowly taking over many of the responsibilities that were once solely Pasqua's. He screamed as he burned his finger, taking the pork out of the oven. Sheets of paper were fanned out all over the orange kitchen counter–cooking instructions that Pasqua had written out for Emidio on some of her good days.

"Papà, we really need to talk about Mamma." Domenico

slouched onto the couch, exhausted. The Fiorinellis had upgraded their living conditions to a two-bedroom apartment in Corona, and Domenico no longer had to sleep in the living room and call the couch his bed.

"Mimi, I left you a martini in the fridge." Ever since Emidio had made Domenico a martini on his very first night in America, father and son had made it an enduring nightly ritual. Whoever arrived home first from work would be responsible for making the drinks.

"Did you know? Did you know about the electroshock treatments?!" Domenico demanded.

Emidio took a deep breath and let out a long sigh. "She can't live like this forever, Mimi; we have to try something. If she keeps on this way, everybody's going to start talking. Do you want people talking behind our back, saying she's crazy?"

Domenico was stewing, staring at the floor, and trying to figure out how to answer that.

"So, you knew. You let that barbarian experiment on my mother?!" asked Domenico.

"Experiment? Stop being so dramatic. It was either that or she'd end up in one of those hospitals, those miserable hospitals. What was I supposed to do, lock her up with drooling, insane people? We don't do that in this family! They said these treatments were safe. Don't you want your mother back?"

Domenico couldn't believe what he was hearing.

"No! They're gonna kill her! I refuse to take her there again!"

"I know you're a big man now, you're the big boss at the factory, you speak English, and drive a big car, but you're still a part of this family!" said Emidio, seeking to take Domenico down a peg.

"Like I could ever escape this family!" Domenico's temper was rising. Both his hands were involuntarily forming into tight fists, waiting for the anger to subside.

"In this house, we take care of our own problems, privately! That's it, end of story!" snapped Emidio.

THE NEXT MORNING, DOMENICO was awoken before sunrise by a frantic Pasqua standing over him.

"Mimi, get up, get up! You need to go stand in the ration lines. If you don't go now, it'll be too late. We won't get any food! Please, Mimi!"

Heartbroken, Domenico decided to make it easier on both of them that day.

"OK, Mamma, I'll go now," said Domenico, placating his mother.

He waited until he was sure his mother had gone back to bed, and then he did the same. He stared at the chipped ceiling paint, attempting to fall back asleep, knowing he needed to wake up for work in an hour anyway. As was usually the case after a particularly bad episode, Pasqua had regressed, reliving past traumatic experiences.

Is this all our life is ever gonna be?

Later that day, walking figure eights around his East Village factory, buzzing with activity, Domenico grew increasingly absorbed in ideas for the future, for his family, and especially for his mother.

He went back to his messy office littered with side projects and doodled on some scrap paper while keeping tabs on the factory floor operations through an adjoining window.

He drew some trees that evolved into a lush green garden anchored by a giant fig tree, its strong branches heavy with fruit. He added rows upon rows of fragrant tomato plants, the kind his father could harvest every August to jar enough tomatoes to keep the family eating their favorite pasta dishes throughout the year. He envisioned an eager assembly line of family members busy peeling, cutting, boiling, and pressing the pulpy plum-shaped fruit. A giant cauldron-like pot bubbling with the fresh *passata* strained from their homegrown tomatoes.

Overlooking the garden, he sketched an enclosed patio, a bright sunroom with giant windows that could swing open in summertime when they'd grill *arrosticini*, the mutton meat skewers popular back home in Abruzzo. He wanted a home where his mother could find calm and quiet, away from the noise and chaos that seemed to transport her to times best left behind.

Finally, he grabbed the metal ruler buried under a tall stack of men's sleeve patterns and meticulously drafted a large modern structure, creating it brick by brick. Encompassing the home, he created a manicured front garden dedicated to *la Madonna*, where she would stand robed in blue, gracefully nestled in the sanctum of her grotto. He imagined a multi-family house where his father could have tenants supplementing his income as he edged closer to retirement.

Domenico paused, embarrassed to believe even for a second

he had actually earned these American luxuries. All the moments that led him and his family to leave everything behind and start anew came rushing back. He thought of his mother, all that she still endured, and all the ways he and his father had failed her.

I've been thinking about this all wrong. Americans aren't ashamed of their successes; they don't think twice before flaunting their good fortunes.

Although he'd decided not to shy away from the American dream, Domenico wouldn't forget the lesson he'd learned long ago–never tell anyone your goals, they'll only use them against you.

He went back to his sketch and added a spacious integrated garage to house his silver Skylark. A separate little house just for his car–this represented success to Domenico. If he could have a garage of his own, he could say he had made it in America. Domenico manifested a family home where future generations could all be raised under one roof in a community. A legacy.

Domenico had been caught lost in thought when an alarm blared on the factory floor and startled him back to reality.

―

DOMENICO USED HIS FOOT to push open his apartment door as he juggled large bolts of muslin and wool fabrics. The aroma of his mother's cooking filled his nostrils, but he instead found his father in the kitchen stirring a large pot of Bolognese sauce on the stove while yelling back at the news blaring from the family's black and white TV set in the next room.

"This son of a bitch; Johnson is worse than Kennedy! Voting

rights and the Blacks; that's all he can talk about. Look! He made it so easy for them. Now everybody can vote. No reading test, no language test."

"Hello to you too, Papà. You've lived here for ten years and still don't speak much English, yet you've voted in every election since you became an American citizen in 1961. I know this for a fact. I've driven you each time, because you don't drive either."

"Oh, I should be like you? Live here, work here, but don't vote? All those people are getting all the rights, voting for you. You think they're gonna vote to make your life better? No. They're gonna vote to make life better for their own kind. When are you gonna become a citizen?"

"Why should I become a citizen? I never even wanted to come here in the first place," said Domenico.

"Oh, with that story again? OK, we'll see what they–"

There was a buzzing sound followed by a loud pop. The room went dark, the TV silent, and the stove ticked as it tried to reignite the pilot. All the power had cut out. Domenico ran to the front window.

"It's not just us; the entire street is dark! Everyone's outside panicking." Neighbors were outside speculating with other neighbors, communicating in a flurry of English, Neapolitan, and Dominican Spanish. Some were heading toward Corona Avenue to see how far the outage had spread, if it affected the businesses. All of Corona had gone dark. Stranded passengers were spilling out onto the street at the 103rd St.–Corona Plaza station of the Number 7 Train.

"Mamma, you have to get dressed!" said Domenico.

"No, Mimi! I don't want to go outside! The people outside steal my dreams. Let me sleep. I want to dream," Pasqua begged in her confused state.

Domenico panicked. If they were in any danger, Pasqua needed to be ready to leave at a moment's notice.

"It's OK, you don't need to go outside now. I just need you to put your robe and shoes on. C'mon Mamma, just do it for me, OK?" Domenico pleaded with his mother.

"The government is doing this!" Emidio chimed in.

"Jesus Christ, not this again. Give it a rest, Papà!"

"You'll see. They're all a bunch of bastard communists running this country now!" Emidio grew more and more agitated and paranoid the longer the power remained off.

"Keep your voice down, will you?! You can't just run around saying things like that all the time. Somebody will hear you!" Domenico was surprised at the words that had escaped his own mouth. Logically, he knew that he was free to say whatever he chose. He'd left Italy and its fascist era behind long ago. He spent his life looking over his shoulder, and his first instinct was still to censor himself and others out of fear.

"What do you mean I can't say things like that? Isn't that what this 'Great America' is for?" Emidio waved his hands around, mocking the politicians' theatrical podium gestures from television. "I can say whatever I want!"

"Yes, they're all a bunch of crooks and thieves–on all sides. When are you going to learn that, Papà?" argued Domenico.

He was going stir crazy, trapped in the apartment with his

parents all night. He'd spent the last twenty minutes staring at the Last Supper wall art mounted on wood as it dangled, crooked, from the wall above the couch, while his father tried to rile him up and his mother lamented decades past.

Look at the three of us. We don't even realize we're still running. We moved four thousand miles away, but we're still running, in our heads.

Eventually, Domenico stormed out of the apartment to relieve the pain of his realization, of what his family had become, and for a much-needed cigarette or two.

Two young Dominican brothers were sitting on the front stoop of their building a few doors down from The Fiorinellis, listening to the news on their battery-operated transistor radio.

"Can I?" Domenico took a long drag from his cigarette and asked if he could listen with them, his words exhaling a giant cloud of smoke. He took a seat on the top step and extended the pack of Chesterfield cigarettes to the brothers, "Want?"

The three men sat smoking cigarettes on the dark stoop, sending halos of smoke up to dissipate in the sky lit by the bright full moon. They listened intently, trying to decipher the barrage of news reports being broadcast in a language native to nobody on their street.

A blackout swept all of New York City tonight, stranding commuters just as they were beginning their journeys home ... The static-filled transmission offered little new information, but still they continued to listen rather than return to their current living situations, made increasingly chaotic by the darkness.

Engineers are working swiftly to get the power back on. The outage has now been traced to a tripped power line all the way up in Ontario, Canada ...

"Mimi? Mimi! Where are you? I can't see you. Come back inside, I can hear the planes coming! Mimi, we have to hide!"

"Goodnight, guys." Domenico flashed two fingers at the brothers, hurriedly greeting them goodbye, as an unlit cigarette dangled from the corner of his mouth.

Pasqua had somehow slipped past Emidio. She wandered aimlessly around their small patch of front garden, calling out and searching for her son, her slippered feet stuttering against the damp grass.

"Mamma! What are you doing out here all alone? C'mon, let's go back inside." Domenico guided his mother back into their apartment. "I promise there's not one plane in the sky tonight, Mamma."

33

STELLA

SICILY, ITALY
DECEMBER 2020

I could feel my chest tighten and a lump form in my throat as the triangular-shaped land mass I'd long dreamed of setting foot on finally came into view out my tiny window.

"*Sicilia Bedda!*" I turned and exclaimed to Michael.

"Are you crying?" Michael asked softly.

"Yeah, shut up," I responded, quickly wiping my tears away, laughing at myself.

"We should go to dinner tonight, a big, fancy, ridiculous dinner!" suggested Michael with excitement in his voice.

"Why? That sounds like something we need a reservation for and–"

"Let's celebrate a year of obsessions and research and sleepless nights–and nightmares–that all brought us here to this amazing trip," said Michael.

—

WITH BURNING THIGHS AND panting breaths, we finally crossed the finish line of our 648-step climb that was carved into the side of an enormous rock. This wasn't our trek to the top of Mount Etna, but to our celebratory dinner reservations at our first stop in Taormina.

"A little head's-up would have been nice, Michael. I would have worn some running shoes instead of these flimsy little ballerina flats!"

The throbbing ache in my feet instantly vanished from my body as I received the reward for my efforts, the most exquisite view of Mount Etna at sunset, and a menu filled with fresh seafood, fished out of the water that surrounded us.

When the waiter arrived with the first course, he looked as if he could buckle under the weight of the gigantic *Crudo di Mare* seafood appetizer I ordered. Octopus and potato salad, raw calamari with fennel, raw oysters, sardines, raw tuna salad, giant red shrimp, and whole-body shrimp that still had its eyes.

"I can't believe I still have a second course coming after this!" I said, already feeling full.

The waiter approached, looking at me suspiciously. "Don't tell me you finished! You haven't eaten anything! Look at the red shrimp! Oh, no, c'mon, you gonna leave those oysters?" he berated me in Italian.

"Oh, I'm just getting so full and I still have more food coming," I said, trying to assure him that I really did enjoy it, switching to my mother's Sicilian. He gave me a look, impressed seemingly, then his expression hardened again.

"No. No, I'm not taking your plate until you eat some more. You Sicilian? You are not Sicilian if you leave all that food on your plate!" He then walked away, leaving me stunned.

"Oh my God, this is ridiculous. Is he serious? Could you imagine this happening in the US?" He would definitely be called into some sort of HR meeting."

I grimaced at all the food, took a deep breath, and ate a little of everything left on my plate.

"Michael, help me so I don't get scolded again by the scary waiter," I whispered.

"Nope, you are on your own with all that raw fish," he said smugly.

I quickly ate the most conspicuous item on my plate—the giant shrimp, sans head, of course, just as the waiter came back around.

"You were right. I ate some more. It was delicious!" I exclaimed, hoping I'd eaten to his satisfaction this time.

"OK, now I'll take your plate!" he said proudly, clearing the table for the second course.

AFTER OUR PRACTICE RUN the night before, I felt ready for the 3000-meter trek up to the top of Mount Etna, the very active, ancient volcano that watches over all of Sicily. The island's matriarch. Mamma Etna, or *Mungibeddu*, some of the ways she's lovingly referred to, has tough decisions to make as the mother of the island—when to nourish and when to send her scorching power bubbling to the surface. When to create, and when to destroy.

If Sicily was fifteen degrees warmer than Abruzzo, then the top of Mount Etna measured thirty degrees colder than almost anywhere else in Italy. I'd never much cared for the sporty look, but I was proud of my carefully curated new hiking outfit. A red and orange patterned windbreaker paired with black leggings and red and black hiking sneakers.

"You look like a volcano," Michael joked as he took a series of cheeky photos of me posing on Etna's Mars-like terrain as the wind whipped my hair around, giving me an electrocuted look.

"All-powerful volcano is exactly the look I was going for!" I yelled over the sound of the wind.

As we continued our snowy trek, I thought about my mom and how close I was to her hometown, the closest I'd ever been. I could probably see it from up here on a clear day.

"As a kid, I asked my mom if it was scary living so close to a giant volcano? She told me giant eruptions were a bit scary when they could see the fire glowing, and sometimes some of the ash would be carried all the way to Rocca Leone. 'But I knew she wouldn't hurt us,' she told me."

"Did she ever make it up here?" Michael asked, as we made our way up an increasingly snowy incline.

"The only place, other than Rocca Leone, that my mother had ever seen was Palermo, and that was as her ship left the port for America," I responded, as I bent down to grab a hunk of black lava rock to stealthily shove in my pocket.

"Deadly earthquakes, a destructive volcano. You come from a tempestuous people," he said with a smirk.

"I suppose that explains a lot, doesn't it? I guess you could say I was born of earthquake and volcano. The great disruptors."

From 2900 meters up, at the *Torre del Filosofo*, all of Sicily and the Mediterranean Sea, a vast patchwork of green, gold, and blue, blanketed everything beneath and beyond.

"Mom, it's not scary at all from up here!" I screamed out as I leaned over the edge of the mammoth lava rock formations. As my voice echoed back at me, I raised my arms over my head to catch the winds that were swirling above me. The warm tears running down my cold cheeks surprised me.

"It's the most beautiful sight I've ever seen!"

My windbreaker was on the defensive against the gusts of wind thrashing me from behind. In an instant, I was jolted backwards, and Michael yanked me away from the edge before I could be swept over it.

"What the hell's wrong with you?! You could have plummeted 3000 meters!" shouted Michael.

"Probably just a couple of hundred meters into one of those craters below." I pretended my heart wasn't pounding with fear. "I guess I was captivated by the moment," I said, wiping the tears from my face. Michael was visibly unamused at my glibness.

"OK, OK, I'm sorry! I didn't realize how windy it would be," I said.

"Alright, fine, it *was* a pretty great moment." Michael finally conceded. "And–I'm sure your mom heard you from wherever she is," he said, picking up his pace ahead of me to avoid making eye contact during this saccharine moment.

A FADED AND DECREPIT sign emerged from the dense landscape of cactus pear paddles and yellow buds of wild fennel along the serpentine road that read *Welcome to Rocca Leone* in five languages. It had long stood waiting to greet the scattered children and grandchildren of Rocca Leone as they made their pilgrimages home to meet her.

"You know, I've never spent a Christmas away from home before," I said, feeling the void of the family and friends we'd left behind in New York.

"Well, you still haven't. Not really." Michael had begun to sound like me when it came to speaking about ancestors and ancestral lands.

"OK, but I've never spent a Christmas without my parents before. Even last Christmas, although he wasn't conscious, we were still able to visit my father."

"Gli uomini passano, le idee restano," declared a giant mural of Falcone and Borsellino, the two Sicilian judges assassinated by the mafia almost thirty years ago, as we continued along the state highway that merged into Corso Umberto.

"People pass, ideas remain." I chuckled, amused by the quick and bizarre responses that the universe had been transmitting lately.

"So, Christmas in Sicily! Where do we start?" Michael asked, rubbing the palms of his hands together.

Swarms of people were traversing Rocca Leone on foot and in vehicles. Enormous panels of colorfully twinkling lights arranged in traditional Sicilian decorative patterns were suspended above us. With the sunroof open, they felt almost within reach. The entire stretch of the Corso Umberto was adorned in these illuminated panels, looming large over the Christmas crowds strolling through the town. The buildings on the main road were covered in flyers that all seemed to be invitations to dozens of different *presepio,* or nativity scenes, on view all over Rocca Leone. We rolled to a stop at a tiny intersection dotted with tall trees covered in bright orange fruit for anyone to pick. I reached my hand out and tore a Christmas flyer that hung on a bulletin board otherwise covered with the townspeople's death announcements. The surnames on the death announcements were all familiar, plucked directly from my family tree.

"I underestimated Sicily at Christmastime," I said, reading the flyer a bit stunned. "What must Palermo and Catania look like right now?!"

"Umm, this strikes me as a quirky, small-town niche event." Michael chose his words carefully, trying his best not to call my people weirdos outright.

I grew up with Nativity scenes decorating our house at Christmas. A cardboard manger filled with hay and little statues of Mary, Joseph, baby Jesus, and a few shepherds and wise men that rested under the Christmas tree–this was not that.

The flyer had the entire town mapped out by *presepio* presentations. Every church and town square was hosting a Nativity depiction in one form or another. Intricately built town miniatures were set up in the church where my nonni were married, Maria S.S.

Annunziata. The children's nativity projects were displayed at the elementary school across the street from my mother's old building. A giant stone grotto, built to fit life-size statues, had been erected in Piazza Carella. Living nativity scenes with the townspeople taking turns playing the roles of Mary and Joseph went late into the night at Piazza Branciforti. Traveling scenes were loaded onto the beds of decorated Piaggio Apes, the small agricultural pickup trucks popular all over Sicily.

"Let's start with the miniatures just up ahead. We can plan all our sightseeing there!" I said.

We approached the long staircase leading into the small and unassuming Maria S.S. Annunziata church, my family's local parish in Rocca Leone. As I climbed the stairs, I imagined my nonna in a white lace head covering and my nonno in his only suit, appearing in public for the first time as man and wife almost ninety years earlier. I pictured all the people who would have stood perched along the narrow staircase to greet the newlyweds—my great-grandparents Arcangela and Giuseppe, my Zia Rosina, and so many others whose names I'll never know. I could almost envision my mother as a child dressed in a homemade floor-length white dress, skipping down the stairs at her first Communion.

I relished hearing the Sicilian language spoken amongst the tight-knit locals—and felt almost disappointed when they spoke to me in Italian. The familiar comforting sounds of open and dropped vowels, their guttural emphasis on R's, D's, and U's, the sprinkled Arabic, Greek, and Catalan words—they were gifts, relics from a childhood surrounded by strong Sicilian women.

A middle-aged woman with a mop of brown curls framing her eccentric square-shaped red glasses had been suspiciously shadowing us since we entered the tiny church. As if tracking our scent, *Eau de American*, she appeared around every corner of the miniature Rocca Leone that we turned. Finally, she approached us at the miniature San Giovanni Battista, the Mother Church.

"Are you from here?" she asked in Sicilian, looking confident that it would trip me up.

"No, I'm from New York, but my mother was from Rocca Leone."

"Oh yeah, what's her name?"

"Sanfilippo, Ma–"

"Yeah, OK, you're one of ours!" she said, sweeping the curls away from her face.

"And my bisnonna was Tamburella, Arcangela," I quickly snuck in. I couldn't help myself. The woman was quiet and still, her eyes grew wide. "No!"

"Stella?" Michael said with an eye roll.

"Did you see that? Did you see what happened when she heard my great-grandmother's name?" I said, maybe a bit too excitedly.

"So, she didn't recognize her name," he said.

"First of all, I'm sure I could place every inhabitant of this town on some distant branch of my family tree. And second, did you see *how* she said no?" He gave me a deadpan stare. "OK, I'll stop. If you admit she'd acted a bit strangely!"

"I thought you were going to show me around this town, Stella."

"OK, you're right. Well, this is *Chiesa Madre*, the mother church, San Giovanni Battista. It's been standing for over four hundred years! This church has seen some shit. It was bombed and fired on in a fire-fight between the Nazis and the Allies during WWII, and look, they even included the damage in this miniature! See the crumbling columns that flank the doors, and the limestone that's riddled with pock marks? That all happened during the Battle of Rocca Leone in 1943. Over thirty civilian townspeople, including my great-grandmother Arcangela, were killed over the two days of battle. Half of them were children."

"Your mother lived through all that as a little girl?"

"Yeah, she had quite the adventure. The history books credit a little boy named Antonio with helping the Allies the night of the battle; there's no mention of the little girl who saved the day, of course. But now at least I know," I said.

"It's crazy your mother never spoke about any of that, but at least you have her written stories now," he said.

"I do." I smiled as we moved on, around the amazing model display. "Oh, and this! This is the crown jewel of Rocca Leone, Granfonte."

We were now standing before the miniature version of the baroque fountain famous for its twenty-four continuously running water spouts.

"Women carried their amphora here to collect water for the household before indoor plumbing, and farmers brought their horses and donkeys here to drink from the trough. And through these arches above each spout, you can see the valley that both the Nazis and the Canadians had to cross to occupy the town during the war."

When my history lesson was complete, we made our way

out of the church, but not before we stopped at the buffet table of traditional holiday sweets and breads. Beautiful and heartfelt presentations of handmade and homemade *dolci di Natale*–cookies, fruit *crostatas*, and honey drenched *pignolata,* all furnished by the locals.

"I would expect nothing less than an amazing spread of local delicacies at a Sicilian event," I said.

"Hey, these look just like your Christmas cookies! *Piccidati,* right?" asked Michael proudly.

"OMG!" I stopped in my tracks at the sight of those large, round traditional Sicilian Christmas cookies. Plump dough filled with a sweet mixture of figs, almonds, and citrus, and then covered with another layer of beautifully carved and sculpted dough. They were topped to perfection with colorful nonpareil sprinkles and powdered sugar.

"You don't understand. I've *never* seen anyone else make them like this, with this method and in these shapes, except my mother and Nonna. I always thought it was their design and creation, made with whatever shaped cookie cutters they had on hand. But it was a tradition.

All those years, the three of us in ritual, moving our hands to the same rhythms and in the same shapes, creating spells together–cooking is a spell. The three of us–maiden, mother, crone–were simultaneously learning, practicing, and imparting unique Rocca Leone traditions. Food traditions that could be traced all the way back to the Arabs' introduction of figs, dates, and citrus to Sicilian cuisine–I had no idea.

I turned to Michael; he'd stopped paying attention to me long ago. He guarded the buffet table, sampling all the various *piccidati* and smiling with his eyes closed, slowly savoring every bite. I finally joined him, biting into an almond-paste-filled cookie as my eyes overflowed with tears.

"They taste like home."

34

MARIA and DOMENICO

NEW YORK CITY
MAY 1973

Maria flashed her beautifully imperfect smile. Her crooked incisors beamed in the sunlight as she swayed to Paul Simon's "Kodachrome" radiating from a nearby portable radio. She playfully twirled around in a white Mikado silk wedding dress with a high-collared lace neckline and lined lace bodice as the women surrounding her gasped and cheered. Maria happily posed for them, gleefully accepting all their compliments.

"Gorgeous!"

"How are they all so perfect for you?!" The delicately translucent lace sleeves gradually transitioned into billowing bell-shaped cuffs, and the train, embellished with lace and pearls, seemed never-ending.

Maria was the perfect sample size for all the wedding dress styles she manufactured; they indeed all fit her impeccably. Her bosses at the Mori Lee factory quickly deemed her the unofficial sample model, doing fit sessions with new wedding dress prototypes before they went into full production.

"When are you going to finally put one of those on for real, Maria?" her co-worker Graziella asked, hunched over her lap, eating her lunch of leftover orecchiette pasta with broccoli rabe, protecting it as if someone could snatch it from her at any moment.

Nina, still dressed in black mourning clothes to honor her husband, pursed her lips and gave Graziella a disapproving side-eyed look.

"Maria, look at all this work we have left to finish today. Stop fooling around!" Nina snapped at her daughter. Maria knew fun and laughter were still difficult for her mother to bear most days. "You know I hate it when all you young women start speaking English. I know you're all talking behind my back."

"Oh, Mamma, nobody is conspiring against you. Besides, everyone knows you understand much more than you let on," said Maria, irritated.

Nina had rejected every man that Maria had ever gone on a date with, or as much as spoken to. She gave all sorts of excuses why they were all wrong for her only daughter.

Georgios, the fabric cutter, "He's Greek!"

Franco, who owned a successful construction company, "He's too short for you!"

Pietro, well, nobody actually knew what Pietro did for a living, but his whole family lived back in Naples. "He'll go back to his family and take you far away from me!"

Gino, who tried to strike up a conversation with Maria on the subway one evening, "No! He looks like a *cafone*. Look at him, showing off that he has a little bit of money!"

"You know, Maria, I actually have the perfect man to introduce you to!" Graziella had brazenly disregarded Nina's rebuke. "You should meet him. He's very handsome and charming–always well dressed. He's Italian, of course. He came here from Abruzzo with his mother and father sometime in the 1950s."

"Abruzzo?! Nobody comes from Abruzzo except bandits and thieves!" Nina said angrily.

"Oh, Graziella, I don't want to get married or have a boyfriend. It all just seems like a whole lot of aggravation to me," Maria said, unbothered, trying to diffuse the situation as she continued twirling and marveling at the giant bell sleeves of the dress.

"Eh, that's exactly what he says when I bother him about getting married. You two are perfect for each other! Did I mention he's a tailor? He owns an honest business, a menswear shop in Flushing. He and his parents own the big house right next door to me; they had it built brand new a few years ago. Very successful!" Graziella was being her typical relentless self.

"A blind date? I–I don't think so, Graziella."

"OK, but you're making a mistake. I know when I see a perfect match. I was the matchmaker in my village! You know how many children exist because of me? Eh!"

While Graziella had been known to often boast of her successes, Maria saw matchmaking as a vestige of peasant villages of the past, and quite frankly, an unnecessary vocation in a huge and diverse city such as New York.

"He's a good man, Maria." The matchmaker couldn't help herself; she had to give it one more shot. "You should see the way he takes care of his mother," Graziella began to whisper, "The poor woman, she's always sick."

That evening at home, Nina couldn't remain silent any longer.

"You put Graziella up to that nonsense, didn't you? You're desperate to leave me, all alone in this godforsaken house, aren't you?!" Graziella had apparently gotten under Nina's skin so badly that she remained silent for the rest of the day. Washing dishes with Maria in their kitchen, she unloaded all her anger.

"Mamma, what are you talking about? That was all Graziella; you know how she is. Why are you saying all these crazy things?"

"Why am I the one who has to make all the sacrifices? I sacrificed my whole life for this family, and everybody leaves me! Who's going to take care of me if you leave me too?" Nina interpreted any attempt at independence as a personal attack.

"At least I know my Carmelo didn't mean to leave me," said her mother.

On the subway the next morning, Maria leaned her head against the scratched-up window, careful to avoid any fresh spray paint. She tried to catch a few extra minutes of sleep as the train rocked and lulled her to sleep. She watched all the different towns fly by, noticing the houses squeeze closer together and the roads grow wider with each passing street that brought them closer to midtown Manhattan. After almost twenty years of this commute, she knew every street sign, every house, and church by heart.

"Oh, Mamma, I forgot. I'll be leaving work a little early today. I have a dress fitting appointment for my friend Anne's bridal party. Don't worry, I'll be home in time to help with dinner," said Maria.

"Fine, I guess I'll take the trains alone tonight," Nina responded dramatically.

Maria turned back toward the window and rolled her eyes.

"You mean the same exact train route you've been riding for two decades now? I think you'll be fine."

"Don't get home late! A woman traveling alone at night; it's not safe."

―

As soon as the clock struck 4:30 pm, Maria gathered up her eyeglasses, change purse, and seam ripper that were scattered all over her sewing table and tossed them into her red leather shoulder bag. She gently placed a hand on her mother's shoulder as she stood up to leave.

"Good night, everybody, see you tomorrow!" Maria shot a quick wink at Graziella, who nodded back approvingly as she hurried out.

Maria climbed the three flights of subway steps with an extra spring in her step and exited at Main St. and Roosevelt Ave. She popped into the massive Woolworth store on the corner to freshen up her hair and makeup. She left with a new shade of lipstick on her lips, clutching a handwritten address and description.

She walked uphill along Roosevelt Avenue, dodging the hundreds of rush hour commuters racing in both directions toward the subways and buses in the popular Queens transportation hub. She slowly approached the address she was searching for.

DonFranco? Strange name for a menswear shop.

She stood outside at the very edge of the store window, peering inside, hoping not to be noticed right away. Two men looked to be about her age, each chatting to their respective clients, set against an infinite backdrop of pristine imported suits and men's tailoring. A younger man, most likely an apprentice, was busy pinning the hem of a businessman's suit trousers. The first man dressed monochromatically in a tan suit. He was tall with light blue eyes and sandy colored hair that extended into a pair of mutton chop sideburns. The other man stood a bit shorter, flaunting dark eyes and what could best be described as an unmistakably Roman nose. He wore a dark suit paired with a striking burgundy tie, which complemented his perfectly styled thick black hair.

"That must be him, that's the smile Graziella described," Maria whispered to herself, working up the nerve to go inside.

She watched the men from the window–their impeccably tailored suits in muted tones, their measured movements, and the stuffy marketing photos hanging on the walls. She looked down at her own outfit–the exaggerated silhouettes and bold colors.

I knew I should have changed my clothes; maybe this was a mistake.

Maria took a deep breath and pushed open the door to the sound of bells chiming above her head, announcing her presence. All the men inside turned to look at her. Maria felt certain they were not accustomed to having women in their traditional menswear store, let alone a woman who looked as if she'd just stepped out of Bergdorf Goodman's. Maria wore high-waisted, navy-blue flared pants paired with a long navy vest layered over a cream bishop sleeved blouse, and red accessories to complete the look.

The dark-haired man's eyes followed Maria as she sauntered her way into the shop. Maria watched as he became completely distracted, ignoring the client still speaking to him.

"OK, Nick, take care. We'll be in touch," said the client, looking at them both, chuckling to himself.

"You must be Maria!" said the dark-haired man.

"You're Domenico?" Maria asked, doubting herself. "Why did I just hear that man call you Nick?"

"Eh, you know some of these big American clients don't want to do business with a guinea like me. It makes them feel better when my name sounds more Protestant, like theirs. So for them, I'm Nick Flowers."

"So, should I call you Domenico?"

"Call me Dominick!"

"OK, well, nice to meet you, Dominick," said Maria.

An irresistible, mischievous smile flashed across his face.

"So, Maria, would you have a drink with me tonight?"

"I'd like that," said Maria.

"Do you know The Star Lounge, just a couple of blocks away? A friend of mine owns it," said Domenico.

―

DOMENICO PLACED AN UNLIT cigarette in his mouth and held the door open for Maria, as the bells chimed over their heads.

He motioned goodbye to his business partner, Frank, in the tan suit.

"See you tomorrow, Dominick. Don't worry. I'll close up here," said Frank with a wink.

Domenico felt relieved he hadn't turned down his nosy neighbor, Graziella's, matchmaking offer this time.

But why did I wear this dark suit today? She's wearing stylish red shoes, and I look like I'm going to a funeral.

He loosened his tie, fidgeted with his gold cufflinks, and lit his cigarette as he and Maria stepped out onto the vibrant street for their first date.

35

STELLA

NEW YORK CITY
JANUARY 2021

We stood shoulder to shoulder in a throng of other passengers chattering in languages from all over the globe. I watched as hundreds of pieces of black luggage on the carousel orbited around the conveyor belt, anxious to catch a glimpse of the red ribbon and *cornicello* amulets hanging from our luggage. We had arrived in New York with one extra suitcase than when we departed. It was the only way to fit all the new souvenirs we had accumulated on our whirlwind trip–*confetti* candies, and Montepulciano wine from Abruzzo, Limoncello and Moors heads from Taormina, pistachio spread and saffron black pepper sheep's milk cheese from Enna, and coppola caps and *mano figa* amulets carved from coral from Palermo.

It was the Epiphany, *La Befana* had completed her journey, so Christmas 2020 was officially over. I had thought Christmas would be unbearable this year, but it turned out to be my best one yet.

"Thank you for taking this magnificent, mind-blowing,

overwhelming, and sometimes truly bonkers trip with me." I leaned over and whispered in Michael's ear.

Tomorrow marked the first anniversary of my father's death. The event that springboarded the highest highs and the lowest lows of this entire past year. I'd always felt as though my father had held on just through the Epiphany for me, so that I didn't have to equate his death with Christmas. He'd been ready to go days, even weeks before. I'd been so preoccupied with my trip to Italy that I hadn't braced myself for tomorrow. Experiencing my parents' birthplaces gifted me pieces of them that I thought were lost to time. I had also brought home pieces of myself I didn't even know existed.

Eventually, we rolled all of our hefty baggage toward the exits, eager to see our cats and sleep in our own bed for the first time in weeks. With every step, it felt more and more as if the walls had closed in on us. The stanchions had been rearranged, creating a narrower path and dictating foot traffic, leaving us only one way out. Men with large guns quietly lined the expansive terminal.

"Hey," I whispered, tapping Michael's arm to discreetly get his attention. "I don't remember there being quite this much security when we got off the plane?"

"You're being paranoid, Stella."

I ignored the incessant buzzing of my phone in my pocket even though it made my thigh vibrate. A woman in an expertly applied full face of makeup and hair blown out and curled to perfection, presumably an influencer of some sort, filmed herself on an iPhone addressing her audience.

"OMG, you guys, the Capital has been attacked! I'm here at the airport, and ..."

"What did she just say?!" I asked nobody in particular. The volume of the nervous chatter in the room grew to a fever pitch. We were being jostled in every direction, thrust forward by the force of the crowd, only to be nudged backwards by the hulking security team. My phone continued to buzz relentlessly–everyone's phones seemed to be dinging and buzzing.

"Stella, check your phone!" Michael said as a stranger wedged their body between us.

The blue light from my phone screen instantly illuminated my face. I swiped through a never-ending scroll of news notifications to find them all reporting the same unimaginable thing. Each source embellished its headline with its own political or social slant, but they all agreed on one thing–The Capitol was under attack. The cult-like supporters of the defeated president were staging a deadly coup of the United States over repeated cries of a stolen election. A mob of conspiracy theorists reacting to a dog whistle. His political opponents in Congress were being hunted, forced to hide in locked bathrooms and behind desks under threat of death. Rioters roamed the halls of the Capitol searching for their prey like canines tracking a scent. The results of the hotly contested presidential election, on the verge of being overturned. Among the sea of American and confederate flags, outlandish costumes, and bedazzled hats meant to distract were the menacing homegrown militias–right-wing paramilitary organizations outfitted in more tactical gear than a black ops team. This violent insurrection was being live-streamed across the globe.

Were we witnessing the next March on Rome? The Beer Hall Putsch? Both were precursors to some of the worst atrocities the world had ever seen. Power grabs by jilted men with homicidal quests for greatness. Weak people who gained power and notoriety by blaming the ills of the world on the othered.

A sharp, startled gasp escaped my mouth,

"It's happening again!"

Fifty years from now, will someone stumble upon their grandfather's red hat, hidden amongst their belongings without explanation? Will it be their *photo in the armoire*? The artifact that sends them down their own path of discovery? If there's anything I'd learned from my deep dive into history, war, and family, it's that people will follow their leaders all the way into their own undoing. History will try to repeat; we are the only thing with the power to stand in its way.

―

"The craziest part of this isn't that it happened, it's that every second of it is immortalized and preserved on video. The entire country watched it unfold in real time, and millions of people will still deny it ever happened," I murmured to Michael.

I was on the couch next to him, curled up in a fetal position, while we both doom scrolled on our phones. I wasn't sure a national emergency upstaging my father's death anniversary was the sort of distraction I needed.

"You know, I can't even decide which event feels more catastrophic right now," I said.

I couldn't look away. I watched and re-watched the footage, scouring the crowds for my cousin Lorenzo. Had he been in Washington DC, storming the Capitol, or did he hunker down and watch from home, aching to join in?

That afternoon, as Michael and I pulled up to St. Mary's, the cemetery I'd been visiting with my family my whole life, I felt like I needed to visit my father alone.

"You know where to find me if you need me," said Michael as he squeezed my hand.

The cemetery looked unusually desolate, except for the leftover brown and brittle Christmas wreaths still adorning so many gravestones. I stood shivering in my cherry red ankle boots as the biting cold air turned every exhale into a giant misty cloud of warm breath. I crouched down and came face-to-face with St. Anthony, the familiar image carved deep into the black granite gravestone. I placed three red roses on my parents' frozen grave, and for a split second, it was my mother's reflection that flashed back at me from the large, polished stone.

I stared back at myself in the mirror-like stone, waiting to see my mother again, but instead, I saw an ominous, traveling dark cloud forming behind me. A chilling sound approached from above. It made the hairs on my neck stand up. I looked up to find a flock of hundreds of blackbirds flying in a low murmuration headed straight over my head and my parents' grave. They then gracefully scattered to land, blanketing the cemetery grounds, only to regroup and fly over again in the opposite direction.

That's totally normal, right? Doesn't mean anything–definitely not a harbinger of some sort? Or maybe it just means it's winter. Not everything has to be a sign.

Once the last of the blackbirds had all moved on, I dug a small, shallow hole in the frozen ground. I carefully placed the vial of Montesciano soil and the Etna lava rock that I brought back from their hometowns inside before filling it back in with the hard chunks of dirt. I tamped it down with my bright red hands, burning and swollen from the bitter cold.

"Mamma, Papà, *mi mancherai per sempre*. I hope all your suffering and sacrifices won't have to have been in vain. I hope we can learn from your stories." I kissed the palm of my hand and then placed it on the top of their gravestone.

I turned to leave, but something kept gnawing at me, something still felt unresolved. I looked at my parents' names etched in stone and remembered the photo that I'd carried around with me for over a year–the photo I'd obsessed over. The photo that led to months of research with a PhD-level fervor. I reached deep into my bag and grabbed it. I crouched down at their grave again.

"What should I do about this? *Dimmi*," I asked them.

The answer came loud and clear. I tightened my black wool coat over my baggy Cure '92 tour T-shirt, patted my coat pocket, and retrieved my father's old silver lighter engraved with his initials, *DF*. I held the photo out over the frozen ground. I flipped open the lighter with my thumb and struck down on the wheel as the blue and orange flame made contact with the corner edge of the photo. I held the photo tight and watched with relief as the flickering red and yellow flames grew hotter and larger, swallowing the image of the man. He finally disappeared, destroyed. Reduced to tiny bits of black ash swept up by the wind in a formation much like that of the black birds. He was nothing. He couldn't haunt us any longer.

I still had no real idea why my father had kept what I'd come to learn had been Grandpa Emidio's photo, but I couldn't be more grateful that he had, given the journey it had sent me on, and all the truths and history I'd been able to learn. There were still the gaps and explanations I hadn't dealt with, but I had more than enough to fill in the blanks. I felt whole, a complete person, who couldn't have been prouder of the strength and resilience of those who came before her and the lessons learned from their extraordinary lives. Maybe it was time to learn how to use a sewing machine?

Acknowledgements

THIS BOOK WAS INSPIRED by the lives of my parents, Maria and Dominick. Although I've attempted to tell this story for as long as I can remember, I'd never before considered telling it with words. I certainly could not have told it without the help of some colorful, impassioned, and sometimes untranslatable Italian and Sicilian words. My parents' native tongues are one of the most important gifts they have left me.

To Leigh Esposito, my amazing coach and editor throughout this writing journey. You have a superpower for inspiring and motivating. I accomplished the impossible while under your mentorship.

To Graham Schofield, my patient editor. Thank you for going above and beyond to ensure this book went to publish as the best version of itself.

Thank you to Sicilian Says, Gen Ziana, and all the people and organizations like them who are working to preserve and celebrate the Sicilian language, Abruzzese dialect, and all the many regional languages and dialects of Italy.

For my husband Pat, who kept my secret. You were the only person besides my editors who knew of this book's existence, and upon first hearing my crazy idea to write a novel you smiled and said, "OK, so what do you need to do to make it happen?" You've always been my biggest fan, my loudest cheerleader, and most persistent promoter of my photography, writing, and solving ancestral mysteries via Google Maps. I can't imagine ever completing this novel without you by my side. Thank you for always supporting my ideas and endeavors—even when I want to build a giant red string board—and for being the first to read this book. Sorry I made you read it three times. I love you right in the face!

To my fellow Italian Americans who have set out on a journey to learn about and educate on our true history, and the history of our ancestral lands; the tumultuous, rich, and diverse history that lies beyond cannoli and spritz.

To all the children of immigrants who were born into the roles of interpreter, translator, transcriber, and advocate; I see you.

About the Author

ESTER MARIA SEGRETTO is a first generation Italian American, born and raised in Queens, New York. She has a peculiar preoccupation with the histories of World War II and Italy's Mezzogiorno. Ester graduated from School of Visual Arts with a Bachelor of Fine Arts degree in Photography and lives in New York City with her husband and their two feline familiars. *Born of Earthquake and Volcano* is her first novel.

www.ingramcontent.com/pod-product-compliance
Lightning Source LLC
LaVergne TN
LVHW091709070526
838199LV00050B/2325